SHALLOWS

SHALLOWS

Tim Winton

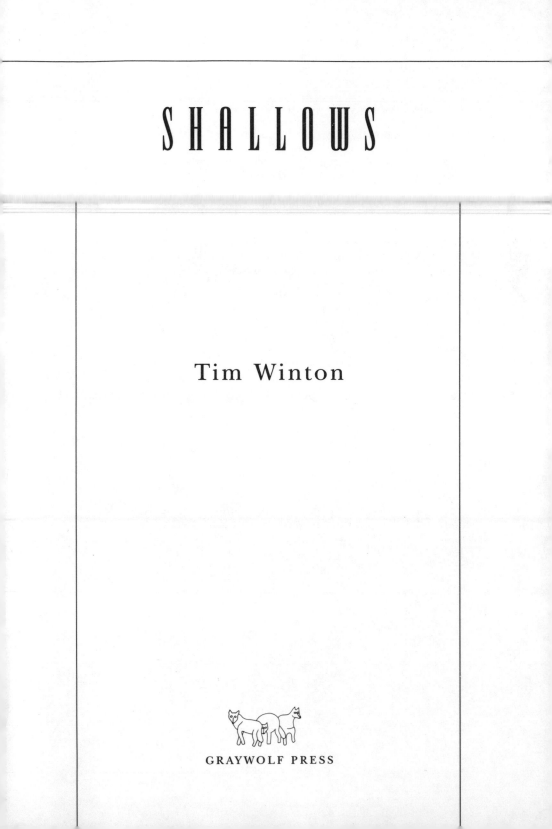

GRAYWOLF PRESS

First published by Allen & Unwin, Australia, 1984

First U.S. publication by Atheneum Press, 1986

Publication of this volume is made possible in part by a grant provided by
the Minnesota State Arts Board through an appropriation by the
Minnesota State Legislature, and by a grant from the National
Endowment for the Arts. Additional support has been provided by the
Andrew W. Mellon Foundation, the Lila Wallace-Reader's Digest Fund,
the McKnight Foundation, and other generous contributions from foun-
dations, corporations, and individuals. Graywolf Press is a member agency
of United Arts, Saint Paul. To these organizations and individuals who
make our work possible, we offer heartfelt thanks.

Published by GRAYWOLF PRESS
2402 University Avenue, Suite 203
Saint Paul, Minnesota 55114

ISBN 1-55597-193-8

9 8 7 6 5 4 3 2
First U.S. Paperback Printing, 1993

Library of Congress Cataloging-in-Publication Data
Winton, Tim.
    Shallows / Tim Winton.
       p. cm.
    1. Women environmentalists—Australia—Western Australia—
Fiction. 2. Whaling—Australia—Western Australia—Fiction. 3. Western
Australia—Fiction. I. Title.
PR9619.3.W58S5 1993   93-8867
823—dc20

To Denise, with love

CONTENTS

So close behind some promontory lie
    The huge leviathans to attend their prey,
And give no chance, but shallow in the fry,
    Which through their gaping jaws mistake the way.

                      DRYDEN *Annus Mirabilis*

those grim travellers in dawn skies
see the beauty—makes them cry inside
makes them angry and they don't know why
grim travellers in dawn skies

                BRUCE COCKBURN "Grim Travellers"

PROLOGUE

HERE—it is 1831 on the southernmost tip of the newest and oldest continent, the bottom of the world. In the wintery gauze of dawn, the American whaler *Family of Man* weighs anchor and leaves the harbour and its search for deserters. An hour later, the Governor of the British Colony of Angelus, a globular man with regally inflamed haemorrhoids, watches the races. Because horses are so precious in the colony, it is the men who race; first the enlisted men, and then the convicts. The enlisted men in their shirtsleeves laugh together in the wild stubble beside the Governor's marquee. They have already raced and bloodied themselves, but their race is but a preliminary event, and with different rules. All eyes are on the shambling figures of two convicts who roll keg-sized stones up the flank of Mount Clement.

The harbour is still as memory, the scrub vibrates, and the granite quarry gapes.

At the foot of the hill the officers and enlisted men and the handful of free settlers cheer as the two convicts grovel up, each inching his great stone towards the peg on the brow of the hill. They toil, pray, push, and find themselves at the same moment at the peg where they let go their stones to race them downhill. Scrub slashes their shins as they career down, and behind them the stones grumble and accelerate and bounce at their heels. The small crowd barracks and bellows: the race is close, man with man, stone with stone, right until the moment Liam O'Gogram trips and falls and is mounted by his stone, leaving convict James Seed to finish amid a disappointed exchange of currency and a distracted avoidance of boulders.

On the outskirts of the settlement, two infantrymen on patrol come upon the wasted hulk of a man on a sand-bar at the mouth of the river. His mad eyes unnerve the soldiers; they are eyes from another world. The man's name is Nathaniel Coupar and his ordeal has left him barely alive, barely a man.

Down on a shelly beach near the entrance to the harbour, a humpback whale lies where it has been jettisoned by the sea, rotting, caving in, rumbling in its decay, left alone by even the sharp-beaked gulls that hunt the lonely shallows for smelt and mullet.

And now it is the year 1978 in Angelus, Western Australia.

The town's station wagons form a metal and glass perimeter around Angelus Oval. Two teams of men slog about in the turfy mud, upending one another, punching and kicking the soggy leather kernel from one end of the swampy ground to the other. The townspeople cheer and jeer from the waxed fenders of their Kingswoods.

Behind the circle of cars, boys play in the muddy gravel, damming up the ochre water, and girls spatter their floral frocks in games of hopscotch, watched by the old woman with the shopping bags who leans on one leg — bun slipping from the side of her head like a cherry from the tip of a melting cupcake — a cathedral of noise in her ears.

After the game, half the town is ushered into the belly of the rickety grandstand for celebrations. Des Pustling, patron of both teams, spits another tooth and sucks his bloodless gums as he signals for the spearing of the kegs. For an hour, this afternoon, black footballers and their families drink with the whites.

In the evening, the pubs are full of talk. Old drinkers in the Royal Albert fling stories and froth and wisdom about; grey-suited men in the London talk through the crooks of their arms and scatter void betting slips. Businessmen in the Amity and the World shout with their heads low to the bar, and at the Black & White words and darts fly thudding into the walls. And down by the waterfront, as he waits for the whalemen to arrive, Hassa Staats, the Aryan publican of the Bright Star, pours watery beers for old men whose fathers drank here, and whose sons will drink here when they tire of youth. His anticipation is boyish, incongruous to his sixteen stone. He almost hops from foot to foot. On the floor, head resting in the sputum and ash of the foot-tray, Ernie Easton, Staats's oldest customer, unable to remount his bucking stool, is dreaming of 1915.

When at last the whalers descend upon the Bright Star Hassa Staats shouts beer on the house and friendly fights break out between crews, and bottles open scalps and spectators clap one another on the back, afraid not to laugh. Ernie Easton, in showers of beer and flying glass, tells himself stories of the sea and reminds himself of his pioneering ancestors in order to coax his eyelids to lift so he can watch. Hassa Staats is so happy.

In the main street an old woman sleeps against the window display of the new Woolworths store.

Off the main street, an old man writes his sermon for the morning, eyes stung to tears by the fumes from a kerosene heater.

Those Aborigines strong and sober enough wander down from the Reserve, caught in the chiaroscuro of lightning, to sit outside the pubs and beg bottles of Brandovino from the white men who fall and fight on the footpaths. On a deserted golf links across town, their sons fight a rival group from out of town with crowbars and reticulation spikes.

A young couple lie in bed. Their house overlooking the harbour from its perch on the side of Mount Clement has stood for generations. The man is thin and whip-haired; the woman is broadbacked with skin the colour of almond kernels. They have not been long married. Marriage has been a surprise for them. The woman is dreaming and not quite asleep. The man is awake and will be for hours. She stirs; she grips his arm, lets go, and settles.

It is one hundred and forty-nine years since the day the *Onan* anchored in Angelus harbour. This town, scar between two scrubby hills, is not a big town, and it has few sustaining industries. But against all odds, all human sense, by some unknown grace, Angelus prevails.

ANGELUS

In a bay east from the town of Angelus, cries resounded in the night. A tent stood silhouetted on moonlit sand and, beside it, the shape of a tractor. The interior of the tent was warmed by a gas lamp. A man and a woman lay naked on their bedding. The man read a musty journal, resting it on the woman's buttocks. She listened to the lovemaking of the whales out in the bay, the sounds of her childhood. She quivered.

'They haven't been here since I was a little girl,' she murmured.

'Hmm?'

'The whales. They used to have a strange effect on me.'

The man shook his long, thin hair from his eyes. 'How do you mean?'

'When they were around at this time of year, I used to have this dream, over and over. I heard. . . .'

'Well?'

'It didn't seem so odd, then. I was only a little girl. I heard the voice of God calling from down in the bay. I got up to the window to look. He was calling Poppa. Quite a patient voice. Daniel . . . Daniel. Poppa didn't come out. After a while He stopped calling and from down in the bay came this thunderous splash and the whole farm shook and in the moonlight I saw this glistening, black . . . whale inching up towards the house. I screamed and fell back into bed and pulled the sheet over my face and there was thunder all of a sudden and heavy rain. When the storm was over I went to Poppa's room and he was gone and the floor was wet and I was

1

alone in the world. I went back to my bed and decided never to wake up. And that was when I woke up. Poppa would be there by my bed with the lamp and a glass of milk. It was God, I'd say. And he'd smile and say, "Yes, I know."'

'This happen every year?' the man asked.

'For a couple of years. Then one year the whales didn't come.'

The man sighed. 'You Coupars!'

'Poppa says the Coupars have always been fools.'

'Fair enough.'

'Fools-elect, or something.'

The man shrugged, closed his book, and turned out the light. He thought he heard the chafe and creak of rowlocks, but there were no boats about. The sound was the old men's noise the peppermints made in the breeze.

Out in the bay the black skins of right whales fresh from the southern ice glistened in the thickening moonlight, their breath settling vaporously on the water.

In the cutting light of afternoon the man and woman walked along the surf-hazed beach to a deep sheltered pool in the lee of the headland. With masks and fins, they plunged in. As he watched her long legs scissoring the water ahead of him, it occurred to the man that his wife ought not to have been born a land mammal. Her lungs were fantastic; she was strong, lithe and quick in the water, and he was sometimes afraid of her. She torpedoed out of the haze to take him by the legs, shaking him as a shark shakes its prey. He saw bold, curious fish, and found their vulnerability attractive. But he could only observe: she forbade weapons in the water. He saw her big body as it went deep again, moving over paddocks of shells in the pellucid light below.

On the beach she showed him the bright, sea-worn objects she had found, pausing to let him wring the brine from her hair. He bit her on the neck.

'Poppa will be expecting us,' she said.

2

II

The same day, as he leaves his sad hulk of a car and gathers the pile of blankets in his arms, smelling the sharpness of their mothball odour, William Pell remembers something that happened ten years ago and he chuckles at himself as he sets out up the winding gravel track towards the Reserve.

A tiny wren alights on a branch before him, turns its head and is gone, the branch not even vibrating under its weight. Pell marvels at the delicacy of it, thanks God for it and moves on with his memories and thoughts. An irony is upon him. A hundred years ago, he muses, these blankets I'm carrying would have been laced with typhoid, and here I am, a century later, still bringing them blankets. He guffaws humourlessly and sighs. Well, they need blankets now, he thinks, so I bring them, that's all.

In the clearing the iron of the humpies is wet with dew and the morning sun offers the scene a forlorn radiance. A man lies immobile on the wet ground by the corpse of a fire. Bottles glow green and gold and brown in the grass. Pell drops a blanket over the man and leaves the pile outside the biggest humpy. Inside the huts the people are sleeping and those awake are possessed by some deep-rooted shame which prevents them from coming out to greet him. Moving back down the crisp-wet track towards his car, the Reverend William Pell nurses his own shame: 1968 creeps back into his mind, how he travelled with the current, negotiating, bargaining with God, and how the moon hid behind a hedge of cloud.

Pell spends the morning at home in his office. He writes a letter to the editor of the *Advocate* and spends time with his clipboard in the spare room that is crammed dangerously full with boxes of food and blankets and clothing. Dust lifts and hovers about him in a grubby aura.

Later he walks down the main street nodding to all those who demand it of him, buys two tins of tobacco at the Wildflower Cafe where the bikies slouch around on the

Laminex with their GOD'S GARBAGE insignia embossed on their leather jackets, and stops outside the office of the *Advocate* to deliver his letter. Each day he rings at the desk he hears the journalists calling to each other.

'And never send to know for whom the Pell tolls!'

'He tolls for thee!'

On his walk to the deepwater jetty in the harbour, Pell is reminded of his age; he is seventy-two and well overdue for retirement. In fact, his retirement has been set for the first of July, little more than six weeks away. Presbytery in the city has decided that the church in Angelus needs a younger man: after all, the Anglicans have one and the Methodists as well, though the Catholics will never again have a young one. The last young Catholic priest in the town was a drunkard who drove his Morris Minor into the sewage treatment plant outside town and drowned. Pell knows the town will welcome Darby, his successor, because Darby is a clean young man who keeps his religion to himself and Sunday.

Without hailing them, Pell climbs down the gnarled wooden steps to the low landing close to the water and sits beside two of his old schoolmates. Dick and Darcy, warm inside their greatcoat, fish, and are mesmerised by the water.

'G'day, Bill,' they say.

'Hello, Dick, Darc. How's the fish?'

Their eyes never leave the sky that is mirrored in the water.

'Well's can be expected,' Dick says. Darcy nods. 'They're there.'

'Good,' says Pell, smiling.

'How's God, then?' Darcy asks, a grin awry on his battered and toothless face.

'Oh,' Pell laughs, 'well's can be expected. He's there, too.'

All three laugh together and the sound is a strange thing to the gulls that stir along the jetty, frightened of the old men's joke which seems as old as the timbers themselves. Pell looks out across the harbour with its flats and torpid shallows where once he and these old men chased fat, lazy mullet and found oysters in the mud and punted about in half-submerged dories, ankle-deep in guano. He gives them tobacco, which is all they will take from him, and leaves them to their reflections with a warmth and a sadness in him.

4

On his way uptown he passes the old Coupar house on Brunswick Street where the old Misses Coupar had lived, where Daniel Coupar himself lived for a short time during the Depression, where Coupar's granddaughter has lived now for a year with her husband from the city. Queenie Coupar is now Queenie Cookson. Pell thinks: a strange fellow, that Cookson, a square peg in any hole. Pell remembers the headlines in an old *Advocate*, EX-JOURNO CAUGHT BARE, and he laughs to himself. Anyone who swims in the raw at Middle Beach in an Angelus winter needs to be arrested for his own well-being, Pell muses. Queenie Cookson had also been naked on that beach that day, but Judge Moorhead Wilkes knew whose daughter she was and she did not appear before the court. Queenie Coupar has always been a curiosity in Angelus. As a child, she was smitten with innocence, unlike her deserting mother, a child who told stories at school that had the teachers wondering, stories about conversations with dolphins and hearing God in seashells, a fear of thunder and lightning which made her seem eccentric to all.

Pell steps into the Richardson Bakery, built in his father's youth, and orders a tank loaf and says hello to the girl who serves him.

'Hello, Father,' she says. He winces.

'Oh, and I'd better have a dozen scones, too, my dear,' he says. 'People always expect scones when they come to my place. And lots of milky tea, for some reason.'

'Yes, Father,' she says, fidgeting with floury hands in the till.

'I'm not your father, girl,' Pells says with a half-jolly chuckle. 'I swear it.'

The girl wraps his order, confused, and thinks what a silly old man and Pell squirms, pays hastily, and leaves.

On the veranda of the manse, in the cool shadow of the old church, Pell suddenly tears a scone from the bag and hurls it at the picket fence; the scone clips the fence, sheds raisin-shrapnel, and bounces into the lane where some passer-by calls out in surprise. Pell slips quickly inside.

Cleaning out his drawers after lunch with dust-motes raining on him in the heatless afternoon light, Pell finds an old manila folder and stops for a moment to read the title. PROPOSAL FOR CONVERSION OF EXISTING OPERATION OF WHALING STATION

AT PARIS BAY, 1972. Riffling through the pages he strikes on a paragraph that he reads.

> . . . as tried and successfully executed on the east coast of the U.S. where old whalechasers and seiners are converted into whale-observing vessels bearing tourists and students who can view these awesome mammals at close range in their own habitat. The right and humpback whales are almost extinct. The sperm, still hunted, could if left alone be replenished and move closer to land further facilitating a venture of this sort. Whale observation might not be as lucrative as whale exploitation, but could be viable enough to sustain employment for many of those seamen and workers who must inevitably lose their jobs when finally the whaling industry in Angelus causes its own redundancy. . . .

Pell drops the yellowed submission into the bin without emotion. 'You're just not a leader,' he says, nostalgic for the days in Angelus when there were wise men and women not afraid to speak out. People who led. Old men like his father; young men like his old friend Daniel Coupar.

From his Goormwood Street office this Monday morning Des Pustling can see the marble slab of the Goormwood Memorial with its recently installed wishing well. It marks the grave of Edgar Goormwood, the first English gentleman to die in Angelus. Convicts died quickly and regularly in those early years. The first free man to die was an infantryman who shot his foot off and died of gangrene in 1892. But gentlemen were rare and gentlemanly deaths history. Goormwood was a sensitive man who, upon arriving in the colony, took to bed and died with a volume of Milton on the coverlet. The stonemason and his brother who acted as an undertaker, drunkards both, buried Goormwood on the wrong day at dawn, too close to the town limits, with the epitaph:

Here lieth Edgar Wallace Goormwood
Died of Greif 16th December, 1832
God rest his immoral soul

The sudden grave and the exotic disease 'Greif' sent the town

6

into a panic and the townspeople locked themselves indoors for a week. Within two years the main thoroughfare parted on either side of the grave, leaving it like a tiny, ugly islet: which within another thirty years became the centre of the town of Angelus. The Pustlings, who arrived a century later, were distant relations to the Goormwoods of Oxford, having been Goormwood-Pustlings themselves until they shed the hyphen and the connection with the advent of the twentieth century. In the 1920s many of them forsook the comfort of England for the opportunity of the colonies. Benjamin Pustling of Surrey found Angelus, Western Australia, and made it his task to prosper and to own.

Des Pustling, without thought to his link with history beneath the wishing well, merely glances across the street to the Presbyterian church and then looks back to his desk-top. Marion Lowell is busy behind him with two handsful of his girdle, like someone trying to stuff too many groceries into an undersize bag, hoisting, hands under his shirt, smelling his deceptive odour of Cryst-O-Mint Lifesavers. She knows not to laugh. She knows the story of her predecessor who paid dearly for laughter. The young woman, seduced into Pustling's vast bedroom by the certainty of the unemployment that would accompany refusal, lay naked on his bed and saw, as her employer undressed, a slip of smeared toilet paper gummed to his left buttock. And she laughed. In a rage, Pustling held her to the bed and penetrated her and dressed her and sacked her and manhandled her out onto his front lawn.

With his girdle in place, Des Pustling sharpens himself to the day's commerce. His office walls are thick with photographs of properties to let, stiff Polaroid shots of leaning bungalows and farmhouses with honest-sounding details beneath in Marion's neat felt-pen hand: PUSTLING REALTY/To Let/ Hacker Farmlet/11½ acres/river views/prime land/bore sunk/generous terms/. Pinned to the wall on his left, a curling calendar with a photograph of a kookaburra that reminds him of Robert Menzies says GOORMWOOD SERVICE AND LUBE. A few early shoppers pass in the street, stare up curiously, seeing only themselves in the tinted glass.

Late in the morning he telephones the Reverend William Pell.

7

'Listen, Reverend,' he says, working a loose tooth over with his tongue, 'can you tell me something about the church?'

'About our church, Des, or *the* church?' Pell answers. 'I suppose I can try.'

'Good. How does a person become an elder?' Pustling grins, gums white.

'What do you mean?'

'I mean I'd like to be an elder. You know, now that I've been coming along awhile. The church needs some younger blood making decisions. I know I'm no spring chicken, but the other blokes are getting too old to tie their own bootlaces, you know what I mean.'

'Yes, I think I'm understanding, Des,' Pell says. 'And they're not all blokes, Des. Miss Thrim, Mrs James and Mrs Galloway don't like to be called blokes.'

'Blokesses, then.' Pustling guffaws. 'Back to the point.'

'The point is that I know what you're up to, Des Pustling. You may not agree with Him, but the Lord set down some fairly comprehensive guidelines for the congregation's choosing of elders. You have to be a—'

'I'll ignore your poor manners, Reverend—'

'Good. I've been ignoring yours for years, now kindly—'

'Just tell me one thing, Reverend.'

'Can I choose which thing to tell you?'

Prickly old bastard, Pustling thinks. Got more spirit left than I thought. 'Who chooses elders, you?'

'The church. The congregation. Current elders act upon the church's recommendation. Not a perfect system, I'll admit, but serviceable enough.' The old man sounds winded.

'Election of elders is when?'

'August the second.'

'Your retirement date is?'

A long silence. Pustling can hear the old man thinking, hear his heart beating between his teeth.

'The first of July. Pustling, if you think you can get control of this congregation to get yourself into some position of what you seem to think is power and influence. . . .'

'Yes?' Pustling laughs.

'Firstly, you won't. Secondly, your reason for trying it will no longer exist. Most of it doesn't exist already. I made a mistake,

8

letting this moment become possible. I made a grave error about your cunning, though I thank God that you've made a worse blunder about mine.'

Pustling stares out across the street, looking at the limestone blocks of the old church on the other side of the road as if the building itself has just hung up on him.

III

With his collapsed gumboots lying like dollops of dung beside him attracting more flies, Daniel Coupar sat waiting, shifting his feet on the veranda rail, farting painfully. It was Monday, 16 May. From below where pasture descended into dried swamp and veldt-grass and dunes, the tractor bellowed like a milk-heavy cow and Coupar cursed that idiot Cleveland Cookson for not knowing the difference between high and low ratios. Sixteen months ago, the city boy had come and stolen Queenie from him. Since then, it had not rained.

Coupar had not slept since the arrival of the whales a few days before; their sounds brought him memories and that feeling of vast time passing and some choleric twitch of foreboding.

The nose of the old Fordson appeared, grinding through the dry bracken near the swamp, jerking in ruts and water-cuts. He saw his granddaughter. She pointed to something across the swamp and Coupar saw ducks rising in a single dark wing.

When the tagga-tagga of the engine stopped, Cleve and Queenie Cookson jumped down, laughing at a joke shared in the protective din.

'You drive like a bloody donkey,' Coupar said, grinning sourly.

'It's the tractor,' Cleve Cookson said, glancing at the festering mounds of the old man's boots.

'Bollocks.'

'Hello, Poppa,' Queenie said, throwing back her tassels of hair, stepping up onto the veranda, kissing him. Coupar growled and accepted the kiss; he noted as she leant over that

9

she wore no bra and he saw down to her navel. It's what happens, he thought dully.

'You've been eating grapes,' she said, picking up an old stalk.

'The last of them,' Coupar said without looking up to the skeleton above. The vine was black with dryness.

The young man went back to the tractor as they talked and untied a hessian bag from the roll-cage. He showed the old man the abalone, each the size of a split pigmelon. The old man stopped speaking to Queenie.

'When I was a boy they were all that big.'

The crisp, brown paddocks ticked like hot metal. Coupar's fences needed repairing and the stock were bony and the cows undermilked. He was growing too old to tend the place: people had said it for years ever since his wife died; but it was only recently that he had lost his will and died a little and realised how old and how repulsive to himself he was. Even the land has putrefied and pussed up around me and worked me to the surface, he thought, and now it's a dried scab and I'm spat out like an unclean thing. Coupar hooked his clawed feet over the rail and farted. His granddaughter looked at his feet.

'Poppa, what have you been doing? Your feet are all blistered.'

'Walking,' he said.

Obviously not working, she thought.

Cleve went inside with the abalone, through the open room with the limestone fireplace, the burst sofa, the browning walls adorned with sombre men and women with fierce, other-worldly Coupar eyes, over rugs that were no longer anything more than multiple series of interlocking threads left colourless from the years, into the cool, dark kitchen with its smells of damp and unbled meat and saddle-soap. He moved a crusty lump of leather with his foot: it was a saddle, hard, furrowed with lack of use and maintenance. Old boots, a necktie, rabbit traps, mildewed books, an axe-head and fowl crap lay on the stone floor. Cleve wanted to belong here. He prodded the coals of the massive stove. He breathed in deep, and he listened to the talk filtering in from outside.

Dusk descended, the paddocks greyed and there was no hint of a dew that might moisten them. There was an unnatural warmth in the air that might once have promised a thunderstorm, but the sky was cloudless, opaque, and heavy with its own dryness. The three sat out on the veranda in cane chairs, drinking Coupar's home brew, listening to the weary sounds of the birds roosting all about, watching and feeling the arrival of darkness,

'The whales are still here, Poppa,' Queenie said, looking down towards the indigo smear of ocean still distinguishable from the evening sky.

'Never thought the buggers would ever come back,' said Coupar. 'Last time I saw the whales in numbers, Queenie, my girl, was when you were catching the school bus from here to town before your grandmother died, before I started feeling like an old man.'

'I remember. They were here every winter.'

Dark became complete, and the Tilley lamp clinked with moths that butted against the hot white glass, their shadows reeling across the ground below the veranda.

'When are you going back to town?' the old man asked, emptying the last bottle.

'Tomorrow,' Cleve said.

'Our anniversary.'

The old man knew only too well, pretended not to hear, and for a few minutes no one spoke. Cleve pushed his chair back, as if making motions for bed, and the old man stirred.

'There's two more bottles cooling down at the bore,' Coupar murmured. 'If you can handle it, that is.' He wanted them to stay up with him even if it meant childish ploys; he wanted to talk with them, these distant strangers, so young, so lithe, so ripe for catastrophe. And he was jealous of them because they were so much closer to the beginning of their lives than he was.

'I'll get them,' Cleve said, rising.

'No, I'll go.' Queenie was already off the veranda and into the darkness. She found her way without hesitation, feeling her infant footprints in the dust.

The old man watched her form absorbed by night.

'So,' he said, without looking up at Cleve, 'you found the journals.'

11

'Yeah.' Cleve nodded, observing the pink rasher of pate showing through the old man's white hair. 'I figured you let me find them on purpose.'

'Read them properly. Read it for....' He hesitated, thinking, the best I can hope for is a disturbance, a stick in the stagnant pool.

'For what?' Cleve asked, tantalised.

'I dunno,' Coupar sighed. 'Read it for the things that aren't there.'

'Oh?' Cleve waited.

'The Coupars have been a proud family.' He thought: They have not loved. Plenty of passion, only no love.

'I know. From Queenie.'

'You don't know the half of it.'

'Well, maybe I'll find out.'

Coupar shrugged. This was indeed a youth before him. He wished Queenie would come. Cleve was beginning to embarrass him.

The water of the bore was cool, cold-hard where the fresh current twisted up out of the ground beneath the solid, memorial spread of the clunking windmill. When she was a child Queenie climbed the windmill to see the whales surfacing in the bay, spouting vapour like gunsmoke. Up there, high above the winter green of the farm, she had thought about the story of Jonah, how the whale was God's appointed messenger, and she had hooked her limbs about the salt-stained legs of the mill and watched the big backs idling, and waited for a message from God, the one she was certain would come. She waited for the whales to belly up to the foot of the mill to attend to her queries. Each winter she climbed and waited, each year the questions were modified; one year the whales did not appear at all.

Queenie Cookson listened to movement in the bracken, the vegetation her grandfather hated so. She loved its stiff greenery, had spent hours, days, lying amongst the fronds, hearing the wind-shivers. At length, she felt around and found the bottles half-submerged by the bank and walked back with them towards the light of the house. They'll be talking about

12

those bloody journals, she thought. God knows, I thought Poppa'd have more sense — he knows what Cleve's like.

Coupar slept dreamlessly on the hard cot in which he had taken solace since his wife's death. In the front room, the Cooksons lay on the big bed, sheets kicked down, and Queenie breathed metrically on her side, asleep with her husband's arm about her and his thumb in her navel. Cleve, awake, restless, contemplated the outline of her back, the same innocent arc he noticed the day of their first meeting when he came upon her lying in a rock-pool on this same beach. He had, a week before, lost his job, the last in a sad string of failures; and he had traversed half the State considering his next move. He had no ideas. He startled her; she tossed her thick hair and snatched him up in her loneliness. At the end of that first day of summer a year and a half ago, Cleveland Cookson still had no ideas, but he had a euphoric sense of flight that shunted from his mind all memory of failure, of cowardice and mundaneness; and flight was enough.

Cleve untangled himself from Queenie's sleeping form and got up and found the lamp on the table in the far corner and lit it and let it burn low. Opening the brick-like volume he cast off his unremarkable heritage.

> . . . And so it was with a great despondency settling upon me that I pulled on my oar on that our final departure from the *Family of Man*, watching her fall sternward, anchor swinging and a few old sailors waving aft, calling ribald farewells mostly lost in the breeze. Someone said then in the boat that he dubbed this place the Bay of Whales. It is a hopeful title. . . .

Cleve read of the setting free of the kangaroo dogs for water, the whiteness of the beach, the pitching of tents, the lighting of fires.

> . . . I am afraid of Finn's crew who all seem to be criminals. Leek their harpooneer has the face of a mongrel dog. Cain their second harpooneer has had his left earlobe torn off in a past fight. Hale our ponderously fat cook tells me that Cain yet keeps the shrivelled lobe in

13

his sea-chest. Hale is taunting me in fun, I am sure. Last night I slept beside him—a veritable hillock of flesh—watching before I slumbered, the firelight dancing upon the canvas. I woke in the night thinking of the dried flesh fused to Cain's earring. I turned over against the protective bulk of Hale and took fright at the dogs whimpering coldly outside.

May 28th, 1831   We are a large party on this expeditional fishery: twenty-five strong, thousands of miles from Hobart Town, our last port of call. I am alone. I make no address to a reader in this journal of loneliness, but merely record emotions and happenings for the sake of memory and mental occupation. Churling is an odd fellow. . . .

Cleve, suddenly feeling the long day's activity in his limbs, closed the journal, turned out the light and went to bed, encircling Queenie and feeling her breasts against his forearm.

Daniel Coupar sat on the veranda beneath the scratch of crows in the guttering. He brooded, looking up to the bare granite cheeks of Wirrup Hill where he knew his granddaughter and her husband had gone. The hill hunkered high over the brown, creased paddocks and the albescent beaches, high over the house and the sheds and the spindly stock. Coupar cursed its smooth, bland face and muttered to himself, overcome by memories. He stomped his feet against the veranda rail and the crows above him scarcely moved. He went inside to straighten the bedclothes on the big bed, leaving his own a rancid, grey knot, and as he shuffled agitatedly around the room he whispered: 'God A'mighty, what's wrong, old man? What *is* it?' He sat out on the veranda again and saw the hill and heard the whales from far below and his body ached as it did with changes of season.

Up on the hill the incline was clotted with small trees growing in the soil that covered the granite foundation, and many of them were as disfigured as leper's limbs, gnarled and twisted. Everywhere, granite knobs, wounds, shapeless extrusions. Queenie picked her way up the gully full of a hopeless hope, every muscle strained towards the waterfall which meant so

14

much to her. It should have been spilling from the bluff in this beginning of winter, but at Wirrup there had been no autumn and before that no summer and certainly no spring, only an unexplained heat. There'll be some water, Queenie told herself; it can't be dry. But there was no water. The fall near the summit of the hill was just a stain on the bluff and the shrunken pool at its base was still, its gangrenous surface pimpled with larvae.

The Coolmans stood wordless. This was the place where they came together, a summer ago. Even then the weather was out of control: it had snowed in the ranges. Then, the waterfall was thick, a translucent sickle cutting at the rocks, and prisms dazzled the bark of trees. Their laughter had tolled in the gullies as, naked, they stood beneath the fall and felt the water on their closed eyes. In the brilliant cascade, they fell and were yoked by the weight of water drumming into their eyes, on their backs. Their pores pricked tight. They sheltered deep in one another, were grafted in water and light, and even when, in exhaustion, they were pummelled apart, they remained fused.

Queenie and Cleve looked at one another. It was inevitable, each saw. They were hungry for that moment. Queenie freed her breasts. Cleve shucked out of his shorts. The soupy green pool barely moved as they ground away with insects on their backs, their eyes shut.

The afternoon sun scythed the dead paddocks with its heat and crows loped across it, low to the earth. Coupar remained inert in his chair on the veranda as Cleve and Queenie prepared to leave; his head ached and his bones pained him. I don't want to be alone in this Godforsaken place any more, he thought. Even the bloody dogs have left me and this land for better prospects; even the dogs, and a dog's about as patient as a bloody Pustling. Coupar did not want the young people to go; he would have shamed them into staying, had he any imagination left. As she came out onto the veranda for the last time, he pressed into Queenie's hands a small calico bag, an heirloom.

'Oh....' she murmured, opening its drawstring neck,

15

'whales' teeth, sperm teeth.' The long curving cones were scrimshawed with the image of a man in the jaws of a sperm whale, the man with a stylised, vacant horror on his face, eyes popping.

'Belonged to Nathaniel Coupar.'

Queenie smiled, hesitant. Cleve beamed, turning the yellowed relics preciously in his hands.

'For the anniversary,' the old man said, going inside, leaving Cleve and Queenie together, dumbfounded, on the veranda.

'Um, I'll get my bag,' Queenie said, going in after him. In the dark kitchen the old man was swinging the stove door open and shut. 'Poppa?'

'Piss off, I'm busy.'

'Listen,' Queenie said soothingly. 'Would you like to come and stay in Angelus with us for a few weeks?'

'In that shithole? With that idiot?'

'He isn't an idiot.'

'What would you know?'

She kissed him coldly on the stubbled cheek and left him.

Cleve revved the Land Rover, pulling his sunglasses down over his eyes. She climbed in and slammed the door.

'Got your bag?'

'I haven't got a bag, you bloody twit.'

He let the clutch out too quickly and stalled the engine, confused.

Coupar watched the dust lift in the distance until it was claimed by the steel-blue sky. Coupar, you stupid bastard, he thought. He berated himself for giving them the teeth. He somehow had the notion that it meant something bad, and he cursed his hunger for goodwill, for affection even, wondering why on earth men ever needed either; knowing full well. 'Don't try me any more,' he whispered. 'Make it rain.'

Nearing Angelus on the road home, the Cooksons listened to the local radio station. Rain was forecast in Angelus and the western south coast, no change in the east. Then began the daily catch report from the Angelus Tourist Bureau: '. . . wish to advise that seven whales have been taken by the Paris Bay Whaling Company and flensing will be in progress throughout

16

the day, so don't. . . .' the announcer was cut short by a jab of Queenie's thumb.

'What'd you do that for?' Cleve protested. 'I was listening to that.'

'Sorry. I don't want to.'

A clutch of cockatoos flushed across the road ahead. On the gravel edges the broken bodies of twenty-eight parrots caught their eye.

'What's the matter?'

'I just don't want to hear how many whales they slaughtered last night, okay?'

'Happy anniversary,' Cleve said.

They drove in silence into town, crossed the tiny Hacker River bridge and saw the birds skidding on the flats near where squatters had moved back to live in the warped shacks built by the failed hobby farmers from the city. They drove past Angelus Oval as dusk fell, past the glare of the pubs and tourist motels to the old Coupar house at the base of Mount Clement. It was clear to both of them: there would be an argument tonight.

IV

Through perforations in the shivering tin walls of the shed, Cleve saw the light of the old men's lamp and closed his Penguin edition of *Moby-Dick*.

He heard the rats outside, on the roof, around the slippery piles, making raspy noises with claws and throats. Two hours before, a pair of bored policemen had sat outside with .38 revolvers picking rats off between cigarettes and station gossip until they ran out of ammunition and cigarettes and had only the gossip to sustain them as they walked ashore. The rats ate their dead; there seemed no fewer rats than before.

Buttoning his greatcoat, he crossed the open-slatted floor through which the water showed in strips, and opened the door and braced against the cold charge of night air. He pulled up his collar and descended the steps to the lower platform from where the light shone. Neither Dick nor Darcy looked up from the radiant, aquamarine water which was alive with the boiling movement of garfish and whitebait and yellowtail.

'No bites?' Cleve asked.

The old men looked at him indulgently from their greatcoat. 'Oh, bites,' Dick nodded vaguely. The old men had no bag or bucket; they sat with their backs to the timber shoring someone had nailed up for them as a windbreak years ago, and they were comforted by the niggling attention the fish gave to their oversized baits.

Cleve had never seen them catch a fish. He sat near them in the lee of the windbreak and watched and hoped that perhaps tonight they would speak to him. He looked out over the water. The deepwater jetty was several hundred yards long and slightly doglegged, underslung with scale-encrusted platforms from which the locals fished. Tankers berthed out on the paw of the dog's leg. A quarter of a mile away, the town jetty was chafed by three vessels from the Paris Bay Whaling Company whose land-based station lay just outside the harbour on the lower reaches of the Sound. The town jetty also protected the sleek shape of the cruiser *Bulldozer*, owned by Ted Baer, world-famous game fisherman, who had this night arrived in Angelus.

'Yer the youngest this jetty's seen.'

Cleve started, shocked. One of the old men was speaking to him.

'Pardon?'

'You must be the youngest watchman this lot've firewood's ever had,' Dick said, muffled in his coat.

'Yeah?' Cleve was too excited to speak. 'Yeah?'

'It's a no-hoper's job, that. Drunks, old sailors, retired cockies, respectable gents like Darcy an' m'self,' he bubbled, half laughing, half coughing, and he spat. The southerly caught the creamy yellow phlegm and hurled it out—two gobbets linked by an elastic tether—spinning into the darkness.

Cleve gathered his wits and spoke. 'You fellas used to do this job?'

The old men looked sideways at Cleve and returned their attention to the weaving needlepoints of fish. At that moment

18

footsteps rang out above and Cleve bounded up the steps and the old men shook their heads.

After he had seen the last of the drunken, randy, foul-smelling merchant seamen out of his hut, having helped them sign their signatures and fended off their mistaken advances and watched them totter dangerously along the final length of the jetty to their ship, he poured himself coffee and opened the journal of Nathaniel Coupar and read.

June 2, 1831 In the past days I have all but lived in this lonely lookout with my eyes fixed upon the ocean. Each day brings poorer weather, more cold, more depressing drizzle and a deathly greyness to the complexion of the sea. I feel some foreboding deep within me, but I cannot make sense of it. No whales have been sighted in this, the so-called Bay of Whales.

If this fishery does not improve we will arrive back at the Derwent deeper in debt and no better off than British convicts.

June 3, 1831 It rains perpetually as though God weeps over this strange, grey coast. There was fighting in the farthest tent last night. That Leek....

June 5, 1831 Huts complete and tryworks much improved: 4 huts; two for boats' crews, one for headsmen Finn and Jamieson, another for shoremen (cook, cooper, carpenter) and harpooneers, and the last is store and galley.

June 6, 1831 Praying that Nowles, who now sleeps above, can throw a harpoon as powerfully as he snores! It is somehow odd to be so dependent upon such unpredictable creatures as whales, and to need to kill them to be redeemed from debt.

June 7, 1831 I write again from the lookout. Ocean impenetrably black. I squat beneath the canvas and the rain whispers. I am a poor lookout.

June 8, 1831 At dawn this morning natives arrived at our encampment in dismal rain. Thin, blue-black men clad in animal skins with spears and curious side-arms. Massacre was prevented by the good wit of Mr Jamieson who prevented Leek from attacking the blackfellows with

19

his lance. Much of this I saw after leaving my post and creeping down through the scrub to observe from a safe and secret distance. Much jabber, some laughter from our men, much misunderstanding and little gained in this exchange forsook for the shelter of the lookout. My heart all but stopped when I reached the lookout high above the beach and saw the distant, twin-plumed spout rising in the bay. I took up my tin tub and beat it like a drum and sounded the alarm. . . .

Cleve sat back with a jerk and listened to the hollow thud of footsteps travelling in the timbers of the jetty, ringing closer for a full minute until he was moved to close his book and slip it into his Gladstone bag. The footfalls came closer. The door swung open.

'Well, don't just sit there gawking,' Queenie said, standing legs apart, big as a sailor in her scarf and greatcoat. 'Sign me on, skipper.'

Cleve got to his feet, hands falling from his pockets. 'What are you doing here?' He laughed, hugging her across the table until she overbalanced and fell onto her elbows. She pulled a greasy flourbag from her coat and a spool of nylon line from the pocket of her jeans.

'Thought I might do some fishing.'

'At this —'

'Too cold for you, huh?' There was water in her eyes. Queenie and Cleve had spoken little since their return to Angelus, avoiding each other, aware of some new element between them.

'No, no,' he stammered, frightened of the tears.

They descended the stairs in the light of Dick and Darcy's lamp. The rain had ceased and stars sprayed light all over the black pan of the sky. The old men looked up when they heard Queenie's voice and adjusted themselves within their coat.

'Hello,' Queenie said.

They nodded and smiled. Darcy's mouth was a black hole and Dick had some teeth the colour of barnacled piles.

Queenie unspooled some line, baited a small hook with a wisp of mussel-flesh from the shells in her pockets, and cast it into the bright, cold water. Her small fingers were blue and the line left white chinks when she moved it in her hands. Cleve watched her hands and the careering silhouettes of the fish and glanced across at Dick and Darcy whose lines were jerking with bites. They sat holding trembling lines, leering benevolently at Queenie.

Queenie caught three herring within a few minutes and the little bodies lashed about inside her bag. She fished as intensely as the old men, eyes drawn to the water.

'You're doing all right,' Cleve said, shrinking into his coat with some inexplicable feeling of unease. 'They,' he called to the old men, 'looks like you blokes'll have to take lessons from this one.'

They grinned, hands jerking.

'Why don't you pull in?' Queenie asked them, feeling their gaze upon her.

They shrugged and Darcy giggled and Dick drew a bottle from the depths of their coat and offered it. Cleve took it, saw it was invalid port, hesitated, and took a swig. He rubbed the bottle mouth and offered it to Queenie who glared at him and drank. It was warm, vigorous, medicine-tasting stuff.

'A lot of fish down there,' she pointed, coughing. 'Attracted by the light, I suppose.'

The old men nodded. The Cooksons looked briefly and blankly at each other. Cleve noticed a lick of hair caught in the corner of her mouth like a fine scar and put his finger to it; she flinched away, watching the fish enter and leave the light in neat, thick schools. In the glare itself the fish were confused and blinded and swam madly.

When Queenie began to shiver they gathered up line and bait and Queenie bade goodbye to the old men and they climbed the steps to the shed.

'Bloody idiot,' one of the old men muttered in his coat as the young couple entered the shed.

'Yairs,' the other said. 'A right one.' They fished and gargled invalid port and the clear sky brought a more intense chill down upon them.

Inside the shed the Cooksons ate stale biscuits and drank coffee Cleve heated in the old jug, and they savoured the steam that rose into their faces and thawed their cheeks. After laying the three little fish out on the floor to see their size, Queenie carefully picked off the transparent scales that had grafted themselves onto her palms and forearms. The shed smelt of burning dust from the old bar heater in the corner, and there was also the more subtle odour of moist fish. All along the platforms and ladders and railings and companionways beneath the whole length of the jetty, the darkness moved with rats.

'I used to fish down here when I was a little girl, when Poppa brought me into town,' Queenie said, looking at her boots.

Cleve cast her a whimsical, knowing glance. You still are a little girl, he thought; you haven't changed at all. I bet Dick and Darcy lusted after you ten years ago on this same jetty.

'Always wondered what was in this shed,' she said.

'Only rats. And me,' he smiled.

Queenie yawned. Why are you watching me so carefully? she wondered, flicking her hair for his benefit. God, I'm so tired of this place. The salt-stains on the walls, the bold shuffle of rats, the smell of the canning factory across the water, the opaque smile of her husband: every sound and sight irritated her. She felt trapped again.

Cleve retracted from her cool, hard stare, even willed himself away from the seductive movements of her hands as they fleeced themselves. Don't blame me, girl, he thought. Your grandfather pushed me into this. This is the only job I can get in this town now. Anyway, I like it; it's mine.

Queenie did not relax her gaze, thinking: Look at you, pretending you're not here with me, as though you're some autistic child. Those old men know I'm here, God, don't they? Queenie remembered this man scissored in her thighs in the waterfall, in the bottom of the dinghy floating downstream. You would have died but for me then, Cleve, in that boat on the water when you cried loving me: you would have stopped living had I jumped out and swum away and left you wanting.

Her coffee went cold; the black surface stained a line halfway down the cup and she saw her own eye in the black.

'Cleve.'

His head wavered; he had almost dozed off.

'I want to know something.'

'What?'

'I want to know why you're reading the journals. I want a decent answer.'

Just like a Coupar, he thought. She demands me to justify

22

my existence, my reading habits, even. He rubbed his palms into his eyes, deliberating behind his palms. Queenie thought: why do you have to float off without us? We don't need any more diversions! You can't leave me alone!

But Cleve only sighed. He loved this woman. There was nothing left that meant more to him. The only happy days in his life had been spent with her. Their love had brought him life, colour, hope; and now he was almost able to stand back and see himself flirting with loss. It astounded him. But he did nothing to arrest it. Reading this journal had given him something more: he was embracing something aged, an offering from the man he feared and loathed and loved— Daniel Coupar.

'Don't hurt us, Cleve,' Queenie said, wondering why she should feel this pity for him.

'It's about your family, okay?'

'Our family's a myth.'

'Maybe.'

'You and me, we're not.'

Cleve shrugged. 'I love you, Queen.'

'That's junky talk.'

He laughed. It was the ambiguity of laughter that drove Queenie to the door. The door slammed and the hut rocked with the force of it. Her footsteps clattered away and Cleve was left to observe the three little fish she had left on the floor, dried crisp as biscuits. He kicked them between the boards and they landed with little smacks on the water below.

... At half past one Jamieson's boat came into view and judging by the briskness with which the men were putting-to at the oars it was apparent that no whale was in tow. As we dragged the boat up the beach I saw empty line tubs and knew a tussle had occurred. The men were in a black mood. I was told that there had been an accident, that Nowles had stumbled over the clumsy-cleat after striking a black cow and wedged his fingers between rope and gunwhale. To prevent capsizing, Mountford seized the hatchet and severed the rope. Someone has said that Mr Jamieson ordered the severance of the fingers and not the rope, but I cannot believe this. Men are not so barbarous as that; we are Americans.

23

There have been crew changes. Cain has become our harpooneer, Leek is Mr Finn's man.

During the flensing of Mr Finn's bull, the natives appeared from the rainy, misty gloom and presented our headsman with tough little roots like lepers' hands which burn hotly and fiercely, and beckoned in return for flesh from the carcass of the whale which they ported back into the bush upon their shoulders.

Half the night men with lanterns moved over the great carcass looking very like Mr Swift's Lilliputians poring over Gulliver. The creature's black gloss danced with firelight, flames boomed beneath the pots fuelled by the roots and natives brought us wrapped in animal skins, and oil glistened on the faces of all.

Sleep is still denied me, for the night is filled with the squirmings and moanings of poor Nowles in the bunk above. How lonely is the sound of a man in pain! There is nothing more solitary; it cannot be shared and a man is isolated in his own sea, the swirling rip-current that is pain. Nowles tosses and pitches his way in the dark. Do I wish to share his pain to ease his burden? No, I am ashamed, but I can only hate him for his pain and his noise and I want him away or dead to leave me some peace and some sleep for what is left of the night.

I am tired and I write with only moonlight over my shoulder. Nowles is calling: 'Gone! Gone!', and now dawn insinuates itself greyly, or do I just imagine so?

At five thirty the shift-siren at the canning factory on the foreshore screamed. Cleveland Cookson woke with his head on the open journal. He spat through the planks into the half-light below; his teeth felt as though they were coated with Campbell's Cream of Mushroom Soup. Gulls scratched the roof. The rats had gone. He nursed his headache for an hour and a half until the day man, a short, porky, drunken fellow whose name continually failed to imprint itself upon Cleve's memory, came to the door in his creased and tired manner to relieve him.

On the lower platform Dick and Darcy lay asleep in each other's arms, the bottle lying uncorked and empty near their feet, lines in the water.

Walking along the jetty towards the shore with its festooning

24

seabirds and brisk-walking shift workers converging on the canning factory, Cleve realised for the first time how long the structure really was. His own house on the hill, so clear in the dawn with sunlight glinting from the kitchen window, was a small square that got no bigger for all his walking.

When he finally reached the gravel path at the end and the dug sand of the foreshore where Queenie had got her mussels, it felt like lunchtime, and the sound of gravel beneath his feet was like the gnawing, scratching of rats.

V

'Twice a year Bill lets me come on these tours,' the robust woman with ham-like arms was saying to her big-chested companion, a woman who ate raisins out of a long, crinkly cellophane bag, 'to let me hair down and see all the natural sights again it just makes yer young and patriotic again Lily like when me and my Bill was courtin' though Bill'd never come on a tour he's got his dogs and the model trains and keepin' the little Eyetalian kiddies from next door off the kangaroo paw and Perth's such a fast city you need a break from it every now and then oh Lily Angelus's such a lovely place all the beaches and bays it's such a beautiful place full of history and things and the people are friendly do you ever see Margie Camberwell no I thought she said Hacker River no I couldn't eat raisins the way you do Lily it would wreak havoc on my bowels bound up a bit are you luv well there's nothing better oh these young people are lovely but so nervous they're like they're on a tour behind the Iron Curtain poor things you know if we were on a tour like this when we was young we'd be havin' a sing-along happy as Larry so much pressure on young people today you never hear 'em sing oh Bill's sciatica's bad Lily. . . .'

Queenie Cookson groaned and glanced across at Barney Wilkins the driver who grinned and winked. Behind the two thick-thighed, bright-haired matrons about twenty people in their early twenties gazed apprehensively through the breath-

25

misted windows at the vast, grey bruise of the Sound, visible as the road wound southward. The young people were a party of students, Queenie decided, observing their art folios, probably on an assignment from the university in the city. They seemed in poor spirits, speaking nervously amongst themselves.

It had been a dull trip so far this morning. Queenie was tired and worn from the silence at home, and this peninsula tour had begun to give her nightmares, dreams in which she starred as a middle-aged, blue-haired, bowel-bound woman like those she tour-guided every day. It would be worse, she knew, when the wildflower season began. The thought of being fifty and incapable of keeping her knees together, her moustache peroxided and her perspiration contained at an age when dignity was all she could conceive to strive for, revolted and frightened Queenie.

At an earlier stop at the Blowholes, Queenie noticed a slightly older member of the party, a man in a cashmere sweater whose face was furrowed with impatience and fatigue. She happened to stand near him when the party gathered around the fluted openings in the rock as the ocean expelled pent-up wind and sent some of them scurrying backwards. She saw his brooding eyes and sinewy features and was puzzled by him. She watched him again at the next stop—the Gap—where the Southern Ocean surged into a vee in the cliffs like the space in a cut cake, and thundered across a flat, submerged shelf, slammed up against the blunt cliff-face sending spume hundreds of feet into the air almost to where the tour party cowered in the wrought-iron lookout on the brink. From her Tourist Bureau Guide's Brochure Queenie recited macabre but compulsory details of horrific drownings and thwarted rescues and she saw her flock huddling together involuntarily as she shepherded them back.

This place always held some mystery for Queenie Cookson. As a child she heard it said that beneath this vast stretch of cliffs, on this the seaward side of the curving peninsula, there were vast caves whose tunnels extended inland as far as the Nullabor a thousand miles away.

Queenie led her party down a path in a wilderness of salt-streaked granite to the edge of the Natural Bridge, an arch of grey granite across a spumescent chasm, and gave them more

26

depressing history and depressed herself further.

On the road to the final stop, as rain blunted itself against the windows and Queenie pointed out marks of supposed interest, the two middle-aged women cooed and tutted, rolling their stockings down a little, and turned to the group of young people behind.

'Listen, loves,' one of them said over the top of Queenie's droll recital, 'you all look so pale and nervy this is a scenic tour which is supposed to be a happy time why don't we have a sing along to cheer us all up?' With that she cawed into 'It's a Long Way to Tipperary' and the people up the back looked dumbfounded and long-jawed.

> 'It's a long way to Tipperary,
> It's a long way to go!
> It's a long way to Tipperary,
> To the sweedest gal I know!'

Queenie recited, despite the singing, determined to retain both control and poise. 'Now we are passing the turn-off to Jimmy Newhill's Harbour. . . .'

> 'Goodbye to Picadilly,
> Farewell Leicester Squaaaare!'

'And now on the left the turn-off to the old quarantine station used until the middle of this century. . . .'

> 'It's a long, long way to Tipperary,
> But my heart's still there!'

'Across the Sound now you can just see Tipper. . . oh, um, Angelus. Oh, shit!'

On the next verse several of the others joined in, and on the chorus Barney Wilkins could not contain his nostalgia; and then the whole bus boomed with raucous song and the young people were laughing self-consciously. Queenie, unyielding, pressed her lips closer to the microphone as the bus ground up the final ascent before Paris Bay.

As the bus crept down the long bitumenised slope, the silver storage tanks and cluster of small buildings came into view and the singing diminished but for the ladies' plangent chorusing. When they felt the silence, even they stopped.

'The Paris Bay Whaling Company has been operating here since 1910 when a Scandinavian group of companies began the venture. In 1918 it came under Australian ownership and has been so ever since. The Paris Bay operation is the last land-based whaling venture left in Australia. Land-based whaling has a tradition in the Angelus region more than a hundred and fifty years old. . . .'

Silence prevailed in the bus for the last half-mile until they rolled into the gravel car park outside the whaling station compound. The pneumatic hiss of the door opening seemed a shattering sound.

Queenie got out of the bus and watched. It took twenty seconds before the small crowd blossomed with coloured handkerchiefs as the stench of boiling blubber descended on them. Let's get on with it, she thought; this is what you're all here for. Just then, as the party moved forward through the gates, the bearded man she had been watching came up to her.

'Excuse me,' he said, with a foreign accent, 'could you tell me, please, where I could find a telephone here? Most important.' He ran the fingers of one hand through the greying spines of his dark beard.

'I'll show you,' Queenie said, walking towards the little museum and souvenir shop outside which stood an old mounted harpoon gun and a nineteenth-century trypot. 'In there.' She indicated the pay phone in the foyer of the museum.

He nodded and went in and Queenie joined the small mob moving downhill with the song leaders in the lead. The students carried their cumbersome folios under their arms, clinging to them as if the wind might snatch them away.

Down at the flensing deck, a long ramp running into the bloody shallows, a whale was being winched up, hooks through the flukes of its tail, chains and cables moving, taut, noisy. Men hosed the platform, standing in gumboots and bloodied singlets. Plumes of putrid steam lifted from the sheds where boilers and furnaces and generators roared. Amid the bitter stench other gumbooted men wandered nonchalantly, waiting with what looked like long hockey sticks. When the whale's carcass was firmly in place and its Gargantuan presence established in the minds of the observers, these men went to

28

work with their hockey sticks and sliced deep into the glistening, black blubber and proceeded to whittle the great body down. Blubber peeled away in long, smooth strips as thick as mattresses. The ladies gasped and went closer. A young man bent over and vomited, spattering the feet of those around. Gulls arced back and forward, feathers greasy from the steam. Steadily, bloodily, the sperm whale was dismantled like a salvaged vessel.

Other whales lay moored and humped out on the water where gulls buried their heads in the huge promontory backs. A launch circled the carcasses and gunshots rippled across the water.

Queenie stood rooted, as always, watching these proceedings she had witnessed countless times since childhood. It was the smell she could not ignore. She remembered the day she brought Cleve here in the first weeks of their marriage, when Cleve had marvelled at the size of the whales and admired the men who hunted and dissected them. That evening they argued while he fried sausages and the argument became bitter and Queenie fled upstairs and he chased her and made love to her as the house filled with the stench of cremating sausages.

'Revolting.' It was the foreigner beside her.

'Hm?'

'It is a repulsive sight to the sensitive.'

'Yes,' she said.

Cameras clicked. Flensers' boots were gummed with blood; their faces, hands, beards smeared with it. Out on the glass water the launch forced up a sturdy bow-wave with an inflated, bird-backed whale in tow. As it neared, the projectile shapes of sharks showed in the water, milling, snouts disappearing into the flanks of the whale which shuddered with the impact. A man with a rifle stood at the gunwhale, shooting into the water.

'The press will be here soon,' the man who had telephoned said to someone Queenie saw from the corner of her eye.

Men moved along the abdomen with their knives and viscera began to tumble out, and soon the flensers were knee-deep. Saws sirened. Queenie concentrated on getting a glimpse of the whale's eye, but the head was obscured by loose meat as it was dragged to the upper deck.

'Soon,' the same man said to the third person. Queenie felt like an eavesdropper.

Sharks broke water all round as the launch idled in. Even gulls were seized as they settled upon the water; Queenie saw a gull's wing floating detached. The towed whale was bunted and buffeted and finally brought to the foot of the ramp, and as it was dragged from the water, tattered black and pink, a shark came up with it, still writhing into the blubber, shaking meat away with every drill-bit turn of its head. The flensers laughed, placing verbal bets, but were disappointed when the shark fell away, tumbling, snapping, down the deck into the water. The two women, handkerchiefs plastered to their faces, shook their heads at the wonder of it. Queenie heard an American accent. More thick blood; more inescapable stink.

'Bastards,' the foreigner said. He looked behind, up to the car park. 'Has been nearly twenty minutes. Now will do. Now!'

Then things began to happen and Queenie felt faint with the shock of it. From art folios all around her Queenie saw sheets of card and neat lettering; folios fell to the ground open-winged like big stiff birds and people were on the flensing deck and lying down in the blood and hosewater and shreds of meat with placards over their chests. Flensers shouted in anger and surprise. The winch ground to silence; the head-saw ceased its coming and going. The only people left standing were the station hands, the middle-aged tourists, and Queenie Cookson, and for a few seconds the only audible sounds were the slow run of water and blood down the deck into the sea and the distant crump of rifle fire. Queenie, for a few moments, could only look. Behind the prostrate, pink-saturated young people with their signs STOP THIS SLAUGHTER and BLOOD ON YOUR HEAD, PARIS BAY and BUTCHERS loomed the colossal bulk of a sperm whale which leaked from orifices and punctures. The great wound in its back exuded blood thick as lava. Queenie heard the middle-aged women shouting.

'Get off there! Go on get off there you silly irresponsible twits my God this is a disgrace I never would have thought....'

The women clenched their fists and shook their big ham-arms; and Queenie saw the flensers fidgeting at one end of the deck, and behind her she heard Barney Wilkins bellowing abuse as he came down the hill. SHAME! a sign said. Queenie

Cookson willed her feet forward and slopped across to where, in his now-bloodied cashmere sweater, the foreigner lay; and she sat, then settled into the pink slush and some cheered. From the corner of her eye she saw Barney Wilkins shaking his fist, she saw the lovable man who had driven her school bus call her names and spit on the ground. Down the hill men were running with cameras and notepads and tape-recorders. Then the young people were singing 'We Shall Overcome' and the old women were choking in disgust. Queenie, without a placard, held up the only printed matter to hand and flattened it across her chest for security's sake.

HAVE A WHALE OF A TIME IN ANGELUS, W.A. the tour guides' brochure said.

Then the cameras were there and then the flensers turned the hoses upon them, and through the haze of her nausea Queenie Cookson heard gunfire.

VI

Born fifty-eight years ago on the bar of the hotel he now owns and manages, Hassa Staats, Reformist, member of the Angelus chamber of commerce, sits back in his father's old swivel chair and shoves the papers on his desk into a ragged pile in the centre. Other men might light a cigarette at this point of completion, when Friday's paperwork is done for another week and the stocks organised and the pools and numbers finalised. But Hassa Staats lives in daily fear of cancer — he sweats in the small hours over it — and instead of a cigarette he draws from his top pocket a twist of barley sugar from which he blows a wad of lint before breaking a piece off in his teeth.

'Mara!' he calls to his wife serving in the lounge bar. 'Ask one of them lazy boggers to fill in for you; I want you to post some mail for me!'

There is no reply from the lounge bar, only a murmur of music and a click of glass. Staats calls again and when no reply is forthcoming he gathers up the mail and strides out into the lounge and is suddenly conscious of the early lunchtime

31

customers and he reins in the shout between his teeth and shoves through the glass doors onto the street. One day I'll beat the livin' crepp out of that woman, he thinks.

Out on the street his spirits rise. The new shops, new cars, new widening roads, soothe him as always; he breathes the town into his lungs: bakery-warm, cannery-sour, Tourist Bureau-fresh, and walks up from his pub near the waterfront to the post office halfway up the street. On the warm brick wall outside the post office six Aborigines sit watching. Staats, deflated, hates them for their black, blunt noses and their shaggy hair and their unmatched clothing and their rough bandages and falsetto whispers; he has always hated them. And they watch him, knowing that he is Hassa Staats the big man of the Bright Star who won't let them into his public bar, whose father sold five-gallon drums of muscat to their fathers and uncles off the back of a utility up at the Reserve, whose employees took payment from their women, and they know him and cut him with their stares.

Staats notes when he pushes the mail into the slot that he has crushed the letters in his fist and left sweaty prints on the envelopes. Passing the Aborigines soberly on his way back, he doesn't even dare spit, and he walks with his fists in the pockets of his Vinyl coat. What right do they have? he asks himself. Look over there at the Town Hall, look at them dirtying the place up with their scabby, sulking looks and jabber-jabber crepp, cluttering the most important parts of town.

Staats is the chamber of commerce member who suggested at the last meeting that the tour buses no longer park outside the Town Hall or the post office and the Wildflower Cafe, and their decision to follow his recommendation has been some compensation for him. It makes him melancholy to see the town poorly represented; he shudders to think how his father would behave if he was still alive in this town. Okke Staats had been a big, pink, meaty, fisty man who sold the Hacker Arms to the Seeds in 1950 because of the quality of clientele it had begun to attract. Hassa still fears him as he fears the distant and featureless God of his fathers.

At the corner of Goormwood Street and Harbour Terrace Staats pauses for a moment to see how work on the replica of the *Onan* is progressing. Down in front of the seventy times

32

rebuilt Residency, now a museum, lumber and pulleys and scaffolding surround the skeleton of the brig's hull. The *Onan* brought convicts and infantrymen and Governor Payne and pigs and sheep and building and agricultural supplies through the narrow neck of the harbour on 2 January 1829. In May of that year she came aground at the mouth of the Derwent River where she sank and lay until 1969 when a salvage team raised her timbers and cannon. The town of Angelus plans to have the replica of the *Onan* built for 2 January 1979 for the visiting Queen of England and her natty husband to admire.

For decades the Bright Star has been a meeting place and drinking place for the whalers. They come in around nine o'clock in the evening when their work is over; they argue and shout drinks, blow up clouds of tobacco smoke, chase women and fight amongst themselves. Hassa Staats, like his father before him, admires these men their freedom and their noble profanity. 'It was the whalers that made this country!' he often roars.

It is six in the evening and Staats has three hours to wait. He sits in the smoke-filled public bar with Ernie Easton, a retired whaleman with whom he often spends the early evening telling and hearing stories and gossip. Ernie downs glass after glass, tantalising Staats with withheld information; he enjoys the discomfort of listeners, an old habit acquired as a seaman

'Yes,' Staats agrees impatiently, 'the *Onan*'s coming along nicely. Make a good boost for publicity.'

'Reckon they'll get it done orright,' Easton says. 'Only hope the bloody Residency holds up another six months; been fallin' down since I was a kid.'

'Before,' says Staats whose father taught him the town's history.

'Comes down like bloody autumn.'

Staats nods. He wishes Ernie Easton would tell him the gossip he is withholding. Sometimes, he thinks, I could wring the little bogger's neck; he's nothin' but a dried up barnacle and he's stuck to this pub as a good lurk. Staats orders him another beer on the house.

'Saw ol' Dick and Darcy yesterd'y evening,' Ernie Easton

says, his squid-beak of a mouth hooked over the glass. 'They sent a cheerio and asked could I get 'em another couple of bottles of VO. Said the fish were bitin' too good to leave.'

'Okay,' Staats says, 'I'll get one of the girls to set you up with a couple of botts.'

'Shall I tell 'em it's on the house?'

'It's always on the bloody house.' Staats scowls. Twenty years he has been the old men's patron, a duty left to him by his father on his deathbed. Some say Dick and Darcy are brothers born Siamese twins, and others say they were fishermen who became lovers, and still others claim they are the same deformed person. As a younger man Hassa Staats lay awake nights contemplating this mystery; but age and weariness and parenthood have blunted his curiosity and left him with other things to keep him awake.

'They was talkin' about that young fella Queenie Coupar married, the one they caught in the raw on the beach,' Ernie Easton says. 'They reckon he's just had his first weddin' anniversary.'

'Yeah, must be a year since she married the stupid bogger.'

Ernie Easton giggles. 'They watch him through the holes in the shed.'

'They what?' Staats says, delighted.

'They say he's readin' old books and he had a blue with his missus. She's — *was* the tour guide for the Bureau.'

'Reads old books, eh?' Staats says. 'What sort?'

'About her mob, they reckon.'

'How do they know?'

'God knows.'

'The Coupars. That girl must've been a lame one to get caught with the likes of him. *Therefore a man leaves his father and mother and cleaves to his wife*...lazy bludger.'

Staats recalls an evening when he was drawn into conversation with Cookson. Being a journalist and a city boy did the young man little good in the Bright Star. Staats remembers the cowed, slack slope of his shoulders, the look of a poorly transplanted seedling. A weed, Staats thought. Staats and Cookson had spoken about local history, about the Goormwood grave, about the whalers, about the Coupars at Wirrup and the old house overlooking the harbour where the old Misses Coupar once lived. They talked about the convict races and Staats told him the Seeds were the alcoholic remnant of James Seed, the last surviving convict before Angelus ceased to be a penal colony. Staats informed the young man that his, Cookson's, wife was descended from Nathaniel Coupar, American deserter, who appeared in Angelus one morning in 1831.

'Settlers put him up for weeks until he was fit and a bit more sane,' Staats told him. 'The ship he scuttled sank with all hands a day out of the Sound. People got suspicious about Coupar. He did some smuggling, some labouring, cut sandalwood, shot roos, sold American grog to the pubs. Got quite a fortune together, they say, and bought that land out east at Wirrup. Seemed a bit funny about the place. Anyway, he made a piece of land out of it. Coupars been there ever since, off and on.' Staats had found himself wanting to slap the boy on the back for marrying into history, but he refrained, overcome by a feeling of distaste.

'Tell me your news, Ernie,' Staats says. 'I've been feedin' you beer all afternoon.'

The pub is filling. Darts thump into the wall. The TV above the bar flashes and winks with city news.

'First the good news.'

'That means there's bad news.'

'Hass, yer a bright one, I can't dispute it. Good news is that Ted Baer has got his boat at the town jetty and he's back in town for a crack at the world record for shark catchin'.'

'Ah, now that is good news. Good for Angelus, plenty of news coverage. Now there's a real man.'

'Yep.'

'What's the bad news?'

'There was a circus at the whaling station today. A pro-test.'

'*What?*' Staats yells, standing, as if to defend himself. 'Didn't anyone do anything? And no one told me?'

'There's more.'

'*More?*'

'Queenie Coupar was one of 'em. She took 'em out on a tour and paraded with 'em. They're foreigners.'

'Bogger me!'

'There's more.'

Hassa Staats sits down shakily. 'How can there be more?'

'Three of 'em are with Queenie Coupar in there playing pool.' Ernie Easton points to the door marked CLUB BAR.

VII

'So who are you all, then?' Queenie Cookson said, fingering her stiff, bloodied clothes.

'We call ourselves Cachalot & Company,' said the man who had introduced himself as Georges Fleurier in the taxi on the way back from Paris Bay.

'Cachalot. That's another name for the sperm whale, isn't it?'

'Yes,' he said, pulling at his clotted beard. His cashmere sweater was black and crusty. Two other Cachalot members chipped coloured balls into pockets beneath a white fluorescent light.

'You're French,' she said.

'Yes,' Fleurier said casually. 'And he's American. The other is Canadian.'

'And I'm an accomplice,' she said.

'An activist,' said one of the pool players, between chinks of ivory—the American.

'Never heard of Cachalot & Company,' Queenie said, sipping her Guinness.

'We are three weeks old,' Fleurier said. 'We came to join some Australians to close down Paris Bay.'

'And,' the American pool player said, 'our Aussie friends have screwed up.' His face was shiny, hard and creased like pigskin. 'Our little introductory effort out there today is wasted because our Zodiacs haven't turned up. And they won't turn up, I know it. If you'd like to know, Zodiacs are inflatable boats, okay?'

'Hey, nice lady,' the other pool player, a short man with a wild sphere of hair said, 'we have a problem. We need a boat.'

'Charter? You? In this town?'

'Yeah,' the hair-mass said, shooting his white ball into a pocket.

36

'You haven't got a chance.'

'You're kidding,' the hairy pool shooter said, conceding two shots to his opponent. 'This is a fishing village; there's boats.'

'This is not a village and you'll never get a boat.'

'We have money enough,' the Frenchman said, sipping his vodka. The hotel had fallen quiet; they didn't notice.

'You can't buy friends in this town,' Queenie lied.

'Can you tell us where we might ask?' the Frenchman said.

'The fisherman's harbour. I could ask for you. No, let me think about it,' she said, annoyed by the pool players, and a little afraid. She had just lost her job with the Bureau, been cursed by an old friend, and washed in a whale's blood; the accents made her dizzy and she felt an exhilaration and a compulsion and some shaft of doubt. As she sat tilting the milky black stout in her glass, the swing door to the public bar slapped back on its hinges and the barmaids stopped pouring, every pool player stopped shooting, and the mottled jowls of Hassa Staats began to work.

It was dark and street lights buzzed and sputtered and tinkled with moths as Queenie Cookson walked uptown with Georges Fleurier. The two pool players walked ahead, talking loudly, looking into shop windows.

'Who are your friends?' Queenie asked, shakily, still quivering with embarrassment.

'Marks, the American—'

'With the face like a wallet?'

'Yes, he is a strandings expert,' Fleurier said. 'Perhaps you would like his credentials?' he said sourly.

'Hope they're better than his pool playing.'

'The other is Brent. Brent is our media organiser, a hippy, a nut, a musician.'

'Marvellous!' Queenie sighed. 'Strandings. That's when whales suicide, isn't it?'

'Suicide? An inappropriate term.'

'I've seen it happen.' Queenie recalled the wallowing bulk of a pygmy sperm grinding through shallows, inching, cudgelling the water with its tail, being forsaken by the receding surf. Had she seen it at the age of six she might have thought her wait over, that a messenger from God had finally come; but she was sixteen and the event struck her as brutal, not mysterious.

'And you still think they suicide? Such an intelligent species? Do you know the size of a sperm whale's brain? Do you know what goes on in that enormous cavity?'

'No more than you, I suppose,' Queenie said, crossing the street with him.

'You are not stupid.'

'Thanks. I'll rest easy now.'

'I mean it.'

She shrugged, suspicious of him; there was a casual rudeness about him that aggravated her.

'Death is a testament,' Fleurier said, holding a finger in the air as though testing the wind. 'One can learn a great deal about the life and mind of something from the manner in which it dies. Marks is a valuable man because he has studied the deaths of many whales. He is man of great compassion.'

'If you happen to be a whale,' Queenie said.

They walked a few moments in silence past a group of Aborigines who sat quietly on the steps of the Town Hall, showing the whites of teeth and eyes and bandages.

'You're going to get trouble, you know,' she said.

'The people are apathetic,' Fleurier said. 'Or perhaps sympathetic.'

'It's the accents,' she said. 'As soon as you try another stunt, as soon as you threaten anything, anything at all—even that bloody stupid grave in the middle of the main street—they'll change. People don't want anything unless it's likely to be taken from them.'

Queenie heard herself quoting her grandfather; he had said it many times. 'You call what happened in the pub apathy? Believe me, you'll have trouble.' She felt a curious and dangerous mixture of feelings: half of her wanted to defend the town against these invaders, the other half of her made her wish she was one of them. 'How did you get mixed up in this game, anyway?' she said, irritable.

'It is no game.'

'Well, why the whales?'

'My father was a diver and I dived with him and I learnt some things about the sea and the balance of life and the

38

possibility of cetacean intelligence. My father was a fool. He dove with Cousteau and Dumas in the Mediterranean. He wasted his life and talent on wrecks and salvage and mystery. He said he wanted to find some answers about Man—as if Hitler and Hiroshima didn't tell us all we needed—and he was looking for Atlantis, the lost civilisation. My father drowned in a swimming pool in Spain when I was twenty. Do you see the irony in that? He was a fool, a dear fool, and he found nothing. He didn't realise that his life was a waste of time. People allowed him to chase relics instead of guiding him towards the future, and our future lies in communication between the species, co-existence with the environment. Not in the follies of the past.'

'You're probably right.'

'Perhaps we think alike.'

'Perhaps,' she said. 'Is this where you're staying?' They stood outside the Angelus Motor Lodge where in the gardens at the front a concrete whale spouted a fountain.

'Yes,' he said. 'We are all here. Our Australian comrades must all be in bed. Did you notice all the concrete whales in this town are smiling?' he said, reaching into his shoulder bag.

'Another irony, I think you'd call it.'

'Yes,' he smiled grimly. 'Here.' He took from his bag a crumpled manila folder. 'Read this. I have ten more, all different. I carry my brain around in scrapbooks.'

Queenie took it and thanked him and walked home, taut inside.

In the warmth of the kitchen with its familiar friendly smells of apples and capsicums, and the sweet furry smell of last season's apricots still emanating from the fruit baskets which made her think of summer and Cleve and indestructible moments of happiness, Queenie flicked through the loose pages in the manila folder: excerpts from journals and newspapers, books and television scripts, government documents, copies, carbons, cuttings in no apparent order.

> ... *Corpora albicantia*: scars on the ovaries of rorquals and humpbacks. Each scar = liberation of one egg....

39

... whereas earlier in whale research, stainless steel darts were shot from a twelve-bore gun into the backs of the whales as markings. To lodge properly the projectile had to penetrate deep into the muscles of the back. . . .

A humpback whale once found with 1,000 lbs of barnacles adhering to it. Humpbacks, it is said, migrating up Africa's west coast will often move close to the coast specifically where the Congo flows into the sea, to kill their barnacles off in the fresh water . . . it is also said that sail-boats were taken there for the same reason.

i. no need of whaling industry ii. mercury levels iii. population studies suspect iv. sperm whale intelligence v. method of killing (150 lb. grenade harpoon).

Paris Bay, Angelus, W.A. Last land operation in Australia. 1975 quota: 1,395. Average size of 42.7 feet. One whale = 3 tons whalemeal (stock, poultry feed, fertiliser), 8 tons oil (margarine, lard, confectionery, soap, candles, cosmetics, textiles, detergents, paints, plastics).

1963 humpback whale protected/recovery 100 years.

. . . even the killer whale has not been found guilty of homicide. . . .

. . . in the Azores found a 47 foot sperm with a 405 lb squid in its stomach, 34 feet across . . . sucker marks from tentacles 4 inches across. *Architeuthis dux*, the largest-known species of squid, known to fight sperm whales.

Humpbacks and southern right whales migrating north close to shore were easy prey for bay whalers who operated in small parties in the early 1800s. . . .

Whales make a variety of groans, ticks and high whistles which, it can be assumed, are used in communication as well as echo-location.

. . . that each whale has a unique voice, as do humans, and that it is theoretically possible for this communication to be understood and interpreted by humans . . . a kind of sensual telepathy. . . .

. . . have always been the objects of superstition. Jonah of the ancient myth, for instance. . . .

Closing the folder, she looked out on the lights of the harbour, the metallic wharf lights, the yellowish glow of the dog-legged deepwater jetty and felt a long way from the homely timber scents and colours and sounds of the old house in which she had always dreamed of living. She put on her coat and mittens; they smelled faintly of damp and mildew. Her stomach was hard as a knot of wet, shrunken rope. She put one of Cleve's woollen scarves on; it smelled of him. Outside it was so cold it made her squint.

VIII

Angelus vibrates with the news this Friday evening, and behind the offices of the *Advocate* the press clatters out tomorrow morning's headline: WHALE FRACAS. Tomorrow the high school debating team will test the issue against good locution, and butchers, as they wrap and snap, will mention the incident at Paris Bay as an addendum to the price per kilo, raising pruned forefingers reasonably to make their point; but tonight there are the meetings. Taxi drivers sit chastised and bitching in the Royal Albert recounting the afternoon's lucrative but forbidden fares. Waterside workers meet to contemplate another strike. The Rotary Club meets, the yacht club meets, the chamber of commerce meets, the meatworkers meet, the Masons meet and the men of the town tire of one another's company as committees are formed, re-formed, malformed, deformed, dissolved.

Twenty miles offshore, ploughing through a heavy swell as the rain thrashes rust from rails and catwalks, three whale-chasers keep desultory radio contact.

Tonight the sesquicentenary has been forgotten: women have suspended the sewing of period costumes; papier-mâché models of placid natives are left wet and incomplete. Tonight the talk is of whales and invasion. Offshore a small pod of humpback whales moves slowly north-west along the coast to warmer and warmer water.

There is a particular kind of unselfconscious manner a man who has lived and dined most of his life alone will employ at table. William Pell displays this hunched over his dinner, chewing, smoking, reading. Were his mother alive, were he still an oversized, taciturn boy on the farm outside town, Pell would have the back of his neck stung with a floral teatowel and his old, hoary father would stare grimly from the end of the table and say, 'Your mother is a goodun with a teatowel, Billy,' and attend to his soup.

Pell's father, born in 1842, lived to be eighty-eight; William's sister Elizabeth was born in 1867, forty-one years before him. She was the only one of his brothers and sisters he ever met, and he loved her above all else. She was a nurse. In 1916 she died in Flanders of typhoid. It was then that William, six years old, decided that wars were not good, that nurses died like normal people, that King George's letters were signed by a machine in red ink, and that his sister Elizabeth was a saint. He told his father who had wept for a week that he wanted to be like Elizabeth. I want to be good, he said. Anderson Pell who had once, when asked by an old swaggie for a pound of flour and a blanket, undressed completely on the veranda where he stood and given the sojourner all his clothes in a bundle, looked up from his weeping and said, quoting by heart: '*He has showed you, O man, what is good; and what does the Lord require of you but to do justice, and to love kindness and to walk humbly with your God?*' William, standing at the dam's edge with his father, watching a long and a short reflection in the water, gripped his father's bony old leg and said: 'Then I should?' whereupon his father took him up in his arms, kissed him wetly about the face and tossed him, with a laugh, into the dam.

Anderson Pell died in 1930 a very old man. Every now and then Pell will remember washing his father's body, helped by his dry-eyed mother. He remembers a lamp burning, cicadas drumming, a thick warm sense of peace. Pell was at theological college in Sydney when his mother died in 1936 and he made the long journey home to Angelus by train, like a man in a vacuum. The white heat of the Nullabor Plain did not touch him. When he returned he found his mother buried and young Daniel Coupar beaten: the Pustlings controlled the town.

Already Pell is tired and aching, even before the sleepless night ahead. Night has come and the air contracts with the

42

promise of rain. Singing floats across the damp lawn from the church hall as the Ladies' Guild strides through Sankey's songbooks. He sits for a while with his big hands around a tiny cup of espresso coffee, listening and thinking. He cannot help but recall the faces in the street today; they were somehow thin and fragile as though underneath there was a force which threatened to craze and shatter and explode the heads from their shoulders. Yes, he thinks, that's how Queenie Cookson looked just now when I saw her pass, as though she might fall to the ground and scream. Poor Queenie, what'll you do with yourself now? The gossip has reached him; the town knows. Sipping his coffee, Pell remembers her as a child, something she once wrote during one of his dull sermons in the safe sixties when the world's problems didn't exist, when everyone seemed to have a job, when the Aborigines were a bad memory from mission days. From the pulpit he saw her intent upon it, scribbling away, and after the service he asked her what she had written that was more interesting than his sermon on charity. She shrugged and gave it to him and Daniel and Maureen Coupar shrugged with her.

'Now where is that?' Pell says, suddenly compelled to find it. 'Such a long time ago.' He gets up with a groan and goes into his office and digs around in his filing cabinets until he draws out a crumpled sheet with a triumphant chortle. 'I did keep it. Well, well. Queenie Coupar, weren't you a girl!'

THE BEGGER

The begger stole my eggs
He cut off his babies arms and legs
The people took pitty
And gave him money, and also some honey,
all in a small paper bag.

Some of the beggers slept out in the cold
Some of the beggers were young or old
Babies with arms and babies with none
This was not thrilling I can tell you now.
Believe me!

Soon the beggers left the town,
without a sound!

43

*Then in the morning we heard not a
word and new that the beggers had
gone, and the town was free to rome.*

'*Queenie C, 10 yrs old,*' he had written.

'*Whoever humbles himself like this child* ... why couldn't
we be born old and grow young?'

Then Pell takes his big body to work. Whorls of dust dance
as he empties his storeroom of its boxes and cartons, carrying
them outside to the rented truck parked at the side of the
house. After three-quarters of an hour, his whole body
trembling with fatigue, he finally loads up the last of it and ties
the flaps of the canvas canopy. The piano still chugs in the
church hall as Pell starts the diesel engine and manoeuvres
inexpertly out onto the road. Within a few minutes he
accustoms himself to the clutch and the gears and the vehicle's
bulk; it has been a long time since he drove pigs to market as a
farmer's son.

Hassa Staats walks without noticing the sound of rain coming
up from the south, conscious only of a constriction he cannot
see, some tautness in his chest. When he felt like this as a young
man he would go for long runs to burn the tightness out. These
days a good run would kill him, so he walks with a heavy,
deliberate gait. Now Staats's chest pain is like nothing from his
youth.

He finds himself, after several minutes' walking, turning,
walking, in Port Park above the miry tennis courts. The park is
in darkness, the gardens are invisible windbreaks, he smells
roses and that dandelion smell of boyhood, his shoes scuff wet
grass. Hassa Staats knows this park well in the dark; he stands
against the ancient cannon, pulls a Coke can from its snout
and a handful of maple leaves. He tosses the can—poink-
poink—across the grass and rubs his knuckles in the wet musty
muzzle-hole. A car passes up on the road, sheeting light across
the gardens and lawns. A drinking fountain mutters, leaking.
Staats walks down to the bottom of the gardens with a view of
the glittering harbour that is barely used, and sits on the big
stormwater pipe where once a freshwater spring gouted. His

buttocks spread on the cold concrete, Hassa Staats is thinking of that night twenty-five years ago when, in the dank, circular dark of this pipe, he and Mara (then a milkman's pretty daughter) grovelled together long and effectively enough to cause the eventual birth of their son Rick. Before Rick was born they were hastily but elegantly married in the Dutch Reformed Hall. Staats remembers the beating his father gave him when he confessed his night in the pipe. Okke Staats might also have beaten Mara Cleekopoorn had she not been five unmistakeable months pregnant. Can't even recall if it was a good go, he thinks. Can't remember a damn thing about it, except the whipping half a year later.

What a day, he thinks, what a day for this town. People coming from everywhere, from *outside*, to tell this town how to live, to shut down *our* whaling station, then having the gall to come into my hotel and drink my beer and play my pool, and the granddaughter of Daniel Coupar among them. People don't even know how to treat their enemies these days. Bad things, this town's coming to. Oh, the whalers, they're not worried, nothing frightens them: don't know if they aren't too dumb to worry. So damned confident, as if nothing, not even God Almighty, could take away the whaling. They're the only ones not afraid of the dole office. This town, this town! I saw them today in the barbershops, all the old timers talkin' about what they're gonna do to these bloody foreigners when they catch up with 'em. We're gonna need more'n old men to get rid of this lot. The people of this town have forgotten how to be strong.

'Oh, God, don't let them take the whalers away,' he says. He is frightened at the prospect of there being no whalers in his pub five nights a week. It isn't the money—he'd give them beer on the house, pour it down their throats to keep them there; but if they were no longer allowed to work as he had always known them to, then they would become has-beens like Ernie Easton, human, sad, silly, soft, and he could have no respect for them as an institution, and Angelus would die for him.

Hassa Staats makes his way out of the blackness of the park and down a rain-slicked path; he pulls his Vinyl collar up and walks, shaking the drops of water from his bulbous nose.

An hour later when the rain has thickened and he is still

45

walking up and down, he sees Queenie Cookson moving down the steep terrace towards the harbour; he knows it is her, he knows that hair. He watches her go hurriedly down in the rain. He cannot think of a foul enough name to call out to her and, in any case, his heart is not in it.

Des Pustling, eating at the Colonial with his private secretary Marion Lowell, finds the sound of the rain soothing. It has been a long day for him and he has worked hard. Thus far, it has been a pleasant evening, except for the mishap of the tooth dropping into his wine glass, about which he is sure his secretary is ignorant. He is wrong.

Pustling is grateful that he doesn't have an ulcer; he prides himself on it. He is the only man of commerce in the town without one, or so he thinks; he considers Hassa Staats, for instance, as too stupid to be able to sustain an ulcer. He is wrong again. Pustling is a poor judge of character and sometimes he knows it, though it never bothers him: he knows his talents.

Ignoring the yellowish lozenge in the bottom of his glass, Pustling sips his twenty-dollar-a-bottle Chablis with satisfaction and looks across at Marion Lowell, a big-boned woman in her thirties who has been in his complete employ for a number of years.

'Enjoying your jewfish?'

'Yes,' she says.

'Did I ever tell you about my father?' he asks, sucking the new tender spot in his gum.

'Yes,' Marion Lowell says, pausing with a spoonful of tartare sauce.

'He was a man who knew the pleasure of competition. Competition's so important. When he came to this town in 1929 he had some pretty stiff competition from farmers. It was a boom time for him — a Depression for everyone else — and the task was to buy up every skerrick of land available. Farmers were crying out for buyers, land was dirt cheap, if you'll forgive the expression. But the excitement for him was the opposition from a small group of farmers led by a young fella, now quite an old fella, called Coupar, who didn't even own a farm at the time.'

46

'Yes,' Marion Lowell says, listening to the sound of rain. Others in the restaurant speak in demure, timid tones; Pustling always speaks louder in a quiet place.

'Oh, they burnt their own farms and slaughtered their own stock like on some Western movie, tried all the tricks, but my Dad bought them all out regardless. Even if he did sell them back during the war,' he says with a wink. 'Nowadays the challenge isn't the same. Been sewn up for a long time and the locals have gotten used to the idea. No challenge, is what I mean. I can see why God keeps the Devil on, you know; it's to stop him from getting bored. Imagine how bored God must get. So I play games — small scale, but fun enough. I mean you can only go up, can't you? Enjoying the jewfish?'

'Yes.'

Des Pustling pictures his dead father: a tall, thin, handsome man. Benjamin Pustling was a man of impeccable deportment and lethal elegance; he smoked a briar pipe and spoke Oxford English and walked like a man on a tightrope. He mourned for years the death of his wife Clarissa who died giving birth to his son Desmond, and he never showed his disappointment with what she had died delivering. You can't blame a messenger for his message, he often said. Within a decade of his arrival in Angelus, Benjamin Pustling became its landlord. In the winter of 1932 a dour, steadfast young man who had been dispossessed of his ancestral land long before, tried to retard Pustling's progress. There was a hunger march, a food-parcel program, a rent embargo, and young Coupar became a threat. Men and women were occupying the idle cannery and sleeping in the church and the Town Hall. Church services were held in the street, on the wharf, and the young man addressed the tattered crowd in his uncertain but plangent voice. Men and women were attracted to him; he kept them angry and they gained confidence from him and he spent his savings on them. It was when he began preaching to them from the Scriptures that the mood changed. Church authorities from the city visited. The townspeople grew suspicious and they gossiped. Pustling reopened the cannery to a few workers to keep the machinery from going to rust, paying them a few shillings more than the dole. Public meetings petered out; Daniel Coupar began to avoid company, secluding himself in the old house overlooking the harbour. To cement his victory, Pustling

47

allowed the old Coupar property at Wirrup to be auctioned in 1939. Martin Coupar had died penniless in 1920 and the land had been sold to pay his debts. Daniel Coupar and his mother were evicted and no Coupar had owned it since. Pustling's auction went as planned. It was no miracle that Coupar's pitiful bids remained unopposed. Pustling himself patrolled the crowd. Coupar was given his land. Pustling was left with his town. For decades, Coupar remained a figure of history, of rumour, and no one saw him. 'Pride,' Benjamin Pustling said to his son, who forgot it, 'is the best thing there is. It has made us what we are. It never fails. It's the only thing the Catholics will give seven out of seven.' In 1950 Benjamin Pustling died. Every citizen of Angelus was present. Old men and women brought wreaths and spat on the coffin.

'How's that jewfish, fine?'

'Yes,' Marion Lowell says.

'Had a chat to a few people about what happened at Paris Bay today. I don't think we'll have any more trouble. Did you know that that Tweetie, or whatever her name is, got involved in it all? My God, we'll have to do something about this town. I've lost another tooth, you know,' he says, swilling the lozenge around in his glass.

'Oh?' Marion says, feigning surprise.

'Yes. There's one there in my glass.'

'Really?'

'Yes. Every time I lose a set I wonder if it will by my last. Frightening.' Since his baby teeth sprouted painfully in his gums and had stayed a while and fallen out and were replaced with adult teeth, Des Pustling has had four other sets of teeth. When he was nine years old his first adult teeth began falling from his mouth like ripe fruit. Children at school were delighted and they changed his nickname from Pus-knob to Pus-gums. He was fitted with a snug set of dentures with which to smile away all insults like his father, but these were soon uprooted by a new set of teeth which seemed to germinate spontaneously and the school's favourite tongue-twister became 'puscusp', often reversed to 'spucsup' or 'spucpus', then 'puscups' and finally 'suckpus'. Pustling's classmates found him endlessly entertaining and he was never without companions. In 1948 when he was studying Law he shed teeth again and left

48

the city for good. It happened again when he was thirty, again when he was forty. 'You don't mind, do you?' he asks.

Marion Lowell sips Chablis. 'No,' she says, remembering the girl with the laugh.

'Good. I think we'll have some fun with Pell in the next month or so. I don't like men who play with my money.'

'He seems to think it's God's money,' she says carefully.

'What would *he* know about God? He's got a demented view of God, a sick man's God. Widows, orphans, aliens, cripples. Whatever happened to the chariots of fire and the floods and famines and fights? Pell is stuck at the wet end of the Bible, I can tell you. Silly old fart. Camels and needles, ah.'

Marion Lowell drinks her Chablis without comment.

'At least I haven't got an ulcer,' Pustling says as a kind of benediction.

In the bedroom of the Middle Beach house built by Benjamin Pustling in 1945, Des Pustling applies himself like a hot poultice to Marion Lowell who twitches and grits. Once, she endured this pinioning out of ambition; now it is desperation. Pustling wallows and totters and sweats and squeaks. Marion Lowell is ashamed and disgusted and pinned and invaded by a viscous but sterile torrent.

She lies awake long after he tumbles off, asleep. He is too horrible to hate, she thinks, his toenails are too horny, his breath too foul, his girdle too pathetic. I don't hate him. But she can not find another word for the emotion she feels as the clock strikes midnight and Pustling farts thunderously in his sleep and the rain falls.

'I was eating rainbow trout, you bastard,' she whispers. Surf breaks down on the beach.

IX

Cleveland Cookson read with the thunder of rain in his ears. Water hissed and the rats scuttled about, agitated. He thought: Friday night, things have changed.

49

June 16, 1831 Nowles is gravely ill with fever and pain and although it should by all rights be another day until my turn to row, I must fill a place in our boat by reason of the accident. Churling, Doan, Smithson and I will take turn at rowing and lookout. Hale does not row; he is considered a disadvantage. I pray God keep me safe.

June 17, 1831 Night, raining, bitterly cold. A ration of rum issued this afternoon, though none sent up to Churling in the lookout atop the hill. When I mentioned this oversight some man muttered that he, Churling, would need no spiritous warming when he returned. This puzzles me. My senses are dulled by weariness and a sort of revulsion for my comrades. Later I will go down to the tryworks to stoke the fires. The stench of boiling blubber permeates all, even in this rain. The blackfellows have left more roots and have hacked pieces from the putrid carcass up the beach.

Nowles stirs and is muttering. The lamplight has a sickly hue this night. Men sit about playing crude games of chance. The dogs howl. Churling must be coming back from the end of the watch. The dogs' howl is not unlike poor Nowles'.

All Cleve felt was the cold rush of air; he heard nothing, but he looked up from the journal and saw Queenie inside the door in her glistening, wet-wool-smelling greatcoat. She was pale and chilled and panting. Rain lacerated the water outside. Their eyes met.

'Hi,' he said, at length, feeling surprise and resentment, yet a longing for her.

'Hello,' she replied.

'Shouldn't you be in bed?'

'Has my reputation in town gotten that bad?'

Cleve squinted. 'Eh?'

Queenie stopped unbuttoning her coat. 'You don't know? My God.'

'Close the door.'

Queenie did so and moved around the desk and read over his shoulder, '*The lamplight has a sickly hue this night*...know how the old bugger feels.'

'Tell me.'

'You won't like it.'

50

'I get that impression. Go on.'

'I was involved in a demonstration today at Paris Bay. I got caught up in it, they were my bus tour—'

'Who?'

'Cachalot & Company.'

'*What?*'

'Listen, Cleve, I'm trying to tell you,' she said, shaking water from her coat. She looked sodden and helpless and hard to blame. 'I got caught up and the *Advocate* boys were there and it got a bit unpleasant and Barney Wilkins just left us all there and—and anyway I got the bullet from the Bureau and I s'pose I'm sort of glad. I feel I've done something useful for the first time in my life.'

'Well stuff me,' Cleve said quietly, rubbing the bristles of his chin. 'And it takes you until bloody midnight to come and tell me. Who are they? What the hell business have they got coming into this town? What are you *doing?*'

'We're planning—'

'We? *We?*'

'—something bigger, much bigger—'

'Queenie, for Godsake!'

She reached a hand out to his mottled cheek but withdrew it, afraid of the look on his face. Rain hammered the tin shed. 'No, for the whales' sake, Cleve.'

'Oh, shit, I don't believe it. This Mickey Mouse show's got you talking like a sentimental twit. You're trying to close down the whaling station right now when there's never been as many people out of work since the Depression, when there's a drought out east and cockies are just walking off their farms. The canning factory—for Godsake—is already working off a skeleton staff and you wanna close the whalers down?'

'It's not so many jobs,' Queenie said.

'It's a lot of jobs to those blokes with family to feed.'

'Cleve, you don't give a stuff about whaler's families; all you're worried about—'

'Listen here, if you want to change things you write to your MP.'

'And do you know what MP stands for in Angelus? Mate-of-Pustling. There's no time to change everything from the top down. The whales are dying out, being exterminated and you

51

know it's a fact.'

'Oh, facts,' Cleve sighed. 'You're not into facts, you're all into emotions.'

'Us all. Us all. You're never met us all. Oh, God!'

'The town's gonna go wild,' Cleve said, shaking his head.

'Oh, the bloody town — who knows? It's just as likely to let it all happen without lifting a finger. Passion and inertia go well together in this town. Anyway, bugger the town, it's buggered us.'

'My reputation blossoms daily.'

'You mean you're ashamed of me?'

'Yes.'

Queenie walked across the hut and slumped into an old cane chair, fingering twists of her hair. 'Well, I've always been a bit ashamed of you, I s'pose. Evens it up. Georges was right, deep down people are arseholes.'

'Georges, eh?' Cleve sneered.

'Yes, he's French. His father dived with Cousteau.'

'Well, the sun does shine out of his arse, then. Permanent spot of sunlight between his heels wherever he walks.'

'Shut up.'

The rain on the water became a menacing sound; inside the hut it was hot, smelly, damp. Their breathing was excited and painful, bringing an ambiguity into the room.

'What is it about these whales?' Cleve asked, not wanting to let this peter out into a vicious silence. 'They're just animals, you know. Okay, it doesn't look all that good on the flensing deck and the smell's a bit ripe; but we both eat meat, it's the same at the abattoirs. Some animals are killed so we survive.'

'And some, you silly prick, don't need to be killed. We don't eat them. Even the by-products are all obsolete. Geez, Cleve, do you know how big a whale's brain cavity is? We could be killing the most intelligent companions we have.'

'You don't seem to remember that we've been killing other people for longer.'

'You sound proud of it.'

'You sound pathetic.'

'I am — look who I married. I thought you'd understand,' she said, bitterly. 'Bugger you, I thought you'd at least listen. You never listen any more, all you ever do is read this crap,' she said, pointing to the journal on the table. 'You can't *do* anything else!'

'Oh, it keeps me out of trouble.' He grinned. 'You should try something your —'

It was then that Queenie got up and swept the journal from the table, snapping it shut as it yawned open, and Cleve grabbed at her and the table teetered and fell and she fenced him away and was suddenly on all fours with the book tight in the space between floorboards with all her weight pushing down on it and him screaming at the thought of years falling away unread, sinking into the Sound. He straddled the fallen table and his fist came down on her back and she went flat.

For a few moments all he could do was listen to her winded gasps and the tick of blood in his own ears; he saw the heaving of her back, the shaking gossamer drops of rain still on her coat and in her hair, the flattened arc of her spine. With each breath she seemed to gain strength and harden. Then he bent down close and saw that her face was tightly screwed, squeezing moisture out. Her cheek rested against the upright spine of the bitter-smelling book. Her tears stained the plank floor and she dribbled like a child from the corner of her mouth. Outside, a splash like a bottle hitting water. Trickles of rain ratted their way down the walls.

'Queenie?' He wished the last five minutes of his life could have been erased. For starters. He felt his testicles shrivel at the memory of those other hundreds of moments, years, he would dearly love to be stripped of.

'I'm sorry,' he said. 'That was stupid, very, very stupid.' He ran his hand feebly through her hair, stricken with a desire to bury himself in it, find a cool, dark hiding place in it.

'No,' she whispered, 'not stupid; bloody unforgivable.'

He did not dare touch her when she left. The journal stuck up out of the floor, wedged between the planks, like a tombstone. The rain stopped and started. He went down to the landing, feeling almost drunk with emotion. Dick and Darcy were staring, befuddled, at a small herring that flipped and turned like a misshapen new coin. It had a big, ragged piece of meat and the hook halfway down its gullet and the old men

53

looked at him as if to say the fish had caught itself, as if to say they wanted absolution from this event. But Cleve was too full, too drunk with shock, to speak to them.

At three thirty, two men stood outside the shed on the deepwater jetty, exhausted. Cleve Cookson opened the door at their knock and reluctantly bade them enter. He knew by their clothes and their accents and the way they looked about uncertainly that they were not seamen. He separated himself from them, moving behind his desk; he didn't ask them to sit. He sat, spread his hands out on the table.

'Someone said we might find a boat through you,' Fleurier said.

'Did...they?' Cleve looked at his hands, surprised by the wide span of his fingers; he had never noticed how big his hands were and he felt the two men were watching them also.

'That you might set us up with a connection, seeing you're well situated here,' Marks said, his big pigskin pores shifting about on his face. 'We need something about thirty-forty feet, fast, reliable, you know.'

'Where?' Cleve asked, sensing a new position of power, enjoying his importance, even if it was only illusion. He had no influence with seamen in this harbour.

'Long trips, far as the Shelf, further, maybe.'

'That's some ride. Fishing, are you? Marlin? Sharks?'

'No.'

'What then?'

'That is our business,' Fleurier said, irritated.

'Listen, buddy, we're not crooks,' Marks said. 'We pay like anyone else. We'll pay good money, ultra-good money.'

'And who'll organise the insurance? What skipper in this harbour would be able to get insurance for the sort of sight-seeing you've got planned? To say nothing about where he's going to live after he does the job. Angelus wouldn't be the same for him, you know what I mean? People in small towns like this stick together. They don't want you here.'

'Are you the spokesman for the town?' Fleurier asked, finger pointing at the soft part between Cleve's eyes.

'Well, I haven't been voted in, but'—he smiled—'I don't

suppose the whales've gone to the polls about you, either, eh?'

'Then you won't help us?'

'Not even if I could, mate.'

'We have a right to be heard,' Fleurier said, hands signalling his fatigue and his desperation.

'My guess is that tomorrow morning you won't be able to buy a Mars Bar in this town. They wouldn't let you piss in a public toilet. People are gonna lose their jobs over you.'

'Well what sort of a goddam town is this?' Marks said, fumbling in his pockets for a cigarette.

'A whaling town, mate.'

'Full of goddam hicks.'

'Look, I don't wanna sit here and argue about bloody whales all night: my answer is no.'

'You won't think about it?' Marks said, dropping the anger from his voice in a last effort.

'It would please Queenie,' Fleurier said with a quiet precision.

Cleve slammed his chair back against the wall as he stood, lifting his hands from the table. 'You ever use that on me I'll kill you.'

'I was told that you were an enlightened and intelligent man, Mr Cookson.' Fleurier smiled. 'Perhaps you are only a violent one?'

'Get out of here before you find out.'

The two men left the hut, slamming the door with a force that shook the walls and silenced the gnawing of rats. Cleve stood in the cloud of smoke Marks had left, still smelling their presence in the room. He listened to their footsteps and observed his own big, shaking, shameful hands. He cocked his ear: something different. The footfalls hammered confusedly, still audible over the intensifying rain. Cleve opened the door and peered outside, but saw nothing; even the irregular floodlights were smothered and stifled in rain. He heard a man's cry. He put his head down and ran into the haze of rain, feeling each jarring step like a surprise blow.

He came suddenly upon the prostrate figure of Marks, a third of the way along, winded, gagging, face-up in the rain. Close by, Fleurier held the rail, weak-legged, coughing and bleeding from the nose and lips.

55

'It seems,' Fleurier said, through his split lips, 'that we have found out what you mean. Only you're more violent than we expected.'

He resisted Cleve's clumsy efforts to help him, moving away from the rail, as if frightened of being pushed over. Rain fell so hard Cleve felt it suffocating him.

Hours later he argued in the darkness of the bedroom, unable to be attentive to his wife's busyness. Her breathing was rapid; the room was thick with the smell of talcum powder, the aftermath of her shower, but panic gave him no time to notice.

'You gotta con them outta this,' he pleaded. 'They'll get themselves knocked around; they already have. Tell 'em to go home, to get outta town.'

There was no answer from her as she moved about in the darkness.

'Look, I don't want to see anyone hurt. God, it was awful out there tonight. Who the hell could have done it?'

No response.

'You think I organised it.' Again only a bustling silence. 'Hell, I'm a thug now, eh?' He got no denial from Queenie. 'Tell them to get out before something really serious happens.'

Queenie stood straight; she knew he sensed it. There was the sound of a heavy zipper.

'They are,' she said. 'We are. And it has.'

She hauled the big bag onto her shoulder and went out the door and downstairs into the twilight. Cleve squawked in disbelief, unable to craft even small words as he followed her down with useless hand movements. Brunswick Street and the harbour and the somnolent crouch of the small town were barely touched by the brushstrokes of the false dawn.

'Hey, what about me?' he called lamely, standing in the doorway as she disappeared into the grey, trafficless street. The house creaked about him; he refused to believe.

X

It is 1978, late in May, night. In the unflickering light of their lamp with the rain folding about them in clean, cold sheets, two old men move inside their greatcoat, giggling. They are winded and panting from their long trek through the dark, smutty labyrinths of the jetty's underbelly, and as they wait for their breath to return they show each other the places where skin is missing from their knuckles and where barnacles have torn their hard old palms. Their bristly chins chafe together as they settle and fend off the rain. The sky is lightening. The small herring at their feet is curled taut. Their lines are in the water and in their tender, split palms, they feel live things touching them. From above there is the sound of a man pacing, and the sounds of rats about their business. And the rain eases and the dawn bides its time.

PORTS

ON the veranda of the house his grandfather built at Wirrup, in the shade of its long, drooping roof, Daniel Coupar crushed grape leaves in his hands, watching the brittle pulp blow from his palms and settle below on the powdery dry earth. June was half gone and there had been no rain at Wirrup, though Coupar was not surprised. He had been sitting on his veranda many days watching the sky without expectation. No one had come in that time, no rain had fallen.

Towards the end of the morning Coupar hoisted himself upright and walked down off the veranda. Unnerved by his sudden movement, the crows stirred on their posts. Coupar's feet hurt in his boots from the long, restless walk the night before. The ground crackled beneath him as he went down towards the bore. He took from his pocket a cube of bread, furry with lint, and he put it into his mouth and felt it slowly dissolve and his belly respond.

Sitting on the solitary green tuft by the bore, he remembered Queenie swimming through bracken mimicking the sounds of the windmill and the songs of the whales. She was an amphibian-child, skinny, shiny-skinned, shimming through bodies of water and vegetation. She bore none of the features of her mother who was dry and savage in her restlessness. Daniel Coupar had no sons, though this had not disappointed him: he was content to be the last in the line, glad there could be an end of it.

He shucked each boot off, one foot against the other, and lowered each foot into the water, observing the wise-looking

58

corns and the innocent pink toes as he swilled about. This was the only green, wet place left. His blistered feet were soothed by the water, and the comfort softened him. '*How beautiful are thy feet*,' he murmured chuckling. With one hand he reached into the water and groped around on the scummy bottom and brought up an abalone shell which he held up so that the mother-of-pearl inside prismed light in concentric twists where the flesh of a living, eating creature had once been. He studied the tiny imprints the conical anterior left in his palms, then he tossed it aside and began wading about in the pool, stirring up ochre clouds. He pulled up more shells and threw them onto the closely cropped tuft of grass, reaching, bending, tossing, until his breath was short and he had to rest. Coupar sat amongst the clutter of shells he had thrown in a few weeks before, and considered them, shells from the sea. Throwing them all in had seemed immensely significant a few weeks ago after his granddaughter and her husband left, but now it seemed ludicrous. He and Queenie had collected thousands of shells once, wandering along the beach below picking over shore-scum, finding things from worlds away. He still had their plunder in boxes in the old milking sheds, hundreds of them, still exuding their salty, exotic odours. When times were hard and rabbits rank with myxomatosis and fish scarce, Daniel Coupar had subsisted on abalone. Those days, it was called muttonfish. Now, people told him, it was eaten in restaurants as a delicacy. It did not seem possible now, as he stared at them, that the contents of these hulks had sustained him.

Thoughts and memories bore down on him. Early in life ideas had weighted him and excited him and punished him with their inconstancy. Always, he was taunted by the shortcomings of his mind: when sometimes he came in sight of understanding, his thoughts faltered, petered out, and he failed to penetrate, as though wisdom had a hide too thick for him. He remained dissatisfied with what he observed and understood, suspicious of what evaded him.

'I am,' he said to the stack of bottles winking near by in the unseasonal sun, 'something. I am . . .' he laughed, 'something.' He had said this many times before, when he was drunk or close to death or prayer; it gave him something aggressive to do

59

with his mouth.

At this moment his mouth was dry and he yearned for the sweet, quenching taste of grapes, to be able to reach out and take and eat. He regretted the long-expected barrenness of his vine, the sinewy old relic of his forebears. There had been other years when it had seemed spent and had lain dormant for a season, only to bear long, succulent bunches the next.

'The old bitch. Wouldn't surprise me if she came good again. It won't. But nothing would surprise me.'

Coupar's attention returned to the bottles, silent, amber things, and he grew suspicious of them. Why had he begun to stack them there all those years ago? They seemed so ugly. He shuffled over and took one by the neck and dashed it against the leg of the windmill. The shattering sound moved inside his ears. He smashed another to repeat the sensation.

'Empty brown bottles,' he said. Some of them, within their amber skins, contained an odour, some the remains of unlucky locusts. He smashed another and shook a splinter of glass from his hair. The movement in his ears was unlike sound. He wondered why he did not recognise any of these bottles individually. Hadn't he drunk each of them on separate occasions? Weren't they all moments in his life? Coupar laughed at himself, scornful of his thoughts. 'Comes from having too much time to think,' he told himself, as if to quell the deep disturbance in him.

He smashed bottles at intervals all afternoon, and the sun burnt the surface of the bore, a heat and light that began quickly to diminish as dusk approached.

'*How long will the land mourn, and the grass of every field wither? For the wickedness of those who dwell in it the beasts and the birds are swept away,*' he said in the twilight by the water.

By the light of a lamp whose wick had long gone unattended, Daniel Coupar held in his hand the final detached pages of his grandfather's journal. Nathaniel Coupar died in 1875 at Wirrup and left the journal to his son Martin who, without reading it, had given it in turn, out of respect for ritual, to his own son, Daniel. Daniel Coupar did not read the journal in its several volumes until after his father's death in 1926. He had read it many times since with growing disgust.

He shuffled the stiff, torn-out pages, and read again the last entries, glad that he had them safe in his hands. For a while he listened to the sounds of the night—grasshoppers rasping across the veranda, kangaroos thumping down towards the bore, the chittering of sheep—before taking himself through the house behind his lamp, feeling the friendly bump of furniture, to his narrow, bowed bed in the back room where Queenie had slept. Beside the bed with its dusty quilt and sheets was the table he had made for Queenie to put her books and shells on. He fancied it still smelt of her, but all her books and shells were gone from it and only his Bible, some papers, and his dead wife's false teeth remained. Coupar rested the lamp on the low windowsill. Some nights years ago, he saw Queenie with her elbows on this sill looking out at him as he returned from long walks, thinking her asleep. More recently —two nights ago—he thought he saw her there still, wincey night gown bright in the dark, beside the figure of his wife Maureen. He saw them there, hair ruffled from sleep, puzzled expressions on their faces, and he slept out on the ground with them gazing out all night.

This night, with the lamp on the sill, he saw only himself in the window, and when he turned the lamp out there was nothing. Much sooner than he expected, Daniel Coupar slept.

In the first light of morning the paddocks and the sheds took on a deceptive, richer hue, which made them look less stark and desperate. Coupar prowled stiffly about his sheds for the last stored feed and found two eggs from hens long dead, and a nest of stillborn rats. He felt the promise of the day's heat everywhere. The faint, insistent cries of animals wallowed up from the bore; they had trodden down the rotten fences and he left them to themselves and their hunger. Later in the morning he kept to the house.

Three times that morning he took up the mean shape of a ballpoint pen and began the letter he wanted to write; but the words were stiff and separate from him, reminding him of his grandfather, and his concentration was impeded by the sounds

61

of neglected stock. Finally he worked his feet into boots and set off across the desiccated earth towards the hill.

Wirrup Hill was the highest point for thirty miles in any direction. To Daniel Coupar, who spent each day with his body close to the finite ground, climbing the hill was like flying, and as he laboured on the sweatless flanks, picking his way up the tiny tracks he had used as a boy, hearing the earth vibrate with the lumberings of kangaroos in the sapless vegetation, the physical effort did not seem a part of him.

Near the summit he came upon the fallen stone walls of the watchmen's hut. Had it not been for the big fire of '56 which tore across the land to the coast, the old hut would have still stood. The fire had consumed every wooden piece: lintels, roof beams, doors, shutters, and left the stones to topple.

During the Second War Wirrup Hill had been seized by the Army as a submarine-spotting post. A small unit of soldiers, mostly locals, were sentenced to four years' of isolation and looking out to sea. They drank sly grog and sometimes attracted an Aboriginal woman or a lonely farmer's wife, and to pass the days they built themselves a small settlement: a stone hut with a deep fireplace, a fortress-like ablution shed, and a great granite throne they called the Looking Seat on the brow of the hill. They dynamited old native waterholes and made catchments and irrigation channels and even a Roman bath. Some of them carved their names and their lovers' names into the granite. Daniel Coupar kept well away from them and heard the blasting from a distance; sometimes he saw their tiny shapes moving about on the bald summit. He did his best to forget them and their war. Only twice did the soldiers report sightings, and both times the submarines were found to be whales westering up the coast on their annual migration. There were no reports after that, not even of specks certain to be submarines: the men were locals and sensitive to ridicule.

As he shuffled about the ruins of the old hut, Coupar remembered his old resolution to restore it as a haven away from the farmhouse. But the year of the fire was also the year of Queenie's birth and Coupar and his wife soon found they were the guardians of their daughter's child, and there was time only for work and the child.

Coupar made his way up to the flat top of the hill and the

62

remains of the Looking Seat. Removing a few fallen lumps of rock, he sat in the generous space between the granite armrests and looked down at the creaming lines of surf on the beaches that stretched away west, one after another, to Angelus, and in particular the beach directly below where his grandfather had hunted whales a century and a half ago, where his father had shot himself, where the ribs and vertebrae of whales and other mammals surfaced each season in the moving sands.

From here there had always been for Coupar a sense of perspective: there was order and sense, each landmark, each familiar plane of light or darkness consistent with memory and history, an immemorial constant around which, upon which, all else happened. To the north, the Ranges; to the east the white sides of Jimmy's Rock; to the west the cloudy tips of Fourpeaks; to the south-west only Bald Island hugging the thin shoulders of Stormy Beach. Ocean. Sky. Dead land.

After resting, Coupar moved west along the spine of the hill, stumbling on its subtle decline, crossing worn patches where the earth and bush had receded like an aged hairline to expose wide, open stretches of granite whose steepness demanded an undignified crab-walk. In the centre of one of these bare spaces, on a level terrace, stood two neat stacks of flat granite stones. Coupar negotiated the edifices carefully, sat down on the lower, seaward side of them, in their shade. When he was a boy these monuments had aroused in him a deep suspicion. The stones, stacked like houses of cards, seemed to generate silence. They looked as though a push would send them toppling. Sometimes at twilight they looked like two men standing together overlooking the sea.

Coupar's father, Martin Coupar, had spoken of them in a puzzled, derogatory manner, as though contemptuous and a little afraid. 'Supposed to be some damned legend about them,' he said, twisting his big moustache, 'about two spirit fellows who lived here and suddenly flew away one day across there to Bald Island. Those dents in Bald Island are supposed to be where they landed. The darkies must have thought it up; Presbyterians around here haven't the imagination.' The young Daniel Coupar marvelled at this and visited the place often to stare out at Bald Island with its spirit-prints, but as he grew older and more sensitive to ridicule, he came to scoff at

63

the stories and his own imagination.

In more recent years he had come back to these structures with renewed wonder, had brought Queenie up to see, had even brought a visiting anthropologist who dismissed them as spurious.

From the stones, the waterfall was a short walk away, farther along the spine of the hill, around and below which grew the thickest bush on the land. Daniel Coupar came suddenly to the brow of the dry fall. He peered over the edge, down at the chaotic gully and the rocks below, a drop of sixty feet. He had seen things at this place that had kept him awake nights.

Twelve years had passed since the death of Maureen Coupar. Twelve years were not enough to diminish the immediacy of the moment in his mind.

For weeks Maureen had been depressed and restless, wandering about the house clutching her gown about her in the night, sitting out on the veranda where thick nets of mosquitoes descended upon her. Coupar, who laboured alone all day and brooded, locked into himself most evenings, was slow in perceiving her state. He began to wake in the night with her flailing about beside him, calling out, sobbing. He found her sleepwalking, tearing her hair. One morning in February he dared to ask her, and his questions sounded awkwardly formal, as though he was addressing someone he'd only just met.

'I have this dream,' she told him without looking up from the breakfast table. 'There . . . there is this little girl swimming like a fish — only there's no water and she's wriggling about in a patch of red dirt — and her ribs are all showing, she's got no clothes on, and you can tell she's hungry, she moves her mouth, it's all swollen and dry and the teeth are black. She wants food. She looks as if she's calling out only there's no sound. Then . . . then she just bites herself and blood comes out like red dust and — ' She looked at him, eyes dark and deep. 'It's Queenie, sometimes, Daniel, and other times it's me. What's going to happen to our Queenie? And me?'

Coupar sat, watching carefully the movements of her face. She was talking to him as though afraid of him, ready to fend off his blows. And she flinched when he reached out for her silvery hair to feel its softness.

64

'Let's have a picnic,' he said.

The previous winter had been so long and wet that, late in summer as it was, the waterfall was thick and boisterously alive. At the top of the fall, at the edge of the still-tumescent creek, they drank beer and ate cold chicken and threw the bones and the bottles over the edge and sang cheery, silly songs that made them nostalgic; they held hands like nervous youngsters. Small birds batted about. The bush whistled and bristled with life, and by noon Daniel Coupar knew that since the summer of 1932 when they had first met there had been a great void.

What had he been doing all these years? Thirty-four years? The realisation almost stole the day's magic from him. Since 1932 much of his life had been spent working hard, hard enough to punish his body, and brooding, mulling over his defeat in Angelus and the nature of his ancestry. And now this was 1966, the year of dollars and cents. Daniel Coupar savoured these moments, then, and tried not to think of the intimacies he had denied his wife, denied himself, those millions of things he had left unsaid.

As the afternoon slipped by they told stories and jokes and shared suspicions and other dreams. They split a watermelon and burrowed to their ears in it, spitting juice and seeds, licking the sweetness from each other, and Daniel Coupar remembered what it was to be frivolous. She danced for him the way Queenie, in town at school, would dance, and they rollicked together in the cool water near the edge where it rushed about their knees; they danced madly as though winning back lost time. Close to the edge they kicked and splashed and were unafraid.

When she stumbled and was taken, Coupar heard her laughter, saw a hand, and was conscious of his trousers flapping from a nearby bough. He heard a shallow sound that might have been her impact or the shock of a magpie leaving a tree.

Now twelve years later, as he made his way around to the foot of the fall, there was a roaring, not of water, but of blood in his ears. The long, granite wall was dry; lichen grew on the rockface like old man's stubble. At the bottom, behind where in plentiful winters the water crashed into the rock, there was an undercut, a cavity that smelt of fox and marsupials. Coupar

65

bent in to see fragments of chewed bone, sharp as needles. At the spot where his wife had opened ripely and suddenly, there was an oval scab of mosquito larvae which came to life as he passed.

Noon was passing when he fought his way down the choked gully with its mutant trees and distorted growths, through clouds of mosquitoes and midges unsated by his thin blood, until he reached pasture and tooled land. Crossing saline, treeless patches towards the house and its tipping sheds, he thought too of last summer and the waterfall and the familiar confusion rose in his throat.

The summer before last, when Cleveland Cookson appeared in his Land Rover, Daniel Coupar felt the beginnings of his loss. Queenie seemed to burst in bubbles of energy, leading the reedy young man about as though saving him from himself and his thin veneer of worldliness. He heard them whispering in the sheds, heard his name, strained, but could not catch the gist of what was said, and he felt his helplessness grow.

It was quite by accident that he came upon their nakedness in the waterfall one afternoon. He had tired of working, as often happened now, and had gone walking, thinking Queenie and her young man were swimming down on the beach. The sight of them—entwined in one another, strained and coiling beneath the hammer of water—had first struck him like a blow; but as he watched and saw he was prevented from crying out in rage by the glow of their torsos, the sincerity of their movements, their clumsy innocence, and an envy that rooted him to the ground and caused him to remember. And he left.

Walking, recalling that day as he came to the fallen fence nearest his sheds, Coupar felt a heat in his cheeks that embarrassed him.

That afternoon, on 16 June 1978, after vainly beginning the same letter again and again, Daniel Coupar dressed in the dark suit he had worn to Cleve and Queenie's wedding, and went out to the shed to the old Fordson. He sprayed the ignition and uttered the foulest curses and cranked until it chuggered awake.

Crows flickered in the scant shade, watching as he passed.

66

He reached the road, breathless from the opening and closing of gates, and he steeled himself for the ride to Angelus. He savoured the breeze in his face.

II

Between the deep, dark swells that march in from the south a launch rolls and twists unhurriedly, engines idling, deckhand vomiting. Ted Baer, unstrapped in his chair, gazes astern along the disappearing glitter of his line out beyond the wake where his baited rig cuts and trundles at midwater. The deckhand, a lad from Angelus who talked himself aboard at the town jetty, braces over the berley bucket and contributes generously to it. The chum of whale-oil, foodscraps, blood and fish waste aggravates his seasickness; he is applauded by the old man at the wheel who steers with a heel in the spokes, rolling a cigarette. 'Keep ladling!' the old man calls, lighting up.

Also taking the swell abeam, the *Paris II*, a quarter of a mile distant, sounds its horn in greeting and cuts away east tracking a pod first seen at dawn nine hours ago.

The same moment Daniel Coupar leaves his gate shut behind him at Wirrup, and within minutes of the moment the two vessels pass one another at sea, Abbie Tanks meets a man outside the Bright Star. The man with the double-knit suit and sunglasses shakes his hand and suggests they go inside. Abbie Tanks grins and hesitates, looking over the man's shoulder to where his friends and cousins sit laughing outside Richardson's Bakery; too timid to lead the way, he follows. Crossing the space between the door and the table the man has found for them, Abbie Tanks sees, with eyes downcast, men he has fought in the street after dark; but as he sits with the scout from the city league team he feels a cool sense of safety upon him. He is immune even from the crimson jowls of Hassa Staats who has only just seen him, peering through the sheets of smoke. Staats's eyes bloom in his head for two seconds before he recognises the big football scout from the city. Abbie Tanks asks for a beer. The scout raises two fingers at Hassa Staats who begins to pour. The scout speaks but Abbie Tanks is only half listening, savouring this moment. Distorted behind the frosted glass of the windows, the shapes of Abbie Tanks's cousins cavort and bob, and he thinks he hears them giggling.

'This is the best day of your life,' the scout says from behind his sunglasses. Abbie Tanks, glass in hand, with an eye on the dartboards and the red-armed men at the bar, nods in agreement.

In the ancient remains of an easy chair on a veranda William Pell wakes to the swampy smell of the Hacker River whose brackish flats swarm with birds. Pell's back aches; his body feels as though it has been beaten. He sees across the water the tiny jetty, the nest of paperbarks below a tilting house where forty years ago he spent an afternoon with Maureen Bolt before she had even met Daniel Coupar. He remembers her bare, rough feet and the black crust beneath her fingernails and the fat bellow of her father from the house above. As he twists in the musty old chair he recalls how he tried to attract her attention to him with witty turns of phrase and the dropping of names and how she kept on regardless, telling him the things she had heard about a footloose young man in town who was organising farmers and tenants in resistance. He would protect them from the Pustlings, she said. They had been burning their farms before walking off. They were singing 'Bringing in the Sheaves', she told him. Pell remembers rolling his eyes and surrendering to the young woman's awe.

Ah, he thinks to himself as a breeze comes muggily up from the paperbarks, the scummy old Hacker brings out the memories in a man. She was a fine woman, too fine even for you, Daniel Coupar.

Pell rests for a moment with his memories. He thinks back over the half-century he has known Coupar; he remembers sitting in church on a hot, fly-buzzing morning in 1919 watching Daniel Coupar, who was older, planting gum under the pews, mimicking the minister's fatal twitch. Pell recalls the time Coupar knocked him down in the locker room at school, and the time he came upon Coupar weeping silently behind

68

the tuckshop. On a camp out at the old quarantine station near the entrance to the harbour, Daniel Coupar had spent a night on the block in the old mortuary, dared by the others. Some boys wagered money; Pell gave him his pocket-mirror, the only thing of value he had. Coupar had kept the money and the mirror and never spoke about the night. Billy Pell often wondered if Coupar even knew what death was. At the funeral of Coupar's father he saw Coupar's impassive stare as the big box was carried across the soaking ground.

Now, as he rests and contemplates his position, Pell wishes that he could speak to Daniel Coupar. When he was a boy he once prayed to God asking that he might become Daniel Coupar.

Mosquitoes fizz about his legs. A hand touches his shoulder and a woman of indeterminate age in a grey frock comes around beside him.

'You've been asleep,' she says.

'Yes,' Pell says, smelling the eucalypt fragrance of her.

'Here's some soup,' she said, placing a bowl in his lap. 'You're not eating enough. When a Pell gets to lookin' comf'table in his clothes, he's not feedin'.'

Pell looks up at the woman whom he has met only once before on a previous run, startled.

'Anderson Pell was a big man,' she says.

'You knew my father?'

'And when you get old I expec' you'll even look like him. A fine man.' She stoops at the edge of the veranda to spit. 'Eat up. You better go soon. The ol' man'll be back an' he'll likely be in a dark one when he finds a box of charity on the doorstep. He'll take charity, but he likes to be alone when he does.'

With a strange sense of exhilaration Pell spoons the thin broth, glancing every few moments at the gaudy truck he has rented and filled with Pustling's money. He feels the stubble on his chin; he has been driving since Monday. A pelican floats soundlessly across the shimmering river.

III

Jouncing down the highway on under-inflated tyres with the hammer of the diesel engine in his ears, Daniel Coupar steered off onto the gravel every now and then to let cars overtake. His eyes stung in the slight wind. Rabbits, bursting from the petrified grass at the roadside, became mallee roots in their fright, only turning and showing their white backsides fleeing into the dead paddocks as he was almost upon them. In a normal winter this road was often under water and the paddocks on either side bobbing and bristling with birds; but this year the low pastures glowered with an unnatural heat and the water lying across the road in the distance was an illusion.

On his left in the distance, the thin coastal hills were never out of sight. The bruise of the Ranges to his right stayed with him.

Over the racket of the tractor engine Coupar heard the braying of another motor. He pivoted in his seat but saw nothing; the reddish bitumen twisted away empty behind. Still he heard the other motor, unseen, demonic. A minute later a black flash whipped past leaving a phrase of taped music and a wave of heat in its wake.

Daniel Coupar shifted his benumbed buttocks. He did not want to go to Angelus. He was afraid of the compulsion he felt in his body; he wanted to disown it.

Daniel Coupar was born on the first day of 1906, a strong-limbed, ravenous baby. His mother taught him to read and to believe before sending him to school in Angelus, and as a boy wandering the farthest reaches of their lonely farm he let the world inform his senses. Sometimes when he lay on the granite breast of the hill above the pastures and the beaches, looking up into the mesmeric blue of the sky, he felt the world swallow him, enfold and engulf him; he felt its milk-warm breath and its sap-sweetness. He learnt to name the things about him with the aid of some water-stained cyclopaedias. His mother read to him from the Bible and he lived and re-lived the magical stories of Moses and Ruth and Jonah. When he dreamt, when

70

he sat out on the veranda watching the sun haul itself up from behind the trees, when he lay by a creek watching the million bubbles tumble past, each with its sealed cargo of white light, he knew that anything was possible, all things were good, and he could doubt nothing.

Daniel Coupar's father was a massive, booming, neurotic man with grand schemes and grander failures. He was a man known in the district by his ancestry and by the things he had tried and failed. His supplementary ventures into salmon fishing and the flensing of beached whales were legendary for their incompetence; they earnt him respect in the district. He often beat his son and wept shamefully afterwards, doubling the boy's punishment. Daniel often heard him in the night pacing, gouging the kitchen fire, muttering, as though cursing or in prayer.

At school, boarding with the other farm boys, Daniel Coupar marvelled at how dry and lifeless his textbooks rendered the world. He longed for holidays and the freedoms of the farm, the hill, the sea, the intricacies of dried watercourses, the deep occasional shadows of whales moving offshore. He loved, too, the work of the farm, jobs that let him think of other things while he worked.

In 1920, in the soft, misty confusion of a winter dawn, Martin Coupar shot himself. He left his wife and son in great debt, dispossessing them of their land. The funeral in Angelus had been paid for before his death. Rain turned the cemetery to mud. The funeral party had to leave the coffin with one end pointing at the black sky as gravediggers discussed the logistics of burying a man too long for his family crypt.

Clouds towered and burnt in the sunset. Fourpeaks was a lighthouse with the white sun behind it. Daniel Coupar bounced through the ribbons of shadows, saw birds settling to roost, smelt the dry-grass smell of approaching night. Torn hulks of discarded tyres began to look like the sleeping forms of children at the roadside. Coupar's necktie slapped his shoulders: pat-pat. In the deep tread of the tractor's rear tyres, the pulped bodies of twenty-eights revolved and cast up an occasional gummy feather. At the Fourpeaks Roadhouse a dumbfounded Herb Hindle looked up from his bowser to see the Fordson trundle past with the unmistakable form of Daniel Coupar in suit and tie poised over the wheel. Coupar waved. Hindle spilt petrol down the side of the black panel van which was full of groping, adolescent bodies.

Daniel Coupar and his mother moved to Kindred, a hundred miles north of Angelus, where he tended horses and she cooked and cleaned for a miserly bachelor. His mother read to him at night when their employer had retired to his room. They shared long, warm silences. Coupar knew the sweet warmth of horse-dung and the benevolent chawing of horses and the gloss-backed beetles on the flags. Sometimes, when he forked hay and crap on winter mornings, hearing the nasal bark of his employer berating his mother in the distance, Coupar was overcome by both love and hate, unable to separate them. He missed the sea and the seasonal passing of the remnant of whales that marked the passage of time.

There were nights when his mother spoke about his father in a way he had never known her to speak. 'Your father,' she said, 'was a man too small for his ideas. He was a blamer: he blamed God, his tools, his friends, his family, his ancestry, for all his shortcomings. I think, deep down, he knew he was small. He envied other people, but he was too proud to treat them like superiors or even equals. Oh, pride! His pride got between him and God, between his fingers even. Made him think that . . . doing away with himself was something he had a right to do. Oh, my boy,' she told him, looking grey and fragile in the lamplight, 'he was a Coupar's Coupar.'

In 1922 Coupar's mother died of pneumonia. On her deathbed she told him what a fine son he had been to her, and he was greatly affected. Till then he had not doubted he was anything less, but his mother's last words stung him with doubt. A week later he was dismissed. He returned soon after in the still of night to empty a bag of horse manure into the old man's watertank.

Coupar spent months idling about the main street of Kindred until he began work as offsider to Shit-Tin Bill, the night-cart man. Shit-Tin Bill had a dark, ugly, eaten face; his racial heritage was uncertain. He had white hair, and blotchy

72

yellowish-brown skin, and a mystical status in the town. He was never spoken to and neither was he badly spoken to. His old mare Lilac farted in time with her roll-lopping gait as he led Daniel Coupar down the back lanes at dusk. Coupar spent his first Christmas as an orphan taking the pieces of fruitcake from toilet seats, drinking port in the first light of dawn with big, black-green blowflies nesting in his eyebrows.

'If they have to shit on me,' Bill told him as they trundled down a potted lane with the sun steaming dew from the ground, 'I ask 'em to do it in winter when there's less flies and a fresh turd'll keep me warm.' Coupar laughed and punched his new-found friend who stank always of ammonia, knowing that he meant every word. 'I am the least and the most,' Bill said, cuffing the wide shoulders of his apprentice. 'They know it, I know, and the Lord knows it, boy.'

It was then, with the tins snattering and chattering, and Lilac clop-*fart*, clop-*fart*ing along that lane between the sagging iron fences and the ivy-thick outhouses, that Coupar vowed never to leave Shit-Tin Bill and Kindred.

When he reached the Hacker River bridge it was almost dark and he saw the silhouettes of pelicans floating down in the twilight. Along the banks he saw the fallen hippy-houses in which old farmers without land had begun to squat. The bridge rumbled. He smelt the reedy odour of the estuary farther downstream and noticed across the bridge, on the Angelus side of the river, how lush the land was. In a yellowish, smudgy cluster, the lights of the Hacker Arms approached and fell behind. Coupar, buttock-sore and red-eyed, inhaled the sweetness from the wet earth and felt his dread retract a little within him. Farther along the road, passing small dairy farms on the outer perimeter of Angelus, he realised that he was speaking aloud, rehearsing lines.

Daniel Coupar left Kindred and Shit-Tin Bill without a word and without hesitation. The last of the Misses Coupar died in 1924, bequeathing the old habourside house built by Nathaniel Coupar to her only nephew and relative. Not once since Martin Coupar's embarassing death had any of his sisters communicated with their next of kin. Martin Coupar's wife was a proud woman. She did nothing to break the silence. Daniel had forgotten his aunts existed until the message came. He arrived in Angelus with the chest of things his mother had left him, a hat and an old broken-down gelding.

In the next six years Coupar worked on roads and boats, on the wharf, at the whaling station, on trucks and trains. He found that he spent little of his money, having no rent to pay and no interest in gambling, and he soon had a generous wad of money in the biscuit tin he kept in his wardrobe. He spent evenings in the Bright Star and the Black and White listening to the whalers and the fishermen talk.

One Saturday afternoon, resting in the shade outside the old Presbyterian church he met a white-bearded, wiry old man who offered him his tobacco pouch and papers and said, lighting his own, 'There's no kindness in this world any more, son.' It was only after the old man left, striding up Goormwood Street, that Coupar recognised him as Anderson Pell, the father of Billy Pell. The old man was dead the next year and Coupar went to the funeral. There he saw the hulking form of William Pell who already looked twice his twenty years. It was the first time they had met in ten years. 'People only catch up with one another at funerals, in this town,' Pell said composedly. They spoke for some time. Coupar felt an exuberance in Pell that seemed unnatural; he suspected it was part of grief.

Oftentimes Daniel Coupar fished in the harbour from an old clinker-built punt. One morning he rowed out into the Sound, past the heads, to fish for sharks. He caught nothing and was capsised by a rogue swell. In a state akin to hysteria or religious ecstacy he swam the mile to shore—*I am the least and the most ... they know it, I know it, and the Lord knows it, boy ... I am the least and the most*—and came floundering into the shallows of Middle Beach, full of seawater and a curious light.

That year Benjamin Pustling found his way to Angelus. Coupar found that men he had spoken to in pubs, women he had bantered with outside the church, began to come to his door at night. As the Depression deepened and people became more desperate and the Pustlings prospered, he discovered that he had more money than most, fewer liabilities and less fear. People twice his age came to him for advice. He told them what he thought. In time they had a leader. During that time he married. Townspeople were forced to sell their land to the Pustlings and to become tenants of and debtors to them. Coupar organised against the Pustlings during the winter of 1932 and heroic and dramatic events occurred. But when Pustling gained control of church and civic leaders, bought the influence of newspapers as far away as the city, Angelus became a quiet town again. Coupar was suddenly alone, and he hid himself in the house by the harbour. He retreated from his newly wed wife, from that immanent light he had known, and for years his isolation remained complete.

It was the summer of 1931 when Coupar met his bride. As he rowed wearily up the Hacker River with the brown light of sunset falling at his feet and the long shaggy arms of the paperbarks reaching at him from either bank, he peaked his oars and rested to catch his breath a moment. The boat was heavy, loaded with food parcels for families upriver. He was startled by a heavy swash near the left bank. He looked over but saw nothing but the hypnotic circles widening on the surface. Then he distinguished a shape in the coppery water moving towards him. Platypus? Crocodile? Neither belonged in the Hacker. He slipped an oar from its rowlock and waited with it raised. When the surface broke just near the gunwhale he gasped: a human, a woman, a girl. Tossing her hair back she blew a jet of air and smiled. Coupar did not smile; he was too shocked.

'You should come in for a dip,' she said, treading water with wide, white movements that flashed in the tea-coloured water.

'I'm busy.' He waved an arm at the boxes in the boat. But it was well after dark before Daniel Coupar resumed his rowing. He sat with her beside the rickety little jetty amidst the faint screams of the mosquitoes and listened to her talk; he did not listen to what she said, only the wandering register of her voice. He smelt the warm, algal breeze, heard the lap-lap of water and the soughing of the paperbarks. They shared a bag of sugar from Coupar's boat, like two greedy children, and when they vomited it back up, they nursed each other and saw each other's face in the milk of the rising moon and became quiet.

Six months afterwards Daniel Coupar and Maureen Bolt were married in the church in Angelus.

Nathaniel Coupar's journals attracted him in the late 1930s. He was reading them in 1939 when, on the eve of a distant war and the birth of his only daughter, Coupar got drunk and rode through and through Angelus on his BSA until he capsized in full sail. As he floated across the new macadamed surface of the road, he had a distinct notion of hovering over darkness which lasted a second or two before he came to rest in a hedge of lantana. Mistaking the Salvation Army hall for a first-aid post, he staggered in, bruised and bloody, and prostrated himself. In the unfocused distance a first-aid man bellowed about Jesus Christ walking upon the water. Coupar, who had seen flies walking on the skin of water, who had only recently experienced a similar sensation hovering above the black road, was unconvinced by the man; he was filled with contempt and a great nostalgia and he passed out.

Later that year the old Coupar land at Wirrup came up for auction. Daniel Coupar went, drunk and reckless, to throw bids at the auctioneer, to goad him. When his bids were untopped he found himself the owner of his father's farm.

The tasks of the farm helped Coupar in his retreat. His wife was kept busy with their child and the domestic chores; she waited patiently for him to mend, to reemerge from himself. The child, Eileen, was of little interest to him. She was not a friendly child, and as she grew from child to young woman she spent less and less time at Wirrup. During one visit home in 1956 she gave birth to a daughter, and within weeks she was gone again and never returned. The Coupars called the girl Queenie, and not even Daniel Coupar could resist her. From the moment she was born, it was constant work for him to remain in isolation.

The Fordson roared and bounced through the lit, rainslicked streets of Angelus. Daniel Coupar took the chill wind on his face and breathed the briny smell of the harbour. Squat houses came and went, windows blue with television. He rolled down Goormwood Street past the memorial, past the Wildflower Cafe and its glossy, parked motorcycles, past bakery, church,

76

florist, the pubs with their ooze of light and noise. His body felt petrified as a root. Turning up towards the old house by the harbour, he felt a disappointment rising in him: Angelus had not changed since last year.

Cleve's Land Rover was in the driveway when he pulled in and doused the sharp stutter of the diesel, but there were no lights on in the house and he knew at once that he had failed. He got down gingerly and felt pain in his feet. He did not bother knocking on the front door, but went round to the back, catching in the corner of his vision the image of Miss Thrim's face between the lace curtains next door. By the back door there were the pungent fragrances of mint and parsley and thyme, and the sweet smell of hanging baskets brimming with flowers. He knelt and felt under the step and found the key.

Inside, the house had the odour of bacon fat and dust, an unaired closeness. Coupar switched a light on. The kitchen was strewn with newspapers and dead matches, flakes of wood-ash and plates pigmented with grease. On the jarrah table there were beer bottles, books—*Angelus: a short history*, *Whaler's Haven: Angelus 1820–1899*, *Whalemen Adventurers*, *Typee*, *Gardener's Almanac*—and blunt pencils. The living-room was strewn with cushions and beanbags, the big fireplace cold and black. Coupar negotiated the narrow, steep stairs cautiously, noting the old creaks at the third and seventh stairs. The hand-smoothed banister was solid and familiar to the touch.

In the spare room there was piled junk: stringless tennis racquets, a folded tent, picture frames, spare mattress, a kite. Coupar was pleased to see the old tapestry of the wind-torn clipper still above the bed in the main room. The sheets on the bed were grey and wrung. Coupar moved about the room, found Cleve's clothes in the wardrobe, but not Queenie's. The empty end smelt of her. Then he sat for a while, immobilised for a moment by a fork of concentration. He looked out through the big window with its curtains aside and askew to the blue wharf lights and the mild blemishes around the harbour. He got up, turned the light out, sat back on the bed.

'Oh, Queenie,' he whispered, 'what are you doing?'

In the mottled dark of the bedroom Coupar saw his hands nested together in his lap; they were his father's hands, probably his grandfather's. At times they seemed separate

77

from him, motivated by another will. There were nights when his hands and arms lost circulation and feeling and he woke, conscious of reptilian things resting on his chest, near his throat; he slid from beneath them, let them fall aside like butchered cuts of meat.

Coupar tried to rein in his thoughts, slow them down long enough to organise and deliver them: they passed him in blurs, the things he wanted to tell Queenie Coupar; they left him breathless and panicky. He wanted to tell her of the pride of the Coupars, their piety, the bloodshed and suicide and disappointment, and he wanted to confess things, but he rambled and confused himself and his stomach clenched in his frustration.

'I was going to write,' he said aloud, 'but the Coupars always write the important things and never say them: it comes from passing too many notes in drawing-rooms and classrooms and churches. So I came to tell you things, Queenie, and bugger me if you're not here. Where the hell are you? God damn you, girl, you should be here!

'Ah, I'm a stranger here. This house, this town, this bloody body. But we all are, your pisswit husband included, poor lad. Aliens. Sometimes I think the Abos thought they didn't belong, sometimes, pining for their dreams. Damn you, I've come a long, long way and you should be listening. Something's going to happen, I can feel it right up my arse. Head feels like a rotten pigmelon, just black seeds, dust, stink. Feel odd.

'Inheritance, Queenie, it's a bugger. Everything done before you by your ancestors, the bad, bad things, even, benefits you and you want to pretend it isn't true. Sometimes I can feel bones underfoot. Dust is like dried blood. People were driven off land, shot and beaten, and now we have land, we have Angelus—roads, cars, houses, parks, beaches—and there's nothing we can do about it. In dreams I go back into the past—it's like a well—and change it all back around, make the past right again and then I wake up and I don't exist any more. My father horsewhipped a man for wanting to walk on his old land again. I saw it, and what am I to do? Yes, I'm ashamed of my father; I'm ashamed of Adam, damn him, but at least Adam lived out his days like a man.

'You have to inherit lots, Queenie, and I don't want you to.

78

You're the last real Coupar. Funny how it ends up being a woman. A woman. To be a Coupar and a woman has never been much of a life, you know. The Coupars treated their women poorly, like packhorses. Your grandmother, too; I treated her like a packhorse and worse. She carried me and the farm, the house, you. Still she had to carry herself and her disappointment. And she didn't even get to see you become a woman. She was a wonderful bitch. Remember the time you came off the school bus trying to hide your mess, your blood? You think I didn't know? Oh, I wanted to laugh and hug you and even rub my nose in it to show it didn't matter, but we both acted like Coupars and never said a word. I bet those other kids gave you shit. Wished I was a woman, meself, that day. Maybe if I was a woman it would've been easier for you—maybe if I was a better man. And your grandmother didn't see the day. She died and there was only me and you.

'I have to tell you about her. I wasted her heart. Ah, I could fill a silo with regrets, Queenie. She didn't die from the tractor; that was a lie. She fell from the top of the waterfall: she was nuddy and laughing and my bloody trousers were in a tree. Seemed sick at the time. Don't know now. I lied to you.

'Oh, there's lots've things I wish I'd never done. There's sins of inaction, too, you know. My grandpa could tell you all about that. Times I wish God'd made it easier for me to live with Him. Wish I could stop everything and start again, feed everyone, heal everyone, make everyone see and understand like I thought I could when I was a younger, better man. *I am the least and the most*...poor old Bill. Why couldn't I have been Bill?

'I wanted to tell you that I saw Cookson and you in the fall. It wasn't deliberate, but I lingered. I wish I never gave him the journals. He worries me. Gawd, he's like me without a background; he doesn't know his arse from a hole in the ground and neither do you, I suspect. But you need him. Can't think why, though.

'I should have been a better guardian. Oh, I'm tired. Feel like I've been fasting all my life.'

Coupar fixed his eye on the cold, blue lights of the wharf. A wind was pacing about the harbour.

'It's having the choices that kills a man. It's the best and the

79

worst. You get to choose and you get to regret. Almost guaranteed to bugger it up. And sometimes not.

'Remember when I used to read to you? Remember all the stories? Remember when you learnt to read? Hell, you were disappointed. All that time in church you'd thought the Lord was saying, "Take Mary and Jesus and the Flea into Egypt". Export the flea, Joseph! Hmph.' Coupar couldn't resist a laugh. 'Oh, Lord, what a child! And where the hell are you?'

Coupar got up, drew the curtains and sat in the blackness for some time before leaving. The third and seventh stairs cried like trodden-on animals. A fine drizzle fell as he mounted the dark, cacophonous shadow of the Fordson. He felt a narrow coolness within and it frightened him. The lights of a whalechaser slid across from the entrance of the harbour.

IV

Des Pustling ushers the advertising executive into his BMW, and as he rounds the bonnet to the driver's side he sees the silhouette of Marion Lowell locking up the office. Behind the wheel, he realises how much he has drunk; such rare irresponsibility thrills him. Slipping down in the passenger's seat, the advertising man from the city belches and sighs. Pustling wonders what is to be done with him; he can think of many unpleasant people whose company he would prefer. Since six o'clock they have been drinking Black Douglas in Pustling's office.

'Ah, all sewn up, Mr Pustling.'

'Des.'

'Des. Sewn like a caesar.'

'Well, I hope your boys are onto the right thing, Phil.'

'Mr Notts.'

'Phil.' Pustling pulls out into Goormwood Street, accelerating smoothly.

'Oh, mind all the traffic, Des. Don't wanna get caught in a traffic jam, now do we? Harf, harf! No, as I was saying, you small-towners have no trust. Probably the hillbilly in you, you know. No offence, of course. Promo is a sophisticated business, Des. This town's hundred and fiftieth birthday'll be a balltearer because of us, don't you worry. Look, you've got a big promo, the Queen coming, maybe even Rolf Harris. You jus' leave it to us, Dezza. My team are making a success of it in advance: 1979 will see Angelus finally on the map of life. The world'll know about it. Your tourism'll go wild. Your trouble, Des—now don't get me wrong—is no faith. F-A-I-T-H. If you had faith you'd be out there now supervising the construction of another five caravan parks, hotels, motels, restaurants, massage parlours, drive-in churches. Instead of a three-month summer peak and the wildflower thing in spring, you'd be all peak—the Matterhorn—full-on boom, like the big bad city.'

'A doubling of tourist trade doesn't make us the big bad city, Phil. And there is a recession and a drought east of the Hacker.'

'But the logo, the motif!'

'No, the whale's fine, Phil.'

'Damn right it is, Dezza. You'll see. This hick town'll see new life; the good life, the bright lights, the good times!'

'Yes, yes,' Pustling says, changing gears.

'The bright life, Pusser. The good lights, the new brights, the...the—'

'Yes, Phil.'

'Bloody hicks'll see.' The man grunts, trying to loosen his tie, half chokes himself. 'Hicks, Hic!'

Pustling winces, converts it to his smile and notices in his rear-view mirror that a long slice of bloodless gum hangs down over his front teeth, and he smoothes it back with his tongue, remembering those awful days at university. On the street today a small boy tapped him on the leg and said: 'Drop something, sport?' The child was pointing to a yellowish incisor on the footpath; Pustling had just sneezed.

Goormwood Street is quiet tonight, even for a Thursday night. An elderly couple walk a collie, coats heavy about them. Closed, lit shopfronts give the pavements a more barren look than even they deserve. Spirals of paper lift in the freshening breeze from the harbour. To think that last year we won Tidy Town award. Pustling thinks. Then, on the other side, rolling downhill, a tractor. Pustling slows, takes a long look at that tractor and its driver, and turns off towards Middle Beach, thinking quickly.

And at this moment Hassa Staats stands behind the bar surveying his regulars. Each man standing in this bar stands where he remembers their fathers standing.

Staats can remember the days when he brought messages down for his father, those special times when he was allowed behind the bar with its glistening pipes and glass and wet wood. He saw the red faces of the farmers in for market, soldiers home on leave, men doing business at tables, the Salvoes shaking tins, the whalemen drinking from jugs. Those brief moments between delivering the message and taking a cuff on the head, he saw and heard things that excited him. The Rrrr! sound of men talking, the chink of glass, the sour, thrilling stink of beer.

Staats wonders if his father felt the same things all those years he stood behind the bar. Only sometimes is it like those days now.

Staats glances about, sighs. He has heard that Ted Baer did poorly today taking only one small shark which broke a trace just before being gaffed. And to add to Staats's feeling of deflation, Baer is reported to be staying at the Ocean View down on Middle Beach. Wonder if I said something wrong, Staats thinks, squeezing beer out of the bar towel. He's always stopped here. He feels the need for fresh air all of a sudden and leaves Mara behind the bar.

Outside in the cold clean wind, he bites off a chunk of barley sugar with a crack and leans against the low, frosted window, hands in the warm pockets of his jacket. From the windy harbour a truck labors uphill, crashing gears. The street looks deserted, shabby; it adds to his melancholy. The tightness in his chest has been with him several weeks now, a constriction like the aftermath of a sentimental film. He grinds barley sugar, thoughtful. He wonders automatically how the whalers went today. He wonders, too, about those bloody foreigners.

He grates his leather soles on the concrete, and his eye, even before his ear, catches the tractor churning down the hill.

Daniel Coupar is down on the pavement, walking towards

Staats before he is recognised. His thinning white hair stands back, windblown into a peak, the suit is smeared with grease at the knees, the black shoes shine ludicrously. Hassa Staats chokes and spits crystals of barley sugar; and Coupar walks right past him into the public bar. Stupefied, Staats stands for a moment, tosses a stub of sugar into the gutter as one would the butt of a cigarette, and lets his breath shoot out in a long, sticky hiss.

'Well, bogger me,' he says, listening to the sudden silence spilling from the bar.

When he hears the talk and laughter resume, Staats goes inside. Coupar, at the bar, has his back towards the door and Mara is pouring him a beer, caught, for once, without words.

Well, thinks Hassa Staats standing awkwardly near the cigarette machine, this is a turn up. What's *he* doing in town? Staats smiles inwardly. This bent old man, ludicrous in a suit, hiding shiny black shoes beneath the bar, is the man his father had called a dangerous rabble-rouser. He looks as pitiful as the last time Staats saw him — at the wedding. Around the room, others glance too casually, talk with false spontaneity, drink too rapidly. Willis Willis, come to buy cigarettes, startles the big, red publican and displaces him from his position by the machine.

'Taken to the ol' Marlboros, eh Hassa?'

'Eh? Oh, no, nah, wouldn't touch the boggers. Filthy habit.' Exposed, he has no choice but to go back behind the bar where Mara glares at him with those eyes he'd swear glowed in the dark like a cat's.

'What's the matter with you?' she says, clawing at the register. 'You look like another darkie's walked in. And he' on his second middy already.'

He scowls, pulling up a stool to rest his bulk, and looks along the puddled timbertop bar to where Coupar hunches over his glass. Ten, twenty, thirty minutes he observes him, and not once does Coupar look up from his succession of glasses.

Pustling dumps his drunken ad-man outside a respectable brothel. As he U-turns to head back into town, he sees the man collapse on the front lawn and the porch light comes on.

Eventually Hassa Staats can no longer bear it; he slides his stool the length of the bar and sits directly in front of Coupar as the old man finishes another glass. It has been a long time since Staats has seen a man drink so much so quickly without falling to the floor, poisoned, and he feels an odd regret at the sight.

'You shouldn't be doing that to yourself, you know,' he says to Coupar, rolling the empty in his hand. Flecks of foam spin out from his fingers.

'Not like you to give a stuff what a man does to himself, Hassa,' Coupar says quietly, with obvious concentration.

'No,' Staats admits with a smile.

'So piss off.'

'But I own the place.'

Coupar motions to Mara for another beer.

'What brings you to Angelus?' Hassa traces figures of eight in the damp surface of the timber.

'The Fordson. Too far to walk.'

Staats grins. Neither man looks at the other.

'A man'd think you were up to no good, turnin' up like this.'

'Leave the thinking to the men, then.'

'Prickly old bastard.' Staats laughs. 'You're early if you've come for Foundation Day, it's —'

'What do I care about bloody Foundation Day? Gawd A'mighty!'

'A man might think you've come to do some rabble-rousing with your girl, then, eh?'

Coupar takes a beer from Mara and looks at Staats. His eyes are bloodshot, his flesh the colour of tallow, his beard wind-thinned.

'Well, she's left town,' Staats says, meeting his gaze. 'With the lunatic fringe. Become a troublemaker, that girl of yours. Comes from bad discipline,. not enough —'

'That's why your boy's been in the city the last ten years, is it? An upbringing so bloody perfect he just had to run away from home.'

'Hopeless bugger, too, but he never caused grief to this town.'

'Only to you and Mara. Doesn't that count? Sides, his father and his father's father did enough grief between 'em.

Why should he worry? Might be he's the best of a bad bunch.'

'Might be I'll have to ask you to leave.'

'Exiled from Paradise. The Bright and Shining Star.' Coupar eyes him from over the edge of his glass. 'When did Queenie leave?'

'About three weeks, I s'pose. And not a moment too soon. Trying to kill this town.'

'It's not young twits that wreck towns, Hassa.'

'That's what Des calls 'em — young twits. But they've got spirit, he says; one day they'll make good decision-makers, good business people; good people. Pah! All I can say is that I admire his patience. Otherwise I'd think he didn't care.'

'Always been a patient man, old Pusarse.'

'But they have to be stopped, and with any luck this union ban'll keep 'em out. Otherwise the old whaling station might be on borrowed time.'

'Always has been. This whole town is. The lot of us. It's always been borrowed time.'

'Ah, you're sounding religious, Daniel.'

'Piss off.'

'I think you've—'

'Piss off! Piss off!'

And at this moment Des Pustling comes in, an expression of mild amusement on his face.

'Will you help this gentleman out, please, Mr Pustling?' Staats says, rounding the bar, taking the old man's lapel between his fingers. 'I think he's had a nudge too many.'

'Certainly, Mr Staats,' Pustling says, eyes sharp as polished precious stones.

As Coupar lets himself be led outside, legs promising to buckle and slide away beneath him, he snatches a dart from the board near the door and calls: 'The beer stinks. Try cleaning your pipes. Your father was scum but at least he cleaned his pipes.'

Pustling unhands him outside. 'Don't mind poor old Hassa. Got the brains of a Saint Bernard. How about some coffee?'

'A cup of tea, Puslips. God, if I ever thought I'd—'

'My car or yours?'

Coupar does not answer. He is thinking. He gets into the BMW and feels it thrust him forward. He feels like a projectile.

85

Pustling lets third gear work awhile, excited, sensing that something is happening. He feels his ennui fall behind.

V

That night, sheltered from the brawling southerly on the water, Cleveland Cookson sat and read. Spreadeagled paperbacks curled their wings at him, face-down where they had been abandoned: *Moby-Dick*, *Ultramarine*, *The Jacket*, *Lord Jim*, books he had begun and scuttled before. Cleve had drunk enough to be reckless and warm—enough to push a sodden road-worker off his stool earlier in the evening. He didn't know why he had unseated him; they had neither spoken nor noticed one another in the hour they sat abreast the bar.

Cleve read, and the browning script seemed to throb with clarity before him.

> *June 20th, 1831* No whales. I spend afternoons walking the length of the beach doling out rope to have it inspected and re-coiled again.
> Yesterday Mr Jamieson sent our crew out in search of kangaroos. We climbed the hills and moved along precipitous gullies until we came to a flat, swampy area where drab birds rose and scattered into the air. We came upon a herd of kangaroos standing motionless as they seem to do. Mountford put a ball into the biggest of them. Cain wounded another in the thigh and the animal staggered about frightening its fellows off. The creature made a frightful noise, and the dogs harried it to the ground. We found it throatless against the broad base of a tree.
> On the trek back we were alarmed by the appearance of a dozen blacks on the top of a ridge—they were such ghostly figures! They made no sign of observing us, and we passed beneath them in the gully without a sound.
> *June 21st, 1831* The only talk now is of black women. Cain and Leek spruik their foul and immoral stories by the fire at night and the rest of the men grow excited and the mood of the camp becomes restless.

Nowles sleeps no better. At night I can smell an
unsavoury odour. In his slumber he often calls out 'No!
No!' and the others in the hut will reply 'Aye, aye, ye
rotting beggar!' I fear there is little we can offer him in his
pain. Hale applies sulfa and rags but this is all.

June 22nd, 1831   Both Churling and myself in the
lookout this morning as I write this. I hope I can trust
him not to report me writing up here. He quakes as if
with cold. I sense some hidden knowledge in him which
far exceeds his years.

June 23rd, 1831   Cain and Leek forced entry into the
rum store last night. After midnight I woke to shouting
and carousal in the other hut. There was chanting and
lewd singing and sounds of fighting. I heard Churling
singing or shouting or screaming. The headmen Jamieson
and Finn were nowhere about.

This morning I woke and began turn at the lookout,
and as I was rising I saw outside in the poor light a
staggering lubra, naked, besmirched and inebriated. She
struck her fists against the door of the hut opposite
without response. Then she proceeded to hammer upon
our door also. Nowles cried out: 'No, not yet!' in his
delirium and the others merely grunted. The woman
staggered away into the bush. I saw drizzle descending,
and, hanging from a bough near our hut, a pair of
trousers — they looked almost too small for a man.

I passed the garment on my way up to the hill without
touching it. There were drops of dried blood on the legs.

Strange, but I dreamt I heard a child weeping in my
sleep.

Noon. Have just seen whales breaching and the boats
are out. I see a lone figure standing on the beach just
now. Where is he looking? It is not out to sea, but across
and upward. A bird?

7PM. Cut the calf from the womb of its mother this
evening. Wading about in entrails sometimes strikes me as
profane. At one moment I found myself chest-deep and
sliding off deeper and had to be dragged out by Mountford
and Doan. What must it feel to be buried alive?

June 24th, 1831   Nowles is dead. His hand, concealed
beneath a blanket these past days, was petrified and black
and most foul. The stench in his bedding has rendered it
useless, though Mr Jamieson has suggested we trade his
blankets to the blacks.

87

Nowles buried at sea after rites on the beach. Mr Jamieson read from the second chapter of *The Book of Jonah: out of the belly of hell cried I, and Thou heardest my voice* . . . . Sealed and drugged, the body was stowed in the stern at Mr Jamieson's feet until we were far enough out in the bay to tip it overboard.

Sat by the fire this night with Churling. He is haggard and pale, like a man whose soul has left him. Is he sick or troubled? I feel it is not my business to offer help until he asks it of me. Altogether an odd fellow. Sometimes he looks quite . . . forsaken? This pathetic countenance causes me to recoil from him, revile him. Never have I seen such a hopeless man.

June 25th, 1831   This morning I saw two naked women tossed from the headsmen's hut. It had been raining and they lay stupefied in the mud as I passed.

The stench grows with each passing day. Up the beach there are rotting carcasses and the sand is oil-smeared and blue. Gulls swarm over the ragged skeletons that lie like hulks in the shallows.

Churling, in the lookout this morning, was like a man with a fever. Once, he looked at me with a feeble expression of disappointment, stared at me until I was forced to look aside. Not a word was spoken. I fear he is mad.

Only seven whales taken thus far with a yield of less than eighteen tuns of oils and some whalebone.

At first Cleve thought the sound was rats. He had begun to fear the rats. But the noise was a wide, regular knocking like something loose in the wind, and the shoreward tin wall moved in and out like a heartbeat; he watched it: an inch in, then back to square, an inch in . . . . When he stood, his head felt stuffed with rags. The noise and the movement of the wall continued. He had heard no footfalls. He moved to the door, touched the knob and was fixed with fear. His mind snagged on that night weeks ago when he ran out into the rain and found two men beaten and bleeding. Revenge? The noise and the wall's heartbeat intensified. He opened the door. Wind rattled through the porous timbers of the jetty. Papers flickered behind him. Half the jetty lights were out. No light from the landing below. He crept along the wall outside, heard the scuttle of rodents, planted each foot fastidiously as he moved. Inched his head around the corner. Waited for his eyes to adjust. Deep in shadow against the wall, a man and a woman locked. He saw a sliver of flesh. Hair. Dark-twisted clothing. Cleve watched. He could have reached out and touched them. A fist fell against the big black back. Growls. The panting.

'You pig, you pig, you pig, pig...pig,' a deep woman's voice said. Cleve heard the words almost breathlessly said in his ear. Blood steamed in him; he stood and watched, mouth wide, until he could no longer trust his breathing. He slipped back inside and heard the thump, the vibration in the timbers like something fallen. Silence. Then a hawk and spit and footsteps. Cleve clutched the corners of his table as the door opened.

'Figgis,' the big man said, running fingers through his waxy hair. *'Prince of Norway.'*

Cleve could only point to the pen and the open logbook on the table. The man leant on one hand and signed; he smelt of pork fat and pipesmoke and some ammoniac odour that Cleve could not identify.

When the man left, closing the door carefully behind him, Cleve contemplated the big handprint stamped dark on the page. He turned the logbook about and put his own hand against the mark. It was wet; the fingers were longer and wider. He smelled his damp palm, curled it into a fist and observed the ivory of his knuckles.

VI

Well into the night, his body and soul chilled almost beyond feeling, Daniel Coupar rolled across the Hacker River bridge, blinded by the headlights of an approaching vehicle. His eyes burnt raw with whiteness; the lights seemed to slow, as though to torment him awhile before passing, then lost intensity for a moment, spearing the bush at the side of the road ahead before extinguishing altogether. Coupar cocked his head, saw in the jaundice of his own lights the parked truck at the edge of the road on the far bank. TRENTS RENTALS, he read in black letters on the high sides behind the cabin. Then he heard the horn and the on-off glare of lights, and he slowed, suspicious. A figure moved down along the gaudy side of the truck: big-shouldered, grey-haired. Coupar braked; the tractor whinnied.

'How are you, Daniel?' Pell asked.

'In what way?' Coupar said, sinking back into the comfortable truck's upholstery against his better judgment.

'Oh, you know, mind body and soul.' Pell lit a cigarette from the lighter on the dashboard.

Coupar sighed, sniffed, and rubbed his chin to chafe up some warmth. 'I reckon I'm about buggered on all three. Me body's pre-Great War, me mind's worthless, and me soul—me soul's anyone's guess.'

'Ah.'

'And I didn't know what the hell you were, for a moment. Been a while.'

Pell drew on his cigarette, features distinguishable for a moment in the ember-glow. 'Funny,' he said, exhaling, 'I was thinking of going to see you.'

'If it's a pastoral visit, don't bother—there's no pasture left.' As his body thawed in the warmth and closeness of the cabin, Coupar felt the thin edge of pain in his head again and the raw bitterness in his throat. Nausea and fatigue from the day threatened to overcome him.

'Never thought I'd meet you coming from that direction,' Pell said, 'at this hour.'

'Give us a smoke, you bugger.'

Pell switched the cabin light on and offered Coupar the packet. Coupar used the light to take a long look at Pell: he seemed bigger, older, stronger than ever before, and there was an acetylene burning in his eyes and lines in his cheeks of jubilance or desperation.

'Been to town, have you?' Pell asked.

'How long you been smoking bloody filter-tips?'

'Since I took up driving trucks again.'

Coupar lit one; Pell switched the light out and they sat in darkness, both men thinking carefully. Pell was awed by the

90

wasted look of him. He looks like an old, old man, he thought; he looks half dead. Coupar wondered about the truck, was determined not to ask about it; the last time he had seen Pell driving a truck was in 1929, and, he mused, the truck was more of a cart with a motor, and he probably didn't even have a licence.

'What do you know, then?' Pell said.

'Me? Nothing. I don't know anything.'

'Heard you've been seeing humpbacks and right whales again out at Wirrup.'

'Don't talk too loud or too bloody soon. Some galah's bound to hear and try to drop the protection law.'

'Make the place feel like home again, I s'pose.'

Coupar shrugged in the darkness. Pell felt the movement.

'Find who you were looking for?' Pell asked.

'Where?'

'Angelus.'

'No.'

'She went a couple of weeks ago,' Pell said. 'There was a barney out at the whaling station. She's taken up with this conservation mob.'

'What are they like?'

This time Coupar felt Pell shrug. 'Young. Half-right. Late.'

'What about him?'

'Cookson?' Another shrug. 'Who knows?'

Coupar sighed, feeling the smoke burn the rawness at the back of his throat. He felt emptier than he had felt before. 'The town hasn't changed.'

'Expect it to?'

'No.'

'Things're bad, though,' Pell said, flicking ash into the tray in the dashboard with a fizz of sparks. 'Recession. This unearthly drought. It's got the weather chaps by the balls. They can't explain a drought like this. Half the town out of work. Little farmers're pulling out again. The noongas live like ghosts. And the council's planned to spend some incredible amount on next year's anniversary. Tourist promotion. Visit from the Queen. Making a replica of the *Onan*, for pity's sake.'

'Least the noongas'll have another place to sleep in.'

'Yeah.' They both laughed a short, sad laugh. 'Everybody's waiting for something to happen,' said Pell. Outside, the bush and the river were silent. A long, watery moon had appeared over the treeline.

'I been waitin' for years.' Coupar felt an immense poverty, a lightness, and tasted the bitterness of vomit on his tongue: a souvenir of that long hour kneeling at the gleaming altar of Pustling's lavatory bowl.

'I was coming out — sooner or later — to ask for some advice.'

'I haven't got any advice,' Coupar said, sucking bitterness from the filter-tip.

'Oh?'

'Take two aspirins and lie down and the world will go away.'

'What about God?'

'Three aspirins.'

'I'm not sure I —'

'Look, don't start on me about the problem of God right now.'

'Why not?'

'We don't get on so well any more.'

'I thought as one got older,' Pell murmured, 'one came closer to Him. You know: wisdom, age —'

'Well, it's not true. Shit, I'm an old man; I can't even find me way down to the bore sometimes, can't even find me fly-buttons — how the hell'm I s'posed to find *Him*? You get farther away from everything. Everybody. Get to be an old man an' realise you know bugger-all. You can't see anything clear.'

'Or you can't see for looking,' Pell said. 'Old men forget, sometimes. Their mind doesn't tell them what body and soul remember.'

'Body and — ?'

'What do you ever know except what's happened to you and what's been promised to you?'

Coupar sighed. 'What advice?'

'What?'

'You said you wanted advice. Thought I'd shut you up before you started quoting.'

'I don't need to quote to you.'

'God A'mighty!'

'Praying, eh?'

92

'Get on with it, Bill.'

Pell moved in his seat; the upholstery squawked. He almost regretted having to come to the point. He wished they could banter all night, two old men enjoying each other's irritable company.

'Pustling's using the church somehow as a financial cover, a tax fiddle. He's trying to get the church working on his behalf, buying land and developing, I s'pose. For the past year he's been making these fantastic donations with invisible strings attached—only we were too awed by the money to think of strings, and in our greedy enthusiasm, thinking of all the things we could do—well. Not often, you see, the church has enough power to implement the things it knows should be done. Trouble is, more often than not, when you get the power—and money is power—it never seems to get done. Comes from being human, I s'pose. The powerless are sometimes more efficient. Anyway, I think he's also bribing us to put in a good word for him here and there next year when all the media and celebrities come. You know, support his promotions, have our name up with his, get the church spruced up for showbiz. He wants us quiet and affirming. Angelus: the clean, honest, Christian town. Maybe he's got some Americans coming from the Business/Bible Belt. I don't know. Everything is unstated, of course. Everything is implication.'

'So?' Coupar asked, irritable.

'So, I'm retiring in a few weeks.'

'And?'

'I won't be in the official job when it all happens. The new fellow'll do anything he's told. They train 'em to be public relations men these days: We Aim to Oblige. Darby's his name.'

'Geez, let him have it. Let some other poor bugger handle it.'

'He won't, that's just it. And the church'll end up another slave of the Pustlings. History all over again. I won't have it.'

'Who cares about history?'

'Listen, if you had fourteen-year-old kids quoting the Crusades at you all the time you'd know what I mean. Anyway, you should talk, you've got history to avoid.'

93

'*Yea. I hated all my labour which I had taken under the sun:
because I should leave it unto the man that shall be after me.
And who knoweth whether he shall be a wise man or a fool?*'

'Now you're the one quoting. Look, I made a big mistake,
and I want to remedy it, if I can, before it's too late. They
retire me in four weeks. I wouldn't be surprised if Pustling's
had something to do with that somehow; I've got a few years
left in me yet. Four weeks. Election of elders is in eight.
Pustling's been attending now for a long time. Now he's
buttering up the soft nominals and some of the senile ones to
vote him in as elder. As elder he gets better control over his
money, sinks more into it, and slowly breaks up resistance from
the rest of the congregation. I mean a church is only people
and — God knows — they make blunders. And I'm not going to
let this one happen. So, I've been spending his money. He had
an account in my name set up a while ago. I've cancelled it and
taken the cash. So far I've spent thousands. There's another
couple of grand in the back — blankets, food, medicines,
books, Bibles, toys, clothes —'

'So you're giving it out. Very Christ-like.'

'No, very desperate and confused,' Pell said. 'Maybe even a
waste of time, who knows?'

'But it makes you feel good, and that's enough.'

'No, it doesn't, and it's not enough, Daniel. Don't come at
me with that rubbish.'

'So what advice, then? Dammit, Pell, get to the point,
bugger you.'

Pell moved about in the dark; Coupar felt the agitation in
the upholstery. Transactions, he thought, a bloody nightful of
transactions.

'I can't keep buying and disturbing indefinitely. Pustling
kind of owns the supply, if you know what I mean. And he's
catching onto my buying out of town. Pretty soon he's gonna
ground me altogether — I can't spend and give fast enough on
my own. I can't set up any chain of distribution or anything;
he'll just break it up. So I'm on my own.'

'The point, Bill.'

'The point is, what am I going to do with the rest? Under
your seat there's a box of cheques, books of account and cash
worth thousands. Can't even bring myself to tell you how

94

much. The point is, what do I do with money and records I can't convert into goods, as they say. Wish I'd learnt a few things about money in my prime. Poverty is much simpler. What do I do?'

'I don't know, dammit, buy yourself a concubine, or a retirement house,' Coupar growled. 'Better still, buy yourself a decent bloody congregation.'

'Don't worry,' Pell guffawed, 'I've thought of that. Talk about temptation in the wilderness.'

'You can't beat Pustling when it comes to money. You won't beat him.'

'Maybe not,' Pell murmured. 'But we don't have to be beaten by him, either. Just because you don't win doesn't mean you lose.'

'Shit, here you go again. Now you'll bring it around to the Good Lord.'

'It's my business, Daniel.'

'And money's Pustling's business.'

'God and Mammon.'

'There he goes.'

'It's nothing new, Daniel, and it'll go on in this town long after we're gone.'

'So what the hell's the point buggerising around playing Santa Claus to the down and outs for a couple of weeks. Why bother?'

'Because for a while I can. And I thank God for it.'

'It won't make any difference in the long run.'

'Not that can be seen, no. *Because we look not to the things that are seen but to the things that are unseen.* Sorry, I'm quoting again.'

Coupar shifted and clumped his feet up onto the dashboard, hugging his knees, pretending that he did not see the moonlight gleaming from his too-shiny black shoes.

'And who knows what effect you had in the winter of '32? As I said, you forget. Specially those things unseen.'

'Listen,' Coupar said, 'I'm going. It'll take me near on another hour to get back.'

'You don't have anything to suggest, then?'

'Jesus, Pell. You come round like a bloody simpering dog, you always have. You know your trouble? You're a worshipper!'

95

'Yes,' Pell confessed.

'Well, I don't want your worship.'

'You don't have it. It's respect you're frightened of, because it demands responsibility.'

A long silence ensued; there was only the breathing of two old men.

'Will you do me a favour?' Pell asked, at length.

'What?'

'Can I hide the money somewhere at Wirrup? It seems to be the only place that Pustling can't penetrate. It would help. After it all cools down I could start using it again. Maybe you could even give me a hand with it. Some people'd take charity from you that shy away from me. What do you say?'

'No.'

'Why?'

'Because it's a waste of time.'

'Why?'

'Because Pustling already owns Wirrup. I sold it to the bastard a couple of hours ago. And the house in town. Coupars have occupancy until the day I die. He has the right to inspect at any time. I'm a tenant like everyone else, Bill.'

A sound entered the darkness, finding its way about the cabin faintly at first, and then broad and deep and rich, and Daniel Coupar, breathless with exertion and emotion, realised after some moments of incomprehension, that it was Pell. He was laughing.

Wind came at him slowly, but with a solidity that worried him, even in his stupor. Coupar felt as though the wind was prising open his ribs, invading him, and no hunching, he found, would protect him. His body felt beaten; his tongue was dry and sore and windburnt. The grease-flecked suit rippled on him. He bent the crown of his head to the wind. Tractor noise bludgeoned him. His cheeks were wet with snot and tears; his fingers hooked, welded to the wheel. Dark wings of sleep descended upon him every now and then—great, flickering shadows that smothered him for a moment or so, leaving him shocked and panicky at the wheel. The day and night cartwheeled about him, made him shiver and disbelieve: he saw water falling and bodies falling and bending, and faces — many faces — and his eyes burnt. As he bobbed eastwards along the lonely road, he felt the wind lose its chill and become warm as blood; he smelt dead land despite the stink of diesel. He moved: he was in yesterday and today, asleep and awake, dead and alive, numb and sensing all at once, and there was no telling between them; his body threatened not to inform him; his mind was at its own mercy; his soul defied him.

He felt some flicker of recognition upon milling through the first gate at Wirrup; he heard the sound of wire coiling and scraping about the rear axle — the hissing sound it made — but he had no knowledge of the second and third as they bowed down before him, and when the tractor strayed wide across an empty paddock, churning across the dust, and teetered and tipped into an old watercourse deep as a creekbed, he was quite asleep.

VII

On the road east the next day, despite his noon breakfast of eggs and toast and coffee, Cleve Cookson felt a sensation in his stomach like hunger pain and, like a hungry man, he saw small objects with unusual clarity as they flashed by, seemed to feel each stone of the road drumming into him as he swept along unsealed stretches. Twenty-eights blurred green across his path. Before the Hacker River bridge he turned off onto a dirt track that buckled through old, deserted properties parallel to the Hacker. The estuary through the paperbarks was a wide, incongruous smile, an arc that swept round to dunes and the sea. At the end of the estuary the water broadened into a cul-de-sac against the flat, wide sand-bar at the river mouth.

Cleve drove out onto the hard-packed sand of the bar between sea and river, and the chassis hissed. Precipitous dunes banked the estuary on either side, wind-smoothed and marbled in ribbed patterns. Over the water, a shag lifted, craning suddenly away. With a flick of the wheel Cleve brought the Land Rover suddenly round; the open tray swung out, spraying a wake of sand as he side-drifted and came to a stalling halt. He switched the ignition off, wound a window down, and inhaled the sweet, mucky smell of the estuarine shallows and the paperbarks.

There, he tried to apprehend a memory. Surf tumbled behind.

The summer they married, the Cooksons came here to swim in the cobalt pools at the end of the beach. The morning was hot and clear, but by noon cloud from the south reduced the air to a chill and there was a quickening breeze from the sea. They gathered hats and towels and walked back along the beach to where the Land Rover was parked, exactly as now, on the bar. Queenie washed the sand from her feet in the estuary, wet legs glistening like polished walnut. She commented on the warmth of the water and continued to paddle about as Cleve stood by the edge. She coaxed him into paddling with her in the warm shoals, and soon they were splashing one another, batting the coppery water about like children, shaking it from their eyes. It was sometime then that Queenie noticed the dinghy upside-down on the bank around from them. Cleve took no notice; he was cautious of ownership and a feeling of dread spread through him as Queenie waded round to the boat. He was afraid of being caught; and then as she coaxed, afraid of ridicule, he took his chances of being discovered and helped turn the boat over, in awe of Queenie's reckless innocence. Underneath there was some rope, a length of anchor chain, two oars, and one rowlock. They launched—gay and awkward—with one makeshift rowlock made with a loop of rope, and began their circuitous route upstream. Neither of them could row; Cleve's father had never taken him fishing as a boy (much to his shame at school) and Queenie had always been reluctant passenger to her grandfather. They took an oar each and laughed and splashed and saw mullet and smelt riffling the surface, skipping in their corkscrew wake.

Snagged in paperbarks a quarter-mile up, the boat confirmed its superiority, refusing to be moved, and one oar floated away through the weepy, tangled trees. They stumbled and cursed; their gazes met and Cleve clung to her and she

98

pulled him to the bottom of the boat and wrapped him in her nut-smelling thighs, wanting him for protection, wanting to protect him, her back bathed in the warm swill in the bottom and her hands in the woody smell of his hair. He could not take his eyes from her face, felt her breasts flattening themselves to him; he ached to dissipate and live in her body, a clean, warm, healing place. He wanted to inhabit the space behind her eyes, the source of her animation. She sighed and the paperbarks soughed and in time he could not tell between them as he made his own helpless sounds. Birds beat their wings afar off, like applause. The gentle rocking of the dinghy sent out a chorus of rings, ripples chasing one another under the flaking forms of the trees out onto the larger expanse.

Later they unsnagged themselves and then the boat and sailed downstream in the freshened breeze, holding spread an orange towel between them. Wind shook white bark from their hair as they went.

Cleve started the engine. He was hungry. His body and his mind growled with dissatisfaction, with pain almost.

At the turn-off, Cleve paused for a moment looking east along the road towards Wirrup. He had a sudden thought: the old man, he'd go and see the old man. He wanted to talk, he wanted to sit out on the veranda with the old man without Queenie hovering over them both. He began to drive east, mind racing. He'd tell the old man about Queenie. The three of them could sort it out.... But on the bridge he braked suddenly, backed up and headed back towards Angelus.

No, he thought. The old man'll think I'm crawling, and I'm not crawling to anyone.

By the time Angelus came into view, his hunger was bitter and it burned acidic in him.

June 26th, 1831   The motto of my companions, it seems, is a text from the prophet Isaiah: *In that day the Lord with his sore and great and strong sword shall punish Leviathan the piercing serpent; and he shall slay the dragon that is in the sea.* The ignorant fellows believe the sperm whale to be the Serpent, agent of the Evil One. No honest fish, they say, has lungs and a teat and a member

99

like a man's. Perhaps it is fortuitous that we concern ourselves only with the right and humpback, the sleepy giants.

June 27th, 1831 At dawn I heard noise and clattering in the camp. Gibbering, threatening sounds and shouting and what sounded like a struggle. There was a single musket-shot, then cries and jabbering. As I rose and peered through the shutter, I beheld Leek in the act of launching a lance, but my vision was narrow and I could not see its destination. Nevertheless I heard a cry, a dreadful scream. I was in the act of dressing when I heard a second shot.

With the others of my hut I went outside to witness the scene. A blackfellow lay convulsing on his back, Leek's lance piercing his throat, letting out blood in great gouts, and another native lay face down with a sorry wound in the back of his head. Men cursed in Cain's hut. We went in. Churling lay naked and stricken with blood upon his lips and a horrible spear wound in his stomach from which still protruded the broken stub. Someone dragged something heavy through the door, and as I turned I perceived that it was the lubra I had seen once before. There was a musket hole in her back and she seemed to be dead.

Some others, drunk, I presume, slept right through the commotion.

We dug shallow holes for the natives as whales breached out in the bay. Finn's boat took a canvas bundle and a Bible and returned at noon with Churling consigned to the sea and a whale in tow. Somehow they contrive to see it as a good omen.

The lamp sputters and my eyes are strained. The wind has backed to north-easterly and blubber steam blows about. For some reason Churling's clothes lie upon my sea chest. They will fit no one else, yes, that is the reason. Excepting his garments, only a waterstained notebook survives him, and that is of little use to anyone here. In it there is but one page of crude lettering which I transcribe below out of some sense of propriety that even I do not understand.

'Eugene Andrew Churling
Lost.
The sand on this bech was once wite.
Myself also. And I thot I might tell him my frend but

100

he is faraway and can not lisen.
He is lost in the Hevens and the Hevens is lost to me.
Flesh. Blod. Sol.
Good thing Mother is in Heven and I to Hell for now I
will not meet face her over this.
For I am ther animal.'

Painstakingly scripted below this is a verse copied from
Jonah the prophet, the favourite, it would seem, of the
whalemen.

Therefore now, O Lord, take, I beseech thee, my life
from me; for it is better to die than to live.'

There is nothing else to tell of Churling. Even the
Testament he has copied from is gone. His garments, like
my own, reek. This shabby piece of written nonsense is
all, and the remainder of his notebook remains a blank
volume.

VIII

Beneath a heatless bolt of sun which angled through her
window, affixed itself to the wall and bristled with angry dust-
motes, Queenie Cookson lay on her bed listening to the
building and, beyond those red, wet walls, the city. Somewhere
a car horn brayed. She would stay in today: the streets, shops,
parks, walking feet, the news-stands, fruit, faces, smells, the
close forward movement, did not attract her this morning.
There had been no news. She was even losing expectation. She
felt winter's firmness and observed that cold bar of sunlight
until an unseen cloud extinguished it.

Queenie had almost given up imagining what the others
were doing; it was difficult to imagine them at all. The anxious
waiting had become a dull anticipation, then curiosity, and
now a bitter taste. She had no idea how Cachalot was
progressing; the papers mentioned nothing, and she could only
presume they were still at their hotel, blocks away, in an airier
quarter of the city, waiting for the Zodiacs that no one would
transport and no one would replace. Without some inside
influence, it looked hopeless. No amount of money would help.

She was glad she had decided to wait it out alone. The trip

from Angelus in the crowded car, the plush hotel, the primal screaming and the parties and hangers-on had been too much. It was action that she wanted, not Brent's sleazy press conferences, not more talk. Waiting was bad enough. Talk made her lonely. She had told herself back then—she could not afford to be lonely. It was what made her need. It was what Cleve liked best and, though she despised herself for it, it was loneliness that she found most attractive in him.

Queenie lay with her hands behind her head, thinking of the past weeks. She had found the guest house in a cheap part of town. The landlady, in a man's threadbare dressing-gown, showed Queenie to her late husband's room which was still occupied by a collection of model railways and war games spread along a wide, laminated table. The room was dark. The mattress of the hollow bed smelt of urine. The big house reverberated with the cough and hock of chronic smokers. The ivy-smothered outhouse was a long walk away, and the lane behind was the territory of fighting cats. The yard snapped and flapped grey with bed linen on long, drooping lines.

Each morning Queenie, not staying for the big fatty breakfast with the other hawking boarders in the dining-room, left her room at the front of the house and sought out new and different places in which to have her coffee and toast, cafes and restaurants squeezed between long nondescript buildings, in arcades and lanes.

Pushed forward by other bodies and an eagerness for exploration, Queenie embraced the city. At first she felt awkward: her skirts too short, jeans obsolete, her accent too broad, her manner dull and friendly and countrified; but she soon learnt to take refuge in the haste and anonymity and the grandness of scale; she buried herself. Boutiques led to markets, galleries, taverns, craft shops, and arcades linked with more arcades: bookshops, cinemas, antique shops, junk shops, theatres; she found parks and restaurants and streets full of American sailors, unemployed youths, browsing matrons, clusters of old men spitting and laughing with phlegmy throats. Chinese, Italians, Greeks, Poles, passed her in the street. She walked blindly into a cinema and found herself watching a pornographic movie with thirty men in business suits who fled when the lights went up at intermission.

In the bookshops she bought new novels and books of poetry she had never heard of. Once, she caught a bus to the beach and walked through the coastal suburb in which Cleve had lived with his parents all his life. She wondered what she would do if she suddenly came upon his parents. She had met them only once. Her walk through the suburb was not illuminating.

Footsore and heady, Queenie returned each night to her room of dusty locomotives and fallen soldiers to read herself to sleep. The bed sank in the middle like a hammock, the headboard was crusty with nosepickings and squashed insects. The hardbound novels, she found, were mostly about the writing of more novels, and the poetry concerned itself with itself, and between them they posed no threat to sleep.

Come on, you bastards, Queenie thought, getting out of bed at last. Let's hear from you. Something must be happening, *something* at least.

IX

When finally the rain ceases, Hassa Staats steps outside onto the footpath under the leaking marquee and draws in the crisp, still air, exhaling cautiously so as not to cough and yield to the itch in his chest, the feeling of having swallowed a burr that will do damage if dislodged. The southerly has blown itself out: the harbour is tranquil and the townspeople pass, unharassed, with armsful of shopping, skirts and coats and hats in proper place. Some of them smile or say hello as they pass, and to those he feels deserve it Staats will wave and grin back between chomps on his barley sugar. Cars hiss by, lifting water from the road, creating their own vaporous rain. This Saturday noon Angelus is peaceful, even dull, but Hassa Staats savours the calm. The empty tour buses parked outside the Bureau up the street do not discomfort him today. It is good to have peace, he thinks, shifting inside his jacket. Everything has its place again today; there is a rightness in the air.

The sight of Marion Lowell unhurriedly dodging the streams of water spilling from the gutters as she comes down the hill

103

from the direction of the Pustling office breaks the spell, though not unpleasantly. As he observes her progress down the street towards him, noting the elevation of her breasts at each step, he is reminded of a matter that until now has belonged to yesterday—Des Pustling's phone call. Pustling had spoken to him about TRENT'S RENTALS and at some length about the future of Angelus. TRENT'S RENTALS is owned and run by Harry Trent who is, by marriage, Hassa Staats's cousin. Pell, Pustling said, had been hiring one of Harry's trucks these past weeks, much to the neglect of his congregation and the commerce of the town. And, Pustling said, the money he was using to hire with was hot money. Embezzlement. Pustling was asking a favour. Hassa was to speak to Harry. Trucks were to cease to be available. All trucks.

It was a shock to Staats to hear such news. Certain though he was about the worthlessness of Pell's denomination and the weakness of the old man's character, the idea of embezzlement surprised him. Instinctively, he thought it a matter for the police, but he would see Harry nevertheless; he was not one to turn aside a favour for Des Pustling.

It occurs to him, as he thinks and observes, that Marion Lowell's breasts must be of considerable weight; he sees them rise and fall like loose pistons and he has a terrible desire to weigh them in his hands. Though he intends to, he has not yet spoken to Harry Trent about this matter of Pell; he is reluctant. Hassa does not like to mix family with business. And this kind of business leaves him uneasy.

'Hello, Marion,' Staats says, as she comes within earshot.

'Oh, hello, Mr Staats,' Marion says, looking up from the pavement, surprised.

'How are you?'

'Um. Fine.' She hesitates, stops a few feet from him. 'Is anything the matter?'

'No.' Staats chuckles. 'No, no, not at all.'

'Oh.' She breaks into a doubtful smile, prepares to walk on.

'Would you care for a drink?'

'I—'

'On the house?'

'Well, I was just going to lunch.'

'A quick glass of sherry, then.'

'Beer will be fine.'

They go into the lounge bar where he steers her to an empty table in a corner and has drinks brought. The pub is beginning to fill. Staats raises his glass. Marion Lowell drinks, nervous; the bulk of the publican, the glowing corpulence of him, frightens her.

'I have a favour to ask of you,' he says, thinking of other favours he wishes he had the courage and the youth to ask.

'Oh?' Her heart shrinks. She does not like favours.

'Can you tell me a few things about Reverend Pell?'

Marion Lowell lowers her glass carefully. 'I'm not an expert on Mr Pell,' she says just as cautiously.

'What about his trips?'

'Well, I hardly—'

'Harmless curiosity.'

'Which trips do you mean, Mr Staats?'

'The ones he makes out to the farms in Harry Trent's truck, for instance.'

'Listen, I think I'd better leave now—'

'Let's be frank, shall we?' Hassa Staats says, laying one pink soup-plate of a hand on the table beside hers, so close she can sense his heat.

'You be Frank and I'll be Marion.'

'You have a sense of humour,' he says, feeling his advantage slipping.

'And a sense of decency, too, I like to think.'

'I need to know—I have to know—what he takes out in Harry's truck. Please?'

'Why do you need to know?'

Staats takes a breath. Why not be honest? he thinks. A bit. 'Because I have to do a favour, too.'

'Favours. This bloody town was built on favours! Hell, what's it matter, anyway? He takes out food, blankets, clothing, matches, kerosene, books, Bibles. That kind of thing.' She sips her beer, disgusted.

'Hot?'

'Hot Bibles? For God's sake!' she says with a tone of amusement that she cannot sustain.

'Well.'

'Well, what?'

105

'Anything else?'

'Why don't you ask the man?'

Staats slides his glass about the laminated table, unable to answer.

'Well, I don't want to spoil my lunch,' she says, rising, thinking: well you've blown it now, girl—on a bloody priest, of all things.

Staats, amused and entertained, watches the tension in her moving buttocks as she leaves and thinks enviously of Pustling. A girl with life, there, he thinks, drinking up. By the time he has finished his glass—and hers—his admiration is replaced by a thin, undefined worry.

He rises and sidles out onto the pavement again where he watches the shopkeepers closing up, cars pulling out, children shouting and evading their mothers. He recognises the thin, awkward figure of Cleveland Cookson emerging from the hooded entrance of the Black and White, and he notices the lopsided gait like that of a man who has recently had an arm amputated and has lost equilibrium; it is the same walk his wife Mara had after her first mastectomy. Staats watches the young man lope off. She's left you for good, matie, he thinks—and I don't know who's luckiest, her, you or us. But even this gives Staats short comfort because he knows that she will be back.

'They never leave for good,' he says. 'Even if they come back horizontal, they come back some time. Even my Rick will be back some time.' And this thought depresses him still further.

He goes inside, feeling his weight and his years, and more.

X

The next Wednesday morning Queenie read a day-old newspaper as she sat in a steamy corner of the laundrobar. She hated the two blocks trek in the rain to wash her clothes in machines used by hundreds of other people. Their pubic hairs, lint, skin flakes, cigarette butts and tissue pulp never ceased to revolt her. She read her paper lightly, keeping an eye on the

Italian boys who stole along the rows of chugging washers with cupfuls of washing powder and collusion on their faces, until a news-story caught her eye long enough for her to read it over and over.

Abbie Tanks, promising new recruit from the country club of North Angelus, has been found critically injured in the car park of Metropolitan Oval. He was found to have massive head and internal injuries and was rushed to Queen Elizabeth Medical Centre where his condition is now described as fair. Doctors said that both Tanks' knees were shattered and his skull and one hand were fractured.

Police said they found the Aboriginal footballer beside his car outside his new home ground comatose and in a pool of blood. They said they are seeking witnesses who might have been in the area between six and ten on the evening of Tuesday 14th June.

It is a major blow to the Metropolitan Club who expected Tanks to play in his first city league game this Saturday.

My God, I know him, Queenie thought. From school. He was the one who used to have his head shaved for lice every summer. He was the one who hit the headmaster back. I know him.

Queenie had seen Abbie Tanks play when she went with Cleve to the football when Cleve was still working for the *Advocate*; both found the game dull, the atmosphere of dreary effort compounded by the weather, but there was always a pleasure in seeing one player do what he did to perfection. She remembered Abbie Tanks winning the school Athlete's Trophy at fourteen, and hearing, the next year, of his expulsion for setting fire to the school. He had been in some of Queenie's classes: thin, quiet, quick. She had never spoken to him.

Schooldays. She unloaded her wet laundry into the wicker basket and hoisted it onto her back. Schooldays. The long rides into and out of town on the bus that Barney Wilkins drove, and in particular she remembered one trip home during her final year of primary school when she sat on Trent Nathan's knee. Trent Nathan was a year older and somehow desirable and Queenie sat on his lap, buttocks contracted nervously, inventing and rehearsing lines of dialogue, ashamed of her

107

plaits and her big brown knees. Other high school boys flicked
snot and spitballs from the back of the bus. Girls sat in clusters
singing songs learnt from the radio in strained American
accents. Across the aisle, a big farm boy slept, a light fuzz on
his chin and a furious pimple on his cheek. Every few minutes
Barney Wilkins stopped at a kerosene-tin letterbox and let out
one or two children who swung their bags into the door
jumping down. Queenie and Trent Nathan looked question-
ingly at one another, and she saw him glance secretly at the
promising lumps in the front of her pinafore. He smiled at her;
she smiled back and realised there was no need for conversation; her happiness blossomed with every mile past the Ranges
towards Fourpeaks and Wirrup beyond. She knew that Trent
Nathan appreciated her sitting on his knee and would ask her
to again tomorrow morning; she also knew that she could beat
him in a fight because he was frail and handsome. Before
Trent Nathan's stop, Queenie felt her happiness and confidence turning into that crawly feeling she guessed was love
and it made her cross her legs. But when the boy's stop came
and she slid, smiling, from his knee, she knew otherwise. Trent
Nathan screamed. Heads bobbed and bent into the aisle.
Barney Wilkins turned in his seat.

'Ah. . . .' Trent Nathan gasped at the black-red stain on his
trousers and then at the patchwork of faces about him. 'Flog a
dog,' he said, near tears.

'Flog a dog!' called the girls up the back.

'Flog a dog,' muttered the sleeping boy with the unhappy
pimple.

'Flogadooorrg!' screamed the girls again.

A spitball hit Trent Nathan on the forehead as he crabbed
down the aisle with his schoolbag over the stain. The bus jerked
away after some hesitation, and Queenie writhed, smudging
the upholstery, with twenty minutes travelling time ahead. She
slid low in her seat, too shocked for tears.

'Queenie Coupar's got the bloods!' the girls called from the
rear. Spitballs ricochetted overhead. The bus moved on
unhurriedly.

From that aftenoon Queenie Coupar forgot boys and turned
back to swimming; she began to train for the school team, and
by the time she was sixteen she *was* the school team. She hoed

108

through chlorine water in carnivals and inter-town meets, winning trophies and pennants that she gave to the school and her bewildered grandfather. Although she hated the smell and taste of it, Queenie loved the colour of the pool under water—the hazy wall becoming defined as she closed upon it, the thud of limbs on the surface, the aquamarine spills of light that fell behind as she tumble-turned for the final lap— because it reminded her of the colour of the shoals at Wirrup and the pastel blue of her dreams. In the pool and in the surf she felt strong and quick and graceful, but in class she felt heavy, thought herself dull and plodding.

Queenie humped her wet washing along beneath the shop awnings, feeling a new sadness in her, remembering those days.

Back on her bed that afternoon, Queenie could not help but daydream. Homely things tormented her: the sounds of wood being split, the smells of capsicums, tomatoes, the combustion stove, the sound of the canning factory siren in the still harbour. She hurt herself with images of firelight and cabernet and jarlsberg cheese—even the thin warmth of Cleveland Cookson; and the thoughts exhausted her, made her so tired, so earthbound. I had to, she told herself. Dammit, I had to leave him. There's no room in him for me. There's not enough time to wait for things.

Through an ultramarine haze towards a distant and indistinct light and tiny sounds like the tinkling the sea makes against rocks, Queenie ploughed on with her heartbeat in her ears. Stippled sand passed below. Cool sea moved between her thighs as she pounded forward into gossamer. Her body propelled itself, willed her on, informed itself, wanted, needed, burrowed onward to that space in the light where she felt the beginnings of a vortex, farther, closer, then the long fence of ivory, and she tipped forward into the cavity, tumbling, then dark. Twilight misted about her as she lay in viscous wetness. Gurglings. The slush had a bitter gastric smell and she felt it begin to burn. The belly of a whale, she thought: this is the belly of the whale. She saw her hands, her knees, the skin flaking, dissolving already; hair came away in her palms as

109

she touched the crown of her head. Acid. A stench of bile. Standing, she whimpered, took a foetid breath and stumbled forward towards the hint of light that came and went. Lumpy obstacles caught her legs, ensnared her feet; the way ahead was arduous. Forwards or backwards? she thought. Mouth or anus? A wave of slush hit her from behind, knocking her to her knees in a nest of entanglements and she saw they were limbs, grey-green, rotted, half-digested, with white peeps of bone and sinew and partially decomposed faces. She saw Staats the publican, jowls dissolving agape, and beneath, Richardson the baker, and the contorted, inflated corpses of Des Pustling, Abbie Tanks, Easton the old whaler, a bikie she once dated, Trent Nathan, Fleurier. And Cleve, horribly incomplete. Queenie floundered forward, burning, legs caught, hands brushing aside papyrus flaps of skin. She heard a scream, the scream of a child, and saw myriads of light.

Waking, she heard the piercing screech of a truck braking outside her window. She heard the landlady fussing in the corridor. She fell back into the mushy bed, stiff and sore with tension.

XI

It is the fifteenth of June 1978.

William Pell wakes after eighteen hours. Still his body tells him it must have more rest. He rises regardless and falls into a lukewarm shower, gazing at his flat toes through the sluicing bars of water, passing coarse soap under his arms, between his legs, over the little pot-belly, and slowly he wakes.

Before his breakfast he empties the refrigerator of curdled milk and anything that has grown a beard, then goes out to pick up the week's copies of the *Advocate* from where they lie—rolled and half composted—on the dewy lawn. He reads the headlines, Wednesday to Wednesday, unravelling.

NORTHS TO HAVE NEW OVAL
EVERY DOG HAS HIS ...
BEACH RESCUE
LOCAL WINES POPULAR
ONAN PROGRESS
LOCAL FOOTBALLER MUGGED
ABBIE TANKS CRITICAL

Pell gathers the wet, curling papers under his arm and goes around the side of the house to the bin, but he drops the armful before he reaches it, grunting in surprise. The truck in his driveway is up on blocks, tyreless. Pell walks over to the driver's-side door and reads the note taped to the chrome handle:

> *Wherever the spirit would go, they would*
> *go, and the wheels would rise along with*
> *them, because the spirit of the living*
> *creatures was in the wheels.*
> Jeremiah.

'Pustling, you ignoramus,' Pell sighed. 'It's from Ezekiel.' He went inside. He needed more sleep.

XII

It was as though there was neither night nor day. Cleve read, drank, ate and slept; there seemed no difference between the jetty and the house, work and rest. At times he found difficulty in distinguishing 1831 from 1978, and it was rarely that he noticed the tin walls quaking in the squalls, or the laughter of the old men below, the emptiness of his bed when he slept without resting in the day. Cleve did not notice the queue running onto the street outside the Social Security office, the milling youths in the lee of the post office, and he overlooked newspapers and heard radio news without listening. He read.

He drove and beat his body as though it was merely an enclosure which housed him, and he retreated within it. He almost forgot himself.

June 29th, 1831   Today at noon whilst chasing a cow we saw the British warship *Keen* drop anchor by the headland in the lee of the easterly and put a boat ashore. We lost sight of the cow in the course of time and soon made for shore.

The Englishmen are leaving in the morning. They make no secret of thinking us disgusting barbarians as they look down their noses at us and speak in their stiff, mannered tones. As yet they have not inquired into the anonymous graves on the beach. They show distaste at the smell all about which we seem to have forgotten. I will be glad when these priggish men take their leave of us for I feel manifestly unclean in their presence.

June 30th, 1831   The *Keen* has departed for Angelus Harbour which is not far to the east from here. It is a penal colony of some sort for the British.

A man from Finn's crew is sick. He screams like an animal in the night and throws furniture about.

Finn's crew took a bull today.

Winter thrashed the town of Angelus. Rain and wind hurtled in off the ocean, jostling the settlement around the harbour. Outside the harbour entrance the Sound was white and broken, and beyond the heads the Southern Ocean moved about like an unsteady mountain range. Few vessels ventured out, though several straggled in from the Bight, wind-torn and waterlogged, to take shelter in the buttressed harbour.

July 2nd, 1831   This evening the most peculiar thing occurred. A light, like a great ball of starlight, moved across the bay and passed over the beach and our encampment. All saw it. We stood speechless and watched and felt it pass. Mr Jamieson says he has seen something similar in the Pacific, but has no scientific explanation for it. The men grumble. Some call it an omen. There is some argument. All are uneasy.

Few natives bring us wood now, and the graves on the beach have been robbed in the night. I fear the blacks are

112

hostile at the present. Daily an expedition is sent out to collect firewood, a perilous routine.

On the eighteenth of this month the *Family of Man* is due to drop supplies or to take us aboard should the fishery prove hopeless. I have resolved to leave this company at the next hospitable port, confident as I am of the failure of this expedition. Desertion of such a party as this can be no sin.

When he was reading Cleve felt a sense of purpose, of control, a forward movement he had felt few times in his life. It was rare that he felt so compelled.

July 3rd, 1831   There being no whales in sight all morning and having executed duties in good time, I spent this afternoon exploring the length of the beach of the first time. I found, to my great surprise and delight, a well formed, clean, dry cave at the base of the westerly headland. It had a rare quality I could not for a moment identify. Then I realised that the air inside was pure, that it did not reek of boiled flesh and fly-blown skeletons. I sat inside, observing the smooth grey walls, savouring the cleanness of it, a veritable haven. Before leaving I memorised the location of my new discovery. I am certain I can find it again.

At dusk today Finn's crew took the lunatic Bale into the bush, returning without him an hour later. They have left him to his own insane nature.

July 4th, 1831   Sealers from Bald Island arrived this morning in a whaleboat, apparently to celebrate. They are mostly from New Bedford and Nantucket.

I spent the evening, dismissed from my duties, in my sanctuary up the beach. The sand is ghostly in the moonlight. I was free from the carousing and revelry of the camp, and I wrote and meditated by the light of a candle. After perhaps two hours I returned to find that the celebrations had soured and fighting resulted. The sealers were preparing to sleep on the beach.

It is late now—perhaps near morning—and I cannot sleep. My bunk has been destroyed in the evening's commotion and the floor is rife with draughts. I write with the illumination of the moon.

Hale is disinclined to speak to me these past days. He

113

mumbles about me keeping too much to myself and has twice called me 'High an' Holy' as though in jest, though there seems to be some sincerity behind his humour. Doan and Smithson, always reluctant to talk, never speak at all now. I am so much younger than they. Perhaps the loneliness of extreme youth was Churling's source of despair.

For Cleve, the realness and aliveness of the journal were precious. Other people's experiences had often seemed more exciting, closer to the truth, than his own: but never before had he felt so close to owning the experience of another as he had with Nathaniel Coupar. He felt he was there, as though his eyes were Coupar's eyes. It was an almost supernatural feeling, as it had been in the dinghy on the estuary with Queenie when he had been filled with wholeness and absence and an exceptional grace which let him feel what it was to be her and himself at once. These were the moments when he suspected there could be a meaning to his existence.

But, too, as he read there was sometimes a vague unease, something more than sadness, like a splinter beneath the skin.

July 5th, 1831 Sealers left early in jovial spirits.
Returning to Bald Island which is west of here.
   No whales.
  6th No whales. Men arguing, fighting.

One night with the sea rocketing about beneath him and the dusty one-bar heater fizzing and ticking beside him, Cleve Cookson shut the journal and stood up, prickling with a memory. It was like the momentary breaking of a spell. He was in the old Presbyterian church, at his own wedding. Hesitant faces all around. Organ music. Coupar ludicrous in a suit. The plodding vows at the altar. His own dreadful words, his lifelong motto: I will (you never do), I will (but you won't you're spineless), I will.... It mocked him. Then out on the pavement he felt the townspeople throwing rice with an alarming enthusiasm, as though aiming for his eyes or wanting to pit his cheeks. They're stoning me, he thought. And there he is, old Coupar, waiting for me to run. Queenie was a white light beside him. He heard her laughter. Her nose was girlishly sunburnt and beginning to peel, her teeth white, and a speck—a grain of rice—stuck to her lower lip as she laughed and held him with her brown eyes. And there was old man Pell, Bible on his hip like a flask or a weapon, eyes narrowed thoughtfully in the sun. He knew, Cleve thought; he knew we would be like this.

At that moment, Cleve plunged out of the hut into the wedging rain, and bellowed into the blackness: 'I will! I will! I am not useless!' There were flickerings of light and laughter from below. Rain stung him like pelted rice. Cleve turned his chin up in the dark. She's ruined me, he told himself; she's made me even weaker.

Next morning Cleveland Cookson bought a speargun. He carried it out of Bill's Sport & Tackle wrapped in brown paper, and the wrapping gave it an even more forbidden feel. He strolled downtown with it under his arm and saw Ollie Fingle the barber watch him pass. The *Advocate* office bore headlines in the window, HOPES DOWN FOR TANKS; they were nonsense to him. He walked home, drunk with excitement.

Around the curve of the ivory beach the chimneys of the Paris Bay whaling station shot steam into the air and it drifted white across the blunt grey of the sky. A few hundred yards out from where flensers moved over the lumps of carcasses, more whales were moored. A launch circled the moored whales. Gunshots did not disturb the busy gulls burrowing into their backs.

Cleve dangled his fins in the dull water; there was a taste of rum in his mouth. He fumbled with the speargun, unused to its bulk and lethal certainty of purpose, and slid with it into the water. His heart flinched at the cold and the immediate fear. Grey water loomed about him. He peered into the unfocused distance. He read the label *Bazooka* on the butt of the weapon, but in the water now it looked to him like a furled umbrella. Thick schools of sweep and herring milled about; each nervous turn they took, each flinch in unison, sent his body to the verge of convulsion. His pores were tight.

I will, he thought.

He dived to the bottom, twelve feet, but it was so cold there he kicked up again immediately, and continued creeping along

115

on the surface. The water felt oily. The rubbers of his gun vibrated, taut, as he moved. Limbs stiffening with cold. Come on, he thought, come on. . . .

He edged out towards the poisonous blue of the deep distance, afraid to blink. I will.

In forty feet of featureless water he hovered, turning in a tight circle, looking, keeping every direction covered. Vertically, he began to turn like the bit of a drill, round, round. Then he heard a gunshot, muffled. Another. He stopped turning for a moment. His body hung. Negative buoyancy.

Then he struck back along the surface towards shore without even pausing to glance over his shoulder. He heard his fins pounding the water.

He slithered up the smooth rocks and lay rigid on his back, gasping.

'Hey!'

Cleve started. The voice came from behind him. He struggled to his feet.

'For Godsake!'

Cleve saw a big man with a deeply lined and tanned face in blue overalls and a crumpled white cap standing on the rock above.

'You must be off your bloody scone, mate! You need protection from yourself. This is *bloody* dangerous water, son.'

'I know,' Cleve said. His jaw ached when he moved it.

'You *know*?' the man yelled. 'Hey, Charlie, he bloodywell knows!' Another man, smaller, whiter, with tufty eyebrows and greenish teeth, appeared on the top of the rock.

'If you know it's dangerous, what were you doing in there?' the bigger, younger man said. His hands, Cleve could see, were like clams.

'Sharks.'

'What?'

'I was after sharks,' Cleve said. It sounded incredible to him now. He shrugged and manufactured a smile.

The two men looked at one another. 'I think the bastard's one of us, Charlie.'

Cleve looked at the big man without understanding.

'Baer's the name. Ted Baer. Maybe you've heard of me.'

'The shark hunter?'

'That's him,' Charlie said.

'Yep. Looks like we're here for the same thing as you.'

'Oh, I—'

'Any time you wanna come out with us, just give us a bell. Know anything about game fishing? Need a bloke with balls. Could even boat you out to good spearing grounds if you like.'

'Well—'

'Spearing sharks, eh?' Ted Baer said thoughtfully. 'Well, you only live once, I s'pose. Any time you wanna come out and see it done my way. Goin' for the record again. Biggest white pointers in the world here, they say. Took a nineteen-hundred pounder here last year.'

'Year before,' Charlie said.

'Had a girth of eight feet, the bastard. Found half a sheep in its guts. Still, there's bigger'n that about. Goin' for 3,000 pound. Ever seen a shark that weighed more'n a ton?'

'No,' Cleve said.

'Well, you won't have to wait long. We're at the Ocean View, Middle Beach. Any time, eh?'

'Yeah, no worries,' Cleve said, through chattering teeth.

'What's yer name, son?'

'Cookson. Cleve.'

'Good-oh.' They left.

Cleve stood on the rock by the dull water, paralysed with shivering. Rifle fire rippled across the bay.

XIII

In the midst of the Friday lunch rush, television and press reporters lounge about by the fountains of Parliament House in the city, waiting for the news event to get under way. While they await the remainder of the cast they smoke, eat meat pies and spill tomato sauce on their ties. In summer they might take off their shoes and socks and dabble their feet in the pools. Rival news teams shout friendly abuse across the lawn at one another, like football teams in the change rooms. Every now

117

and then incurious public servants and Members of Parliament pass with their hands in their pockets, stretching their legs while the weather permits. Today is warmer than yesterday, they tell one another, one eye always on the weather.

The big woman on the steps of Parliament House is ignored. For five days she has eaten nothing, sleeping beneath an oily tarpaulin. Her placard has run in the week's rain and is now buckled, illegible and pulpy. But she is still speaking, MPs step over and around her.

Suddenly cameras are seized and cocked. A group of men and women marches across the asphalt car parks, through the gardens, between trees. The newsmen are on their feet, filming, and now the words of the large woman on the steps are recorded by crouching sound men. Two or three uniformed policemen appear at the rear of the mob.

CACHALOT SUPPORTS THIS HUNGER STRIKE ON BEHALF OF INNOCENT CREATURES AND MOTHER EARTH, the first placard says.

'Who?' reporters ask one another.

SUPPORT SALLY MILES
REDEEM YOURSELF: SAVE THE WHALES

A man climbs a tree, captured on film like rare wildlife. At the foot of the steps a large plastic parcel is laid on the ground and a tyre pump appears. A youth fits valve to nozzle and commences to pump. Fleurier stands behind him. Beside Fleurier is an impassive Marks. Brent, up in the tree, is nailing a cardboard placard to the trunk. Someone interrupts the big woman on the step and hands her a loudhailer which squeaks and pops.

'How do you use this bloody...oh.'

Sound men wince.

'I am Sally Miles...'

Ragged applause.

'...and I am here on a hunger strike to protest against the continued slaughter of the sperm whale in our own waters by our own people. It is time the slaughter stopped. It is time the whaling industry owned up. I will not eat until these things happen....'

118

Reporters nudge one another knowingly. Sally Miles weighs fourteen stone and they find it ironic.

'. . . because the whaling industry is obsolete. It is inhumane. It is causing the extinction of what may be the most intelligent creature on our earth. Therefore it is immoral!'

Cheers. Clunks and whirrs of cameras. Signs up.

STOP IT, NOW!

'Join us!' Sally Miles cries. 'Fight Paris Bay. Fight this government!' A great inflated whale is dragged up the steps and Sally Miles hugs it by the flukes. 'This whale is my brother!'

Cheers from supporters. Nudges within the press. Reporters are beginning to be bored; they doodle and their cameramen pan the crowd without shooting. The plastic whale obstructs the main entrance to Parliament House. MPs wait outside, bored, still eyeing the sky. An irritable public servant kicks at the smiling head of the whale, provoking the crowd. His white hair suddenly turns red and the shoulders of his pinstriped suit are saturated. Other blood-bombs, condoms full of sheeps' blood, rain onto the steps, drenching Sally Miles and the whale. Cameras roll again. They swivel as another mob swarms across the car parks. The crowd cheers, then falls silent as the placards come into view.

HIPPIES GO HOME
YANKS GO HOME
WOMEN GO HOME

And four men carrying the vast, snaking banner: AMALGA-MATED STEVEDORES DOCKERS CARRIERS SHIPWRIGHTS BUILDERS' LABOURERS CATERERS PUBLIC SERVANTS SHOP-KEEPERS METAL, ROAD AND MISCELLANEOUS WORKERS' UNION (AUST.) There is a shocked silence. The State Secretary of the ASDCSBLCPSSMR&MWU (AUST.), whose brother lives in Angelus working as a deckhand aboard the *Paris II*, takes up position on the steps with his own loudhailer.

'We believe it is the right of every working man in this country to work, if he so chooses, brothers, and you greenie bludgers are sacking good men. Go home to your rich mums

119

and dads and let the workers alone. You're worse than scabs. Paris Bay,' he says to the newsmen, 'Paris Bay have hired these people to help them retrench workers. It's a smokescreen for a conspiracy!'

A sound like gunfire. On the steps of Parliament House the bloodied public servant is slashing the whale with the paperknife he uses to cut his lunchtime apple. Shreds of plastic come away in his hands. Sally Miles wails. Cameramen cluck, delighted at the symbolic possibilities. A blood-bomb mutes the union loudhailer. Police arrive in vans. Mobs clash. Cardboard is torn.

Later a camera crew hovers about filming significant shreds of plastic left here and there, and a press reporter stands with an MP who chuckles goodnaturedly and says:

'Of course I understand the situation. I'm a keen amateur fisherman myself, you know, and I know the value of a whale oil slick. Caught my first marlin with it, you know. No, the industry is indispensable.'

Above them, on the tree, is nailed the sign:

HUBBA HUBBA!

XIV

Queenie began to sleep late. Lethargy threatened to overcome her completely. Her will, her anger, waned. On a Sunday morning she had a dream, a static dream like a still photograph with a one-hundred-and-eighty degree panorama. It was the view of Wirrup from the top of the windmill on a winter's morning. The house in the mid-distance, covered in a fleece of vines, was sharply defined. Thick pasture was broken only by the vermicular trails of sheep and the creek twisting down from the hill beyond. At the side of the shed nearest the house, her grandfather held a hen by the feet, axe leaning against his leg. The hen bled from its headless neck, and, framed in the doorway behind the shadowy veranda,   her

120

grandmother, arms akimbo, weight on one leg—a pale but distinct figure—watched with a mouth that was curiously awry. To one side there were the fat backs of sheep. To the other side, a solitary cow, udder gorged and swaying in the grass behind a dozen mild steers. Queenie puzzled over the expression on her grandmother's face. Her slouching posture suggested contentment, but that mouth was questioning. Before she could understand, Queenie woke.

If something did not happen soon, she knew her will would break. Old things pulled at her. She had an urge to ring Wirrup, but there was no phone there. She did not write letters. I should be back on the farm, she thought. I shouldn't be here, I don't want to be here. I haven't turned out. It's not right.

Somehow the waiting had to stop.

That afternoon, Queenie moved out of the guest house.

A party raged on the fifteenth floor of the hotel. Queenie was let into Fleurier's room by a very drunken Brent who breathed whisky and Lucky Strikes all over her. She followed him, stumbling over prostrate bodies in the dimness. The suite was full of smoke and people and music. Eventually, Brent found her a corner and a drink. With his lips close to her ear, he babbled about the *I Ching* and the reincarnation of Jim Morrison, telepathy, the Grateful Dead, Hunter S. Thompson author of *Bleak House*, until he fell comatose to the floor. There was a small metal badge on his soiled Mexican poncho which said: *A Turnip Is Your Brother*.

With a sigh, Queenie got to her feet and picked her way through the crowd to the door, thinking: my God, this is enough, no more. She wrenched the door open and found herself face to face with Marks. He smiled, a little awkward.

'So you're back.'

'Well actually I was just going.'

'Oh?'

'Brent has just been drooling on me.'

'Ah.' Marks grinned, seaming his big leathery face. 'You're lucky he didn't tell you about the time he saw a whale.'

'Why?'

'Because then he would have been lying through his gold-plated teeth. The closest he's come to cetacea is a childhood of watching *Flipper* on TV. Wanna drink?'

'Okay.' Good God, why not? she thought.

In the next suite Queenie stretched out on the divan and Marks sat on the floor. Two sleeping mounds occupied the double bed. Geez, Queenie thought, it's like a rock'n roll band—groupies and everything.

'What are you with this mob for?' she asked him, sipping on another drink. Music thudded through the near-side wall.

'The whales,' he said. 'You?'

'The same.'

'Not to escape a tyrannical husband?'

'He's not like that. I'm in it for the whales. It's more than you could say for some.'

'What do you know about whales?' he asked, swivelling ice about in the bottom of his glass.

'Just what I've seen them do. They used to pass by the farm every winter. They used to tell us what time of the year it was, remind us of what we did the year before. They move west along our coast and then around the capes and up this coast northwards, and back again later in the season. Watching them is a family habit. A vice, you could say. I used to watch them when I was a kid. Then there were years when there was nothing. And this year they're back again.'

'Right whales?'

'Humpbacks, too.' Queenie warmed to the conversation; it had been a long time, and she felt a renewed purpose, an enthusiasm.

'What about you?' she asked. 'Aren't you the strandings expert?'

'I guess so.'

'Why do they do it? If they're so intelligent, why do they beach themselves? I saw a pygmy sperm do that once—it was horrible.'

Marks sighed. 'How long you got?'

'All day.'

'There's a heap of theories, you know,' Marks said, scratching his chin. 'The echo-location faults are the most popular at the moment, like the whaletrap theory. You see, when a pod of whales is moving north along a complex coast with inlets and coves and deep bays they sometimes come into a bay which is so deep and so big with a sweeping headland that in order to get out again they might have to swim south for a distance. You know, exactly in the opposite direction their migratory senses tell them to. Their whole beings compel them to move north — to escape they must move south. They get distressed, hesitate long enough in the swell which is often heavy — or the tide — and they can get caught in the shallows.

'Whales don't operate their best in shallow water. Very flat, long, shelving beaches are traps. The water is warm in the shallows — they like it — but their sonar gets hazy in that kind of uniform terrain. They can't identify it properly, make mistakes, get frantic, they're stuck. And all this complicated loyalty. If one goes, all go.

'In a harem stranding juvenile males are often kicked out of the pod by the older cows who look after the nursery. Sometimes, if they exile a young bull near the coast he goes off upset, gets himself into difficulties, lets out the distress call, and, being loyal, loving creatures, they'll all go to help and get caught like him. Being a whale in shallow water is a godawful business. Navigation is ultra-complex.

'If a pod leader, for instance, gets into trouble, there's almost a certain stranding of the pod. They will follow him anywhere. Hundreds of them, sometimes, on the beach. You can tow them right out to sea again and they'll go right back in. They just throw themselves up and die. Unless you can kill the leader. Lately, it looks as though the only way to save stranded whales is to kill some. If you kill the leader and stop the distress signal, you have a fair chance of towing the others out and having them re-grouping and moving on, with a new leader maybe. I guess the bulls fight it out. Once in New Zealand when we first tried it, we were only guessing which was the leader. We got there late. We shot a lot of whales. God, there was blood and mucus, suffocating whales, gunshots — like a battlefield.'

'Did you feel you were interfering or something, you know, in a natural process? I suppose whales've been beaching for years.'

'Yes, we were doing that. But with the situation so desperate

123

for whales, you have to intervene on their behalf. You have to redress the balance. Man has been interrupting a long time. That's what this Paris Bay thing is all about. Redressing previous interruptions with more interruptions. Man, I want my children to grow up to see whales; I want them to know their place. An ocean without whales is like a wilderness without trees. No matter what kind of people they are, whether they appreciate it or not, I want them to know what the world is really like; they have to know good, bad, big, small. They have to have more than half a world; they have to be more than half people.'

Queenie nodded. Yes, she thought, yes, yes.

'Anyway now,' Marks said, stretching. 'Where was — oh, yeah . . . whaletraps, harems, follow-the-leader . . . and there's sickness, too, you know. I guess whales get sick like anyone else. They get parasites and all kind o' things.'

'And there's stress. I guess one day there'll be cetacean psychoanalysis. After they prove cetacean intelligence. You see once they get called intelligent they'll also be neurotic.'

'Are you kidding?'

'I hope so. But you should hear them talk.'

'The whales?'

'No, the goddam theorists. Jesus, if only they spent more time and money protecting them and less time trying to make the poor bastards talk and do Rorschach tests! Like, they think, if we can prove they are intelligent then we'll have an excuse to protect them. All this morality crap.'

'Don't you believe in whale intelligence?'

'I don't give a shit about it. They are inhabitants of the earth — they need protecting, that's all, because they are meant to be here. Needs no justification.'

'Meant to be here? Who meant them to be here?'

'Geez, Mother Nature, Father God, Brother Darwin, pick your poison. A thing doesn't have to be intelligent to need a reason to be. Retarded children, buffaloes, phytoplankton. It belongs here, it should stay. Goddam intelligence freaks,' he muttered, 'they'll want whales joining the UN and the Club of Rome. How many whales wanna say 'Mumma' and 'Dadda' in morse code? They've got along fine without it.'

'So,' Queenie sighed, a little bored, 'they're the theories.'

124

'Oh, there's more. That's just some. The easy ones. There's stress theories, too. You know the idea that people can do amazing things under stress. Even dogs — you ever seen a dog run up a wall?'

'No,' Queenie replied, 'but I've heard of people jumping out of the way of cars.'

'And that story about Ernest Hemingway carrying that Italian soldier without noticing half his own kneecaps were shot away. Impossible. People can talk in different languages, breaks iron bars, fly. They say it comes from stress making you regress to a forgotten, primitive part of the brain. Someone called it the Reptilian Complex, I think. God, I'm no scientist.'

Queenie nodded thoughtfully. Music seemed to vibrate, incoherent, in the whole building. The sleeping bodies did not stir. 'My grandfather did something like that, once. My grandmother was driving the tractor. She got caught on a slope, hit a stump that lifted a wheel. It rolled and she got crushed underneath. He was an old man even then. He suddenly knew something was wrong, came out of the sheds, saw the wheel of the tractor up in the air, and ran. When he got there he saw her legs sticking out, all bloody. He did his block. And in his rage he somehow lifted the tractor and dragged her out. It was no good, though. She was dead. But I'll always love him for it.' She saw it all as she spoke, as though she had been there, observing from the vantage point of the windmill. It had become her personal memory.

'Yeah,' Marks said, steepling the fingers of his hands together. 'Well, likewise. If a whale is sick or being chased or anxious, it will do similar things, like try to get up out of the water and walk away like its ancestors must have done. They want to be what they used to be. I guess the old myth of the Immortal is what people must flick back to in those situations. You know, be Adam or Eve for five seconds, and then back to real life.'

It struck Queenie as a bizarre thought, that her Poppa had the strengths and virtues of Adam for those seconds during which he freed his wife. That's what heroism is, she thought, people saving each other's lives, memories of Eden. For a second or two. But for whales? Did they have an Eden, or a Fall? She tried to remember the Sunday School stories, but

125

nothing came to mind.

'You got kids?' she asked him.

'Nope,' he said, rolling his empty tumbler in his palms.

'A wife?'

'Used to have. Why?'

'Dunno,' she shrugged.

'I guess Brent would call me pelagic.'

'I suppose it makes me pelagic too,' she said.

Marks scratched his tanned chin, dubious. No, he thought, you're anchored all over the place, girl; it's written all over you.

She found Georges Fleurier out on his balcony with a bottle of Chardonnay and a glass like a rosebud. His eyebrows lifted perceptibly when she joined him at the rail. Lights came on along the freeway and around the river. The air was still and cold. They were alone and the music from inside was muted by the glass doors and the heavy drapes.

'Well,' she said.

'Hello,' Fleurier said, glancing briefly at her.

'Another party.'

'Yes.'

Queenie took his bottle and swallowed a mouthful of the wine which had a dry, metallic taste, and she looked out across the river to where the lights of the old mill had begun to burn. 'So, what've you been doing these weeks. Nearly a month. You didn't answer my messages.'

'We were frozen. The unions have a ban on us. No one will transport our Zodiacs from Sydney. No one will supply to us here for fear of strikes. Nonsensical. They broke up our demonstration at Parliament House—did you see it? You should have been there. A fiasco.'

'This whole thing's a fiasco, if you ask me.'

Fleurier poured himself more wine.

'Four weeks,' Queenie murmured. 'A whole month. Nothing. That's what I'd call a balls-up.'

Fleurier sipped.

'I mean some poor sod has donated money, more than one I s'pose—and what for? A first-class holiday and all-week parties. That's expensive. And bloody wasteful.'

126

'In terms of life, yes. They have been killing five whales a day, sometimes eight, off Paris Bay.'

'I meant money,' Queenie said.

'Of course you did.'

'Well,' she waved her arm behind, 'who did you justify all this to?'

'Nobody.'

'Oh, come on, now. Surely there's a Foundation or something. This is big money.'

Fleurier sighed. His impatience was audible. 'I am the Foundation, Queenie, and it is peanuts money.' He permitted himself a graceful smile as he rubbed the bridge of his nose between thumb and forefinger. Queenie let out a long, thoughtful breath.

'Well,' she said at last, 'where do you get enough to spend it like this?'

'Hardly a polite question,' he said.

'Well?'

He smiled, humourless. 'I have many interests.'

Queenie took another gulp of the wine; it warmed her stomach. There was a great doubt welling in her and it made her fearful.

'What are you in this for?' she asked.

'Oh, fame, fortune —'

'Be serious.'

'Well, only a deep sincerity about this cause would keep me stranded in this little town, I should think. Not one of the world's most compelling cities. Not one of the world's cities, for that matter. I have enough money to be elsewhere, you know. It is summer in the northern hemisphere.'

'Well, why spend all the money at all? Why not stay in France?'

'I haven't been to France since I was sixteen. We are here to stop Paris Bay. The whales, remember?'

'I was beginning to think I was the only one who did. What are the whales to someone like you?'

Fleurier smiled; it was a savage smile. 'You mean someone with money? The whales have become my life. They are the most amazing creatures alive. They have intelligence, wit, compassion. There is much that is mystical about the whale.

127

One day, if we keep them alive long enough, we will discover it, and perhaps learn something about ourselves. They are almost magic, the friendly giants of our childhood dreams. Think of the things the whale has seen, the civilisations coming and going. They are observers, perhaps even recorders. They pre-date us. They are the biggest things in existence; there is nothing bigger than the whales. We take all our measurements of size from them. They harbour secrets. I want Man to know them one day.'

Daylight was gone. The lights of the night marked the expanse of the city. Queenie was struck by the beauty of its glitter, its size and strangeness. The air was cold. She felt her skin prickling beneath her pullover. The alcohol left a smooth feeling in her head. Something far away told her lightly that she should be worried. She had listened to Fleurier with a forced scepticism, wanting to sneer, but remembering all the time those dreams of the whale lurching up across the paddocks, spiracle whistling like wind in the eaves, to take her Poppa from his bed, to bring a sign from God, to crush their fences and roll through the swamp.

'Well, sitting around having parties seems like a pretty hopeless way to save whales and discover eternal secrets. I can't see much hope.' She sighed.

'My God, I thought tonight of all nights your hopes would be boundless.'

'Why tonight?'

She saw his face in the faint light through the drapes, puzzled, a little unsteady from the wine.

'Hasn't anybody told you?'

Queenie squinted, sniffed.

'Someone anonymous has supplied us with Zodiacs and motors and all the rest that's still in Sydney. That's why I thought you were here. Tomorrow we leave for Angelus.'

Looking out across the lit city, Queenie felt a surge of hysteria. Back. She found herself counting and suddenly recounting the days since her last period.

128

XV

Drizzle descends lightly, silent as dew. Des Pustling puts his
tongue out and takes from it the ugly yellow molar he has
worried out of his bloodless gums in his reverie. Below, the
mustard surface of the Hacker creeps downstream.

Pustling shakes moisture from his hair and turns his collar
up. He remembers the time his father brought him to this
bridge the year before he died. Those times were the
beginnings of prosperity after the war and even these small
properties had begun to yield consistently. 'Keep an eye on this
land, Desmond,' his father had said with his polished pigskin
shoe up on the rail. 'This will be the place to come to. Watch
these people. A lot of old dreamers squat out here on these
banks mulling over their lost years and fortunes — even their
innocence, I don't doubt. They're a useless lot, but restless at
times. You're best to leave them be useless as they are now
because bad times'll see them itching. I remember farms
burning out here, with only the river safe. Made the whole
place black and ugly, uglier, for a good time, though it did
help with clearing shanties and bad fences and the like. One
day you'll change Angelus, son — you'll make a permanent
mark on it. If you can't change the name or the history, change
the geography, move the town away from itself. God knows,
nothing will get them away from their houses around the
harbour with its stinking flats. It's as though they believe the
Second Coming or the Loch Ness Monster will erupt from the
harbour itself and they daren't move an inch. No, you can't
change the people. But you can find new blood, attract people
from outside the district, perhaps, I don't know. I'm an old
man. Ah, these people're petty and proud, bred of bad stock, I
suppose, and Angelus shows all the blemishes; but it's ours,
and that counts, Desmond. It's good for a man to build and
create, good for a man to reap. Reap and sow, Desmond, for
we are the reapers.'

Des Pustling does not regret being childless, heirless. Since
learning of his own birth and his mother's bloody, pale death
during it, the thought of childbirth has repelled him. And the

129

idea of passing Angelus on discomforts him. As a young man it took him some time to resign himself to the siring role of sex, from which he was saved during his university days by his dropping teeth and foul breath; the women he paid in parks and backyards were merely receptacles on their knees in the dark, nothing like the pale flesh and blood he saw in photographs of his mother. The image of Marion Lowell's naked belly comes to him. He shakes moisture from his hair. There's prime acreage, he thinks coolly.

Pustling has never been certain of his sterility; he has never consulted a doctor for a final opinion, preferring to gamble with the awful possibility of linking himself with childbirth. But it is a safe gamble, he knows — more than safe, and he likes the odds. Odds, he thinks, are something else to compete with. A little minor competition — like Pell, he thinks gloatingly — is good for the system. Innocents: they take life so seriously! Old Pell will have it all on my desk within the week. Competition, safe competition, is grist to the mill, he thinks, turning, walking back along the bridge to where his BMW is parked. Like these other innocents, he muses wryly, and their rubber boats that cost me a small fortune to procure. If they only knew. Safe competition to activate the town a little. And people say I don't have the affairs of Angelus at heart. Good grief, they forget it's my town!

In the car with its windscreen wipers screeking, Des Pustling takes one last look at the Hacker in his rear view mirror as he heads towards Angelus. He thinks of the housing estate he has in mind, and the thought comes to him: 'The only competition you have, Desmond, is the ghost of your old man.'

XVI

Cleve passed two days inert. He read little, slept less. Much of the time he imagined himself bitten in two, torn, mauled. His daydreams were full of speeding shadows. At home on the third day, Saturday, he watched yachts straining across the harbour in a dying wind, and he worried about his meeting with Ted Baer. All my life, he thought, there's been some bugger mistaking me for the real thing. At school Cleve was one of those students upon whom teachers pile their hope. He tried, but he was barely mediocre. At university his manner led tutors to believe he haboured great potential and they marked him mercilessly in their disappointment. Employers picked him from the queues, seeing in his eyes speed and capability. There were many employers, many queues.

Still, he thought, I did last two minutes in the water

That night Cleve went back to reading in earnest. It was a busy night on the jetty, though, and he did not begin to read uninterrupted until after midnight.

July 7   I asked Hale some questions concerning Churling this morning, and he acted in a most peculiar way asking me to 'leave us alone'. This evening he was found too drunk to cook supper and has been locked in his hut until he sobers.

July 8th, 1831   No whales today.

July 9th   Nothing.

July 12th   Fighting. Leek has knocked out the front teeth of Mountford. Headsmen have taken no action. They are drinking our rum.

July 13th   Hale always drunk. We eat poorly.

July 14th, 1831   Last night I dreamed the white light returned and took the camp up in a sudden flurry like the Rapture and left me on the beach asleep. I woke with a start.

July 15th, 1831   Whales today. Woke to find a small pod couched in the lee of the headland. The boats worked all day. In the afternoon I rowed. We stalked a cow and her calf around the bay, maneuvering and plotting until near dark when we caught them in shallow water near the western headland. The cow threw herself on top of her young to shield it, and while she was thus exposed Cain reared up and sank his harpoon deep into her. A brief but spirited tussle ensued, and she was lanced in an exhausted lull and died quietly with a sign and a slick of blood. Wearily, we towed her in towards shore and the

131

fires on the beach, and were astounded and appalled to see the great carcass slide away and sink slowly in eight fathoms, almost taking us with it. There was enough rope to play out to the beach where we fastened it. We will wait for her to putrefy and bloat and rise again to the surface whereupon we shall haul her the distance to the shore with the windlass. By which time she will smell most foul.

July 17th, 1831 Hale rummaged through my kit and stolen Churling's clothes and his notebook. What drunken foolishness in this?

The *Family of Man* is due tomorrow. There is a feeling of gloom in the camp, the men feeling certain she will not come. Behaviour these past days has been quiet enough, though sullen in the main. The natives have not been seen. No one speaks to me. Mr Jamieson smiles when I am near. He thinks me a fool, I hear. Perhaps it is this diary which makes them hostile. I spend more hours each day in the lookout where even here the stench of excrement pervades all. I am doing a poor job as lookout, writing here as I do, but at least it is safe from taunts and glares, and whales do not interest me.

All I yearn for is the return of our ship. I will desert, but where? Hobart Town? New Zealand?

We have become animals. No — they. Filth, and hopeless barbarity.

July 18th No ship. Much rain.

July 19th Rain, whale sighted but lost.

20th Rain. Daren't write more.

21st Rain.

July 22nd Cain, Leek and four other men from Finn's crew have deserted. They stole the muskets, shot, powder, flour, meat, salt, sugar and tea. Hale of course in a drunken stupor offered no resistance when they broke into his hut. There are sixteen of us left, enough for two crews, but Cain and Leek were our only remaining harpooneers. Our food is almost nil. Please God bring the *Family of Man* soon!

July 23rd, 1831 We will eat whalemeat, it has been decided. There being no weapons, we cannot kill kangaroos for none of us are skilled in hunting or snaring them otherwise. Fish are being caught in only pitiful

numbers. It is obvious that Cain and company will strike
out for Angelus Harbour, surely several days' journey on
foot. One would think their needs to have been better
suited by stealing a boat and sailing west.

Jamieson and Finn argue about who will be headman
and which boat will be used. With the *Family of Man*
overdue they have become nervous, loath to use both
boats. Most of Finn's men are gone or dead. I'll wager
Jamieson will be headsman and Finn will wield the
harpoon.

July 24th, 1831 This morning we hunt our first meal of
whale. As I predicted, Jamieson is headsman and our boat
is to be used. And I must go for that reason. Smithson
and Doan are lookouts. It must be a long time since Finn
aimed and threw a harpoon. I cannot ignore the great
feeling of doom in my bowels. It is raining. We will be
called any moment. Why do I feel the need to stow this
diary and my other belongings in my kit? Deliver me,
Lord! And I do not want to eat of Leviathan.

So the journal ended. Through the cracks in the tin walls signs
of light showed and became more insistent. The harbour was
veiled in a mist that moved close to the water catching brief
strains of sunlight which withered in the oncoming cloud.
Cleve stretched and yawned until his ears seemed to split.
Makes no sense, he thought blearily.

The remainder of the leather-bound journal was empty
yellow pages. Cleve ran his finger along the groove where pages
were missing, or was it just the spine beginning to break? *I do
not want to eat of Leviathan.* Something ominous about it all,
he thought. Must be another volume somewhere. Cleve paced,
waiting for the arrival of the day man, all his nerve ends
strangely alive.

Gulls stirred from their pickings of bait scraps and pollard as
Cleve approached. Cleve ran at them, chased a mess of wings
along the jetty, yaahing, kicking at them, pleasantly stimu-
lated. In the weak dawn of 19 June the harbour water was slick
and jetties, wharf, seedy flanks of ships, clouds, were lightly
brushed with the gentle tones of a watercolour. Behind him,
down on the oiled surface of the harbour, the *Paris IV* slit the
water's skin nosing towards the harbour entrance.

In the kitchen Cleve made himself a cup of tea from the kookaburra tin his mother had given him: the brew was the one he had been raised on. Stirring sugar into it, he read the labels of Queenie's exotic blends—Jasmine, Lemon Grass, Alfalfa— teas she bought from the corner of Richardson's store where all the eccentric goods were kept: chopsticks, taco shells, copies of *Bagwhan's Breakfast Moments*, home-brewing kits. He snorted.

A ship's siren and the shift siren from the canning factory keened a duet.

'Nathaniel Coupar,' Cleve said, listening to the strangeness in his voice.

In the darkness of the attic his mind was alive with thoughts; each pillar of rising dust seemed to unearth a new query, more questions to put to Nathaniel Coupar, about Bale and Churling and the others. He lanced the torch into the darkness, turning over old prams, blinds, shoeboxes, curtain rods, hatboxes, flags, rat skeletons, open crumbling boxes of Biggles books and Enid Blytons. The black dust filled his lungs until his chest was heavy with it and he was driven back down the ladder to the kitchen and more Bushells tea.

A tug moved across the harbour. Small craft made for the harbour entrance. Traffic stirred in the town. Cleve sat, grime-faced, by the window, lost in thought.

I saw drizzle descending, and, hanging from a bough near our hut, a pair of trousers—they looked almost too small for a man. . . I passed the garment on my way up to the hill without touching it. There were drops of dried blood on the legs.

He poured himself another cup and stirred it langorously. You knew whose they were all the time, he thought; you knew, you bugger. They were raping him, and you knew. And never did a thing.

He drank his tea down in one gulp.

It took him just over an hour to find—a rat-eaten, mildewy lump of paper, torn and wrinkled. He wiped it down and took it below.

Before opening it—he knew it was the journal, the binding

134

was the same, the same dull heaviness, it made the same heavy feeling in his bowels—Cleve washed himself clean of the black dirt and went downtown to buy some groceries. Goormwood Street was empty, except for the few cars parked outside the church. The delicatessen was open. The Bright Star was unofficially open, swing doors ajar. He returned home with a loaf of bread, a pepperoni and a flagon of invalid port. The bread was warm and he broke it open with his hands and ate it dry, squeezing it into pellets in his fists. He unscrewed the port and took a long draught. Then he opened the old book.

XVII

William Pell watched television. He was too tired, too old, it seemed, to do anything else. The news program showed footage of Angelus Harbour, and Pell recognised the robust outline of Ted Baer's launch *Bull* moored at the town jetty.

'The mayor of the little harbour town, Mr Herb Higgins, said today that the whole town was behind Mr Baer's effort. He said the townspeople had a great affection and admiration for Mr Baer who has visited Angelus each year since 1967. The mayor said that if this year brought the world's largest caught shark to Angelus, then the town would run riot with celebration.'

Pell turned the television off with his foot, thinking maybe he wasn't too tired or too old after all.

I can still pray, he thought. There may be nothing else I can do for this lunatic town, but I can still pray.

He shuffled into his room, feeling his body so far away, and his God so close.

XVIII

Cleve drank port from a beer mug as he flicked through the loose sheaf of papers inside the cover of the book: drawings of boats, sketches of men and scenery, monograms, doodles. In

135

the corner of one page was a stylised representation of a man in the mouth of a sperm whale, a look of terror on his face. Cleve got up and went to the mantlepiece in the living-room: it was the same design as the scrimshawing on the whale teeth Daniel Coupar had given them. Sitting again, he drank more port and turned to the first page. The handwriting was more leisurely, long fluid strokes that gave the impression of confidence and age. To his surprise, Cleve found the first entry was dated 22 July 1875. Forty-four years, he thought, blowing away the fine pollen-yellow dust.

July 22nd, 1875 I write this as a man past his middle years having worked too hard and seen too much and understood too little, and have resumed this journal, abandoned through circumstance and grief many years ago, because now I have some leisure time and vacant moments I fill with thought and speculation. My life has never brought the fulfilment I expected of it, even though I will not die a debtor like my parents, or a prisoner like so many before me in this colony, or a squalid whaleman breathing the ocean into his lungs at the end of a long swim; but I discover a difficulty in even showing gratitude for my survival. Since the days I came here as a young man, since my marooning, I have ceased to live, continued merely to exist. Life has disappointed me.

The period since July 24th, 1831, has until now remained unrecorded. It will be useful to ponder in these my declining years. The value of a man's labour in his prime is that it saves him from excessive contemplation.

The morning of 24th July, 1831, we decided we would eat whaleflesh. Kangaroos were elusive and fish were scarce of a sudden. We rowed out into the bay. There was little wind and the rain had for a time abated. As we rowed, Finn and Jamieson argued over strategy. Despite my sense of foreboding, I felt drowsy. When they breached with an almighty hiss not forty yards from us, I almost dropped my oar. The man behind me cried out in fear. Jamieson sent us about as the whale sounded unseen. We peaked for a moment whilst Jamieson found his bearings, and then we followed the smooth, marbled patches on the surface which give mark to a whale's movements; but there was no need to give chase, for in a moment the whale erupted from the water directly ahead. Although I could not see it, facing the stern as a man

136

rowing must, I surely heard the water rolling from its brow like a waterspout. I saw our own steady wake and the clamped jaw of Jamieson at the sweep. We pulled hard at his barking.

So hard did we pull, our speed rammed us right against the beast and we came aground on its back; and as it reared, we lifted free of the water, oars tipping, a chorus of frightened bellows, above which came the plangent, anonymously spoken word: 'Sperm.' Even before we smacked back into the water upright and afloat, Finn thrust out, off balance, sending his harpoon deep into the back of the monster.

There was no time for a change of men for lancing. This was not the flurry of a sleepy right whale. Finn was suddenly in the water, falling behind as the line hissed out and I felt the wind of it against my shoulder. The keel seemed to be breaking up, such was the speed at which we raced through the steely water, clutching at our oars, clutching at anything. From my position amidships I saw the whitened face of Jamieson who held the sweep arm as though it were his only connection with life itself, as though it might not be of such desperate import that we kill this creature for its flesh, but that his fight was a duel of steerage with the Evil One himself, that his soul was in the balance.

With good manila rope disappearing by the fathom into the deep, we skated out towards the dark line of rain-bearing weather near the horizon. The sperm, unwavering in its dash, carried us like a sleigh full of grim travellers right into the very teeth of the approaching darkness. No one made motions to sever us from him. We sat like dead men, like shades. Rain lashed the water and contributed to the deepening swill at our feet. I feared we would begin to spring timbers as I held on, feeble youth that I was, and we took more water as the monster bore round to the west, leaving us to take the seas on the port beam. I yelped when a large sea lifted us high and sent us skittering into the trough of the next, all but burying us in seawater, slowing us to a creep and catching all hands unawares with a sudden resumption of our former velocity. Hence, Mountford's unfortunate end. I had no time but to see his hat bob once in the tempestuous wake. Oars rattled away, mine included. I resorted to bailing and summoning the attention of the Almighty.

Before dark another two men were lost. The hurried

137

fastenings of the rope to the stem-post had by then tightened into a steel-hard knot, an unalterable connection. The hatchet was gone from its niche, though none of us would have had the mind to use it and free ourselves of this tireless beast had it been there, I am sure. No lantern was lit, and likewise no other provisions were brought out. It was as though we were all entranced, stunned into inaction.

Once when the whale's pace flagged conspicuously the trance weakened and an effort was made to retrieve rope in the hope of gaining an upper hand, but the effort was clumsy and weak-willed as though all hands believed that it was more than a whale pulling us and fighting hopeless. Within moments the rope went taut again like an iron bar and we were all thrown into the bottom of the boat.

We travelled on in darkness and rain and thunder and lightning as storm and craft converged. Land was long lost to us as were hope and—it seems to me these years later—commonsense. We cringed and held on.

At a sudden change of direction, or collision with a freak sea (or perhaps a lightning strike, I was in no condition to make distinction), all of us were jerked from our seats once more and I found myself jammed against the underlip of the port gunwhale on my back. I felt nothing, heard nothing. The final, distinct wakeful (if there was ever any such thing) memory I have of that longest night of my life was an odd recognition of the absence of Jamieson at the sweep, and for a long time I held in my gaze a hand—or more correctly, five white fingers clutching the timber of the gunwhale above my head. The fingers curled from outside the boat, nails denting the wood. I made no move to go to the aid of the fingers as I could not tell whether it was they that pulled us along or whether they wanted to stay with the boat or whether they were there at all; and in any event I could not move myself. I do not recall when the fingers let go and disappeared, and I cannot tell whether I laughed or cried or was asleep or dead when I noticed them gone....

Cleve paused for a moment, drained his glass, refilled, whistled through his teeth, shook his scraggy head, and read on.

Perhaps it was the blow in falling or even a momentary madness of circumstance, but my sleep that night was

138

lunatic. Few details have remained in my memory. There was a return of the white starlight of many nights previous above me, always ahead, and the recurrence of a scream, the highly pitched wail of a young man or woman in distress. That night I inhabited the spaces between life and death. It was as though I travelled aloft, unafraid of the sometimes indistinct forms below. The indistinctness plagues me — I saw, but I cannot identify. What did Lazarus tell his family after his resurrection? Did he describe such a half-world?

Why did I not call out like Churling and his Jonah for deliverance, tied like a babe to the furious Cachalot? Had I truly begun to think of this beast as the Beast himself, like poor ignorant Hale? Is that why I, like the rest, made no real attempt to break free? I fear I must then have given up all hope of Salvation.

I woke to light and the low sounds of groaning and snorting, and I crawled from the bottom of the boat to look about me. Alone, I floated in the calm shoals of a tiny inlet. The empty boat was almost full of water, and what at first appeared to be a reef beside me I suddenly recognised as the crippled and dying whale, its great back clear of the water, flukes flopping up and down idly. Its groans were pitiful and each breath showered me with pink vapours of blood and spittle from its blowhole. Finn's harpoon quivered in the air, trailing fathoms of tangled rope which floated in the shallows like an armada of seaweed blown in by a great storm. Rain began to fall and between thunderclaps I heard the whale die; and when it was over I waded, blubbering, to shore.

To be brief, the next days were ones of agony. I did not think to take provisions from the boat. I did not, I think, make a rational decision as to where I was headed, though deep in my delirium there was a destination and a conviction.

Who knows how long I shambled about?

After a journey lost to the world of dreams and madness, I eventually stumbled upon the beach of our encampment, met with desolation, huts and tryworks dismantled, oil barrels gone, whalebone gone, windlass gone — even the flensing ramp. Not a soul was left. The *Family of Man* had returned, taken all survivors off the beach, and given our crew up for lost. I must have been gone a number of days. I fell to my knees and cursed them all, cursed the sky and the wind and the fish of the sea, berated and spat upon their Creator. Of all men, all our company, *I* should have been saved. Hale and others had been taken and I had been left.

Rotting caverns of bone lay in the still shallows near the shore and their stench overcame me. Only ruins and rubbish were left on the beach and it was through these scattered piles of litter that I fossicked in search of food, of life, discovering a bag of infested and water-hardened flour, some greenish biscuits and, ridiculously enough, my journal. Into a piece of rag I tied these things and hauled them onto my blistered shoulder, turning as I did, to walk back west. Back along the beach I noticed something protruding from the sand, and when I finally came to it, wondering how it was I had not noticed it minutes before, I saw it was a native's spear upon which a blanket was impaled. The stench of it told me it was the blanket beneath which Nowles had rotted and died. I walked on westwards along the beach towards the headland, thinking only of the sanctuary of the little cave I had found weeks before.

When I reached the cave, my quiet, clean place, I found the petrified form of Bale, the lunatic, his face grizzled but not tormented. In fact, it bore, despite the disfigurement of weathering and death, a look of bliss, and the chafed waste of his hands appeared clasped in his lap and his eyes, worried by ants, were frozen upward in their sockets.

I left the defiled place and made my dream-like way west. Did I inhabit a trance, or did a trance inhabit me? Many things happened, though whether they are dreams or reality I cannot tell; nevertheless they did occur.

First. At some time during my trek I found the remains of the four deserting crewmen who had accompanied Leek and Cain. They were by fresh water, a greenish place with stones smooth as skin. Much of the men's flesh had been taken, not savaged as if by wild dogs, but butchered with some grim deftness. Their throats were cut, black and vile with infestation, but their heads were intact, though ant-ridden and eyeless and I felt no amiable stares from them as I had had from poor Bale. The remains were naked except for two whose feet rotted inside boots and one with a wide-brimmed hat still plastered on. Muskets lay about and it was clear to me what had happened: ammunition

140

gone, they had fought or argued and Leek and Cain had
somehow killed the others (in their sleep perhaps?) and
butchered them, I can only assume, for food.

Second. One night, *some* night, when food was gone,
birds descended upon me (crows?) and dropped into my
mouth a substance that was neither meat nor bread. They
cawed and I ate and was satisfied. They returned and I
drank from their red beaks, felt the cool breeze made by
their black wings. Then a pack of hounds came up from
out of the earth, wet-mouthed and howling with the voices
of men I knew, but they were chased off by the birds who
returned with the dogs' eyes, which I declined to eat; but
the birds left and returned with more, eyes that tumbled
down at me until I was almost suffocated with them and
blinded by them, warm bloody marbles. A single bird
alighted on my chin and uttered a single word: 'Fool', and
raked my own eyes with its talons and departed. I rose,
half-blind, and went.

I remember not marvelling at this. This happened. You
know it did, Coupar, you will die before you deny it!

Third. I saw black shadows at night, natives perhaps.
They made no sound as they flew.

Fourth. I found the inlet at which the whale and myself
had come aground and heard the sounds of decomposi-
tion, haunting chemical groans, and found in the snagged
boat a firkin of water, some dried biscuits and rum. I
used a thin piece of stone to hack the rope anchoring the
boat to its putrefying anchor, bailed out as much water
and sand as was possible with my hands, and launched
hopefully from the inlet with a sail I could not manage
and a single oar. During the journey of an incalculable
time, I had the recurring vision of the white fingers above
my head cutting into the timbers.

Two soldiers found me near the then unnamed Hacker
River where it meets the sea.

These things happened to me, Nathaniel Coupar, son
of respectable debtors, fool runaway to the sea, observer
chiefly, whaler, survivor, smuggler, shopbroker and
latterly farmer, husband, ogre it seems. They all occurred;
nevertheless I doubt them all. I am an old man already. I
have survived but not lived. Married, begat, built. My
wife fears me, my cries in the night, my burning tempers,
my otherness. My son and my daughters fear my presence.
And still I must bully this sullen soil. Mull things.

141

I have looked Evil in the eye and have been confounded since.

You do not sleep at night, Nathaniel Coupar. Sometimes you are at the brink of all knowledge, others you creep along the crumbling bank of all ignorance. I have no guilt. Some men speak of their guilt as though it is a valuable asset, like a potent stud ram, and the more the better, the richer the man. Rubbish.

How strange to write this all into a journal to keep in an old sea-trunk: as a youth and as an old man, the most constructive and the most useless labour of my life. Why do I not *tell* these things to Ellie, my beloved? Is it fear? Not shame. I am not ashamed. Perhaps, like a fool, I hope she will read this when I die, or stumble upon it by accident in my room — I often leave it open here on my desk for that reason, but she is an incorruptible woman and it is such a puerile notion. No one has known me, not my wife, not my children. Except God. He alone must know me. He must.

Some nights Leek and Cain come back for me, for my flesh and for my soul. I am tormented. Perhaps I could tell my wife.

Port was sweet and hot in Cleve Cookson's mouth. A little spilled from the side of his mouth. He raced through the last pages of the journal.

July 24th, 1875 If I was Leek or Churling or Hale or Cain I would have got down on my face and called to God for some measure of mercy and grace. If I was.

July 25th A man is not responsible for his company. I suffered in resisting barbarity. I did not participate. I am innocent.

July 27th, 1875 'Are you also still without understanding?'

July 28th Grave doubt.

July 29th Whose hand? Once I understood these Scriptures, but now they scramble in my mind, and sometimes I doubt God, I doubt his judgment.

And these are only memories, after all, and I was but a child in 1831. What can one trust of childhood memories? Ah, but remember the sound of the gate in the evenings when father returned from his club? Remember the sounds of saddle-leather and horse-breath in the streets of Salem? These are, too, childhood memories. All true.

I hardly see the whales in the bay of late.

July 30th, 1875   Why the others?

July 31st, 1875   A man has only himself and his cunningness and stubbornness, brute strength and wit. He has no need of forgiveness. And, should I have need of it?

Cleve stared at the final page, too drunk and confused and excited to notice the stub along the spine where pages had been torn out.

Arrogant old sod, he thought with admiration. It's sixty miles from here to Wirrup. Stubbornness and courage. You old bugger.

Cleve sat for an hour in the kitchen as his thoughts jumbled hurriedly. *We need blokes with balls....* He saw a little boy with his penis in the teeth of a metal zipper. He saw an emaciated man hobbling into a searing light. He saw himself in the long shadow cast by Queenie Coupar in the afternoon sun. He saw his naked name on the front page of the *Advocate*. Saw a white-fingered hand. Saw himself shivering in the rain, treading water in circles like a drill-bit. A shrivelled ear. *One of us....* His fist crashing down on her back, his back, backs.

He slid low in his chair until all he could see was the jarrah grain of the table, like a brown sea, like effluent, oil, leather, skin, windows, nothing.

At three o'clock in the afternoon Cleve staggered out to the Land Rover and, unsteadily, made his way through town to Middle Beach. An offshore breeze licked the tops off the incoming swells and an archipelago of surfers took advantage of the conditions. Old men fished from the beach with long fibreglass rods and retired couples strolled along the cold white sand. Cleve parked outside the Ocean View Hotel and got out into the chill. The low sky foretold rain. His head was dense with alcohol and confusion; he walked without grace.

At the reception desk a balding man in his mid-thirties scowled at him. 'What can I do you for?'

'Er, is . . . Ted Baer in, please?' Cleve managed to say, wrestling consonants.

'No. Sorry,' the balding man said, looking as if he was itching to pick his teeth, 'Mr Baer doesn't have visitors.'

'Oh, I'm not a visitor,' Cleve said, rocking gently, 'I'm a colleague.'

'Listen, mate, if you're from the press you'll have to book an appointment by phone. You can go outside somewhere to a public phone and ring from there.'

'I'm not from the press,' Cleve said. 'Do I look as if I'm from the press?'

The desk clerk eyed him critically. 'You look like you're from the Boongs' Reserve. Out!'

Cleve stared, dumb. 'Hey, listen,' he said after a moment, 'I've been invited to go shark fishing with Mr Ted Baer—'

'You look like you couldn't catch a dose of clap, let alone a shark. Now get out, or I'll have you put out.'

'Listen, mate, I drink here, you know!'

'Looks to me like you don't care where you drink.'

'Now listen here—'

Cleve found himself in a half-nelson in the company of two men with thick sideburns and bad breath, walking, bent over, out of the hotel. He was amazed at such behaviour and before he could unhand himself he discovered himself face-down on the grass verge.

Nauseated and angry, Cleve drove back through town and out to the Paris Bay road. He overtook tour buses and strayed several times onto the gravel edge of the road. At a roadside shop be bought a hamburger, the meat of which slipped from between the buns and into his lap as he drove off. He opened a warm bottle of beer that had rolled about under the seat for weeks, and drove with it between his legs.

Half a mile before the locked gates of the whaling station at Paris Bay Cleve turned off the sealed road and bounced up a track that led to the beach. Sleepy, he sat for a time above the place where he had dived and met Ted Baer. He listened to the radio and in time the ABC announcer lulled him to sleep.

When he woke, Cleve was thirsty and the sun was heavy on the hills. He drank the remainder of the warm beer and started the Land Rover.

144

A few miles along the road towards Angelus in the national park, Cleve was confronted by a huge kangaroo that stood in the middle of the road, turning its head from side to side in a gesture resembling arrogance. Cleve sounded the horn; it did not move. Cleve sat with his fist on the horn, stopped directly in front of it. When at last the creature sniffed and lumbered off to one side, Cleve was seized by a sudden urge.

He pulled off the road to one side, cut the engine and got out. From the tray in the back he pulled out the speargun, tightened the spool of line with his palm, and went into the dense bush where the kangaroo had entered. Light was worsening; the bush was low and in the lee of the coastal hills. There was no sound except for the wind and Cleve's footfalls. He stopped for a moment, braced the butt of the speargun on his hip and pulled back the heavy jelly rubbers to load it. He picked his way through the noisy banksias, stalking, surveying the bush slowly and with care. For seventy yards more he stalked, pointing the diamond head of the spear about him. His head ached and his throat was parched. Twilight, sudden winter twilight settled and the air grew colder. Cleve became angry, frustrated, embarrassed by the very idea, and he turned to make his way back. Out of the darkness beside him came another dark which brushed him aside, floating like a black cloud. As he fell, Cleve felt the spear jerk free, heard the rattle and the thick grunt. He lay on his back, dazed, the spool spinning beneath him. It took him a few moments to realise that he had not speared himself but the kangaroo. The bush was awake with pounding and crashing.

He grabbed the empty stub of the barrel and tried to stem the unravelling of the spool. As soon as the line went taut he was jerked to his feet and then back to his knees. He swore, realising it was almost dark and *he* was connected to a struggling, wounded kangaroo in a national park. He was dragged a few feet on his knees, cursing; farther along a stump caught him in the shins. He made hopeless efforts at wrapping himself round flimsy trees, but they broke and slashed his cheeks. The animal was in pain; in the darkness he heard its weight, its impact against the logs and earth.

'Lie down and die, you bastard,' Cleve muttered in his desperation.

145

And then the barrel was jerked free from his hands, the butt catching him sharply on the chin. He heard it rattle away. For a few yards he followed; it was always a little ahead, snagged on rocks and bushes. The animal lurched on, coughing.

Cleve was doubled up by his own sickness and he vomited until he could breathe again. When he stood it was totally dark. The horizon was about eight feet away. He abandoned the hunt and turning, and turning again to return, realised that he was lost.

He blundered for an hour. He found the road, but in the darkness he could not tell in which direction the Land Rover lay. He shouted at the dark to save himself the indignity of more tears. A car passed, slowed, break lights glowering.

STORMS

MARION Lowell moves about in the fluorescent light of the empty office, looking now and then down to the deserted street that is salmon-pink in the dawn and silent but for the wind rushing in from the harbour, lifting papers, stirring muck in the gutters. She opens filing cabinets and drawers, jerking them out. Something catches her eye every time she changes direction — the kookaburra on the Goormwood Service & Lube calendar, head back in ridicule, eyes unblinking these past six months. All year she has been watched by those eyes as she marks off the days with a felt pen as she has done all the years before. And now she takes up the pen and strikes the twentieth of June through; and pauses for a moment before blackening the kookaburra's eyes with a hasty pair of sunglasses. She scoops up an armful of files and takes them to the shredder in the back room.

We Buy, We Sell, the plaque says. I know, I know, she thinks. The sound of the shredder all but cancels thought; she looks about her with care.

HAVE A WHALE OF A TIME IN ANGELUS,
150 YEARS OLD IN 1979

ANGELUS: HISTORY MADE AND IN THE MAKING
PIONEER TOWN, 1979

JEWEL OF THE SOUTH: ANGELUS '79

The new posters on the white walls left by the drunken

147

executive almost a fortnight ago still make her uneasy: she can almost hear them shouting over the noise of the machine; too many smiling faces and rich colours. How long? she thinks, returning to the office. Oh, Marion, you've just been too stupid and too greedy. She feels the calendar in the recesses of her vision as she gazes out into the street: *150 Years Old in 1979*. Yes, she thinks, I feel as though I will be, too. You should never have thought you could climb in this town, dearie. Should have vamoosed to the city with all your friends. This place isn't right. It drove the old man away and Mum's sickening from it. And your efforts at ripping the place off have been a laugh. Oh, the first one, Johnny Weldon, wasn't too bad; and I did all right out of it. Could've married him and had the lot. Pity the poor old bugger had to die and leave me out in the open. And this. Five years, this. Five years of being a septic tank for Pusface's effluent. God knows I'd have married the animal once, but I was hungrier then and it didn't seem such a high price. And if and when he died — well I had hopes. That night I picked his keys out of the shoebox in the trophy room I knew what I was doing; after all, there's only one BMW in this town. A septic tank. Well, Desmond, you disintegrating piece of crap, you can spill your beans elsewhere because my drains are blocked well and truly and God do they stink. Feel that, Marion, feel the skin under your chin. Even your hands look like your mother's. All this year on the keys they've looked like someone else's. You wash them too much. Those mother's hands rubbing his pimple-headed back. You're someone else now. A loser, woman.

Down the street a milk truck hauls its rattling load uphill past the Bright Star on the corner outside which a curled figure sleeps. Marion Lowell is tired. The thickening light reminds her of the long night's thinking and deciding.

Well, that's about it,' she says aloud. Her bag is full of her personal stationery, coffee mug, box of tissues, and the ugly paperweight someone forgotten once gave her.

She types a note and leaves it in the machine.

As of today, 20 June 1978, I am no longer in your employ of any kind. Records concerning Pell no longer exist, so leave him the hell alone. Don't try to contact me. If you

148

threaten me I'll do some talking in the pubs and maybe a few bedrooms and even the Presbyterian church about your business interests and your sexual interests, and I'm sure the town will find them very interesting and probably very very funny. I'll also tell them about how your sperm is as fertile as cold sago pudding if I get the urge. I hope you won't do anything that'll make me get the urge.

Before leaving she turns the heating up to the maximum level, turns on all the taps in the kitchen, switches on every light, two transistor radios, the electric typewriters, the colour television, the telex, the electric shaver in Pustling's drawer, the electric fans, the empty kettle, the private burglar alarm transmitting to his home. She drags out the movie projector, choosing from a catalogue of blue movies, and splices one up and sets it into motion with the image smudging all over the wall. Then she opens a window and turns up the sound. Finally, just as she is about to leave, she opens the long cabinet beside Pustling's desk and drags out a soiled girdle.

Out in the street she walks into the wind, cheeks painfully alive. She stops beside the Goormwood Memorial with its wishing well and pulls the girdle over the head of the monument. Then walks away in the wind.

Two men stand beside the urn in the office of the Angelus *Advocate* talking over the muted clatter of press in the rooms behind.

'Today,' one says to the other.

'Then it's on?'

The first man nods before returning his attention to the telex. A telephone rings. Another. Calls from two hundred miles away. They ring all the morning as the press clatters.

II

Immediately the convoy of vehicles trundled down the hill at Paris Bay the gates of the whaling station compound were swung shut and padlocked. Flensers continued to work. Some workers in their lunch break walked up the gravel drive to the gates to watch the cars and a microbus disgorge strange young people. Faces, arms, hands, voices. The workers smoked nervously. Placards went up, held above the ranks that rallied into a rough formation in the muddy car park. Then silence. A camera crew arrived and settled on the bonnet of a car. People sat on the roof of the microbus.

Out on the bay the launch towed an inflated carcass towards the ramp. Gulls followed the listing hulk. People held handkerchiefs to their faces. A loudhailer appeared, glinting in the weak light. Over the murmurings of the launch came the sound of an outboard motor in the far distance. Feet scuffed the mud.

When the Zodiac inflatable came skittering into sight, smacking away a sudsy wake, nosing up in the breeze, the crowd came alive. A television crew arrived in a station wagon and another car poured out reporters. Telephoto lenses traversed the water like gun muzzles, following the tiny craft across the Sound and into the bay. Moustachioed men in sports jackets fiddled with cameras and microphones, combing their hair.

The workers at the gate were joined by others. A loudhailer barked at them. They raised their fingers at the crowd. Queenie Cookson, standing beside Brent who shouted into the loudhailer, raised hers in reply. A ragged chorus of 'We Shall Overcome' got into motion, and pressmen moved amongst the nervous young people, sucking peppermints, thinking of angles. More cars arrived. Townspeople who had followed the convoy out of curiosity stood, at a distance, on their car bonnets, pointing, horrified, at the inflatable skating across the bay. They were soon joined by their share of reporters.

From the distance, back in the hills where the road wound through the national park to the township, came a sound like a squadron of bombers echoing in the abating wind. It grew louder every moment until the procession of Harley Davidsons topped the hill above, greeted by a cheer from the crowd of young people. As the bikies dismounted the cheers dwindled to a collective moan. *God's Garbage* moved through the crowd distributing Paris Bay leaflets and hostile stares before taking

150

up position on the seaward flank, flexing their tattooed arms and long bellies. Reporters left them unmolested.

Queenie cringed and sank back into the crowd, terrified that the bikies would recognise her. Which one did I go out with? she wondered. Geez, I must have been game. Oh, God. But none seemed to pay her any special note. Then she saw the Zodiac turning in a wide arc and a figure in the bow holding a banner and she tried to sing with the others, but she could not get enough air into her fluttery lungs and a man in a sports jacket stood too close and blocked her view.

'Are you aware that those men out there in that rubber boat are in grave danger? The locals say the biggest sharks in the world inhabit these waters. Are these protesters irresponsible, do you think, or heroes?'

A notepad flapped in Queenie's face. Sharks? Oh, shit, the *sharks!* Rubber boats . . . how could I . . . how could we not . . . ?

'Well?' the man prompted, turning his pencil as though it was a small dagger. His eyebrows worked up and down belligerently.

So bloody stupid, she thought. 'Heroes,' she said.

'And is it true that Gil Cranes, ex-Deputy Prime Minister, is coming here to support your protest today?'

'Yes,' she said, hoping it was so because no one had told her. The reporter moved on, leaving Queenie hollow. The long night, the tiredness welled up in her. Bloody hopeless, she thought.

She recalled the long night before driving hard from the city in an atmosphere of jubilant expectation, arriving at dawn to discover, on the cold, white sand of Middle Beach the Zodiacs—left by their anonymous and expensive supplier— that no one knew how to assemble. Fleurier assumed Marks knew. Marks thought Brent knew. Steam rose from their quiet hissing. All morning, to the jeers of a growing mob of onlookers, they read instructions from a manual and fended off reporters who seemed to appear from nowhere, until finally Marks struck upon a method that worked and the craft took shape and the cameras were allowed near.

Queenie kept her fists in her pockets as the Zodiacs made arcs across the pink lake at the foot of the flensing deck.

151

Bikies spoke through the fence to workers, friends and brothers-in-law, passing tobacco and papers.

The outboard buzzed and raced. The singing of 'We Shall Overcome' was pale: word had got around about the sharks. A dachshund floundered through the crowd between legs. Another car pulled up. Gil Cranes, ex-Deputy Prime Minister, climbed out in his denim jacket and tweed pants, but he went unseen because at that moment a murmur went through the crowd as it mouthed the word on the banner held in the bow of the Zodiac.

SHAME!

Queenie Cookson pulled her hands from her pockets and threw them into the air with a cry. 'Shame!' Others followed her lead. The loudhailer whined. The bikies booed, and down on the deck a silver curve of water shot out from the firehose towards the inflatable. And then a unified gasp. Fingers pointed to where, beyond the moored whales, a mass of dorsal fins broke the oily surface.

'Sharks! Sharks!' the people called.

No, Queenie pleaded, oh no.

Near the moored whales the dorsal fins split into two groups and began to curve in towards shore. The crowd became hysterical. 'We Shall Overcome' expired completely. The bikies fell silent. Gil Cranes lowered his fist and got down off the bonnet of his car. And the men in the Zodiac zigzagged for the cameras.

It was several moments before something tripped in Queenie Cookson's brain, as if all sound and movement seized for a second and only the benign, familiar shapes of the dorsal fins burnt into her senses.

Dolphins. Bloody dolphins, she thought. 'Dolphins,' she said to Brent in the silence.

'Eh?'

'They're dolphins!'

The crowd was still for a second, teetering between relief and disappointment. Then people were shouting 'Dolphins! Dolphins!' as the grey-blue backs hooped out of the water in an unmistakeable movement. 'We Shall Overcome' wound itself up again. Notebooks flapped.

And then, before it rained, a faint rainbow appeared over the Sound. Queenie began to laugh. 'Aah,' the crowd murmured. Yes, she thought, yes!

III

Cleve Cookson was given his dismissal that morning over the telephone. Haggard and hungover, he drove down to the town jetty, seeing as he left the glance Miss Thrim cast at him, and he returned her stare as one would return a baited dog to its owner. He saw, too, the ugly stubble and greyness of his face and winced. Last night was a nightmare now, just a part of his drilling headache. He had been hours late for work, drunk, delirious; he had wept. An empty beer bottle rolled about under the clutch pedal as he drove downtown. The harbour was flat, gleaming, becoming still as the southerly died.

He parked in the gravel patch at the end of the town jetty. Already he had heard of yesterday's catch, but he had not seen for himself. He walked out slowly, carefully, because of his head and his fatigue, and as he went he was seized with a sudden fear of falling through between the planks. He slowed, made each step with the utmost precision.

At the end of the jetty he joined the small congregation around the towering carcass whose sharp, ammoniac smell made him even more light-headed. A fourteen-foot white pointer hung by its tail from the gallows. Its skin was dry and tearing where the chains held it. The huge guts had fallen forward, bunching grotesquely behind the head, and weepy juices drooled from the mouth. There was little of the shark about it: it looked to Cleve more like a gigantic leather trunk full of stinking wet laundry. Organs even protruded from the mouth, forced down by their own weight. On the grey flank the catch weight was written in chalk: 1,993 lbs. Its girth was the equivalent of a middle-aged jarrah tree; two men could not have locked arms around it. Beside the shark Ted Baer, tired and hungover himself, posed for photographs for the steady procession of townspeople. Someone dragged a hose across and played it about over the planks near the open mouth. Cleve sighed and was about to leave when Ted Baer caught his eye and beckoned him over. Cleve hesitated. He felt others watching him, even heard the startled blood ticking in his ears. He went closer.

'Not bad, eh?' Baer said, smacking the emery flank with gloved hands. 'Not a record, but a nice fight. Forty minutes he was.'

'Yeah,' Cleve said. Tell him it's bloody disgraceful, he thought; tell him what you think of hanging it up like that going out of shape, stinking like a . . . 'Nice.'

'Shoulda been there, mate.'

'Yeah,' Cleve said. Like hell, he thought.

'What about comin' out next time? See how broad yer skills are, eh?'

'Well—' My God, what's the point of it, Cleve thought, where's the sense in it?

'You can sell what you catch.'

How? How? When you let it go rotten like this? 'Well, I've got sort of business commitments this week,' Cleve mumbled.

'Today's Monday,' Baer said. 'There's all week.'

'Well.'

'Okay, okay,' Baer laughed, with an eye on the gathering. 'Second thoughts. Woman's prerogative.'

There was a nervous titter, and Cleve left, full to bursting with the smell and the anger of it. Slits of sea loomed up between his feet. You can piss off, mate, he thought, you and all your men's shit.

The long walk along the deepwater jetty did nothing to dispel his fear of falling between the planks. The water was twice as far down and twice as deep; the journey out seemed like an endless crossing of precipices. A great rust-scaly tanker shouldered the last section of the jetty beyond the security hut. Across the harbour cars wended their way out along the peninsula. He felt nothing but contempt for Ted Baer and his sack of soiled meat.

Cleve's humiliation on the town jetty receded in the pride he

154

took in walking away. Best thing I've done in a long time, he thought. He thought it odd that he could not remember the last time he had done something well, something good for himself or for someone else. His life seemed such a ludicrous jumble of non-events, memories with great troughs of blankness between. Most of his memories seemed to be disappointments. To distract himself from his fear, he sifted through them for moments of joy, fragments of pride to value, to cherish. Before he reached the watchman's shed he had those moments in the palm of his mind. They were moments worth living for, he knew, and he also knew that they couldn't be repeated, though perhaps, in kind, they might in some way be revisited. It's her, he thought, there's just her. And her grandfather, the old bastard, much as I hate him. Cleve knew then how much he wanted to be wanted by them. He felt like nothing.

A cardboard box of books and pencils, a rolled poster and a pair of seaboots stood outside the door of the watchman's hut. Cleve hesitated at the door and decided not to knock; instead he took the box under his arm and went down to the lower landing to where Dick and Darcy fished.

'Fishin'?' Dick asked, without turning.

'No,' Cleve said, sitting. He watched their boots dangling over the edge. Look at them, he thought, they heard it all last night, they know what's up — somehow they always know what's up.

'Wanna guzz?' Darcy offered his bottle, but Cleve shook his head.

A storm in every port, he thought wryly. He sensed them watching his box and he looked at the slate water, thinking. 'Either of you want these boots?' he asked, pulling them out and holding them up. He couldn't think how he came to have them; they had always been in the hut and he had never worn them.

The old men shook their heads. Neither did they want the paperbacks or his poster of John Lennon.

'Shouldn't be wastin' yer time here,' Dick said, looking at his jiggling line in the water. 'I hear there's another barney on out at Paris Bay. And that granddaughter o' Daniel Coupar's was in town this mornin'.'

'What?' Cleve almost shrieked.

155

'But I'm just an ol' bludger,' Dick murmured. 'Could be jus' another rumour.'

Cleve leapt up the steps and left them chuckling. Water blurred beneath his feet as he ran down the jetty.

Other cars seemed to be idling along in the same direction, unusual for a Monday, and he overtook them on the winding road around the harbour and along the peninsula.

From the hill above Paris Bay, with his engine ticking, Cleve saw the crowd below outside the compound of the whaling station waving placards and cameras and fists and inflated toys. Cars and black motorcycles were parked all over; a minibus, roof thick with young spectators. A man stood on the bonnet of a car, denim arms waving at the inattentive crowd. An inflatable boat sliced through the red field of water at the base of the flensing deck where the open guts of a sperm whale beaconed in his vision and a great murmur went up from the mob. Steam oozed up from the chimneys, rolling in the breeze like smoke from cannons. He heard singing. He scanned the crowd again painstakingly and he saw a bulbous head of hair beside which he saw the blonde colour that burned into his senses, into his stomach; the recognition quickened his heart.

Driving back with the image of Queenie Coupar's aureate hair sharp before him, Cleve knew he was afraid. But it was another kind of fear. A persistent prism, a tiny rainbow glowed in his side mirror. A hard and dark rain fell as he reached Angelus.

IV

Even turning the blotchy pages is an effort. Pell reads the occasional column of interest, resting his eyes frequently; he is tired and today, again, he feels like an old man. In the lane next door he can hear the thud of a football as boys play in the rain. Gutters gurgle and grottle and moisture creeps down the windows. And Pell sees his own name in a lonely column between advertisements for pantyhose and harvesters.

156

Another citizen retiring from service this week is the Rev. William Pell, a familiar face to all in Angelus whose work in the Presbyterian church here has spanned several decades. Mr Pell (68) will preach his last sermon this coming Sunday 26th June and his ministry will terminate officially on 1st July. Mr Pell has been active in pastoral concerns throughout the community and in the native community for many years and the *Advocate* wishes him well in his retirement.

'I'll bet you do, boys,' he says, turning the page.

Pell feels nerves springing in his arms and legs as he lights a cigarette and throws the newspaper aside. He remembers yesterday's service, the hymns, the long, long delivery of his sermon, and Des Pustling down there in the congregation smiling, nodding. The bone colour of the walls were the same bone colour of Pell's childhood and probably, he thought at the time, the same colour as the convicts made it those years ago. It occurred to him as he preached how little the old building meant to him. There were small memories like his initials in the pew up the back on the right dating back to 1914, and the pews under which he had, over the years, planted gobs of gum—they were still there, fossilised lumps—and the special pews from which he had glutted on the sight of the naked necks of girls and their mothers, pews on which in moments of meditation he'd overheard whispers of pregnancy and divorce and pledges of pubescent love. He even remembered, as he stood there, the time Mrs Bray, the late organist, took a fit mid-way through 'Be Thou My Vision', dentures a-rattle. And yet he knew as he preached, feeling himself outside of himself, that these were small, whimsical memories, and that the place he would truly hate to leave was the manse, the place where he hoarded his supplies, his memories, his prayers, his reserves of strength.

He had seen astounding things under that roof, people healed and broken, people dead and some born. The manse was a place of doubts, and on occasion a place where people had held certainty between their teeth. Men, women, children had come to vent their doubts; they doubted themselves, the existence of God (others wondered whether He knew what he

157

was doing), the existence of existence. Pell looked back on those times with nostalgia: it was a curious sensation to have while preaching from the pulpit. He knew the value of doubt, and he saw the lack of it in the faces of so many of his congregation as he spoke, the malevolent calm in the faces whose minds and spirits had gone warmly stagnant and grown a water-skin upon which his words were only insects dancing.

Pell rubs his eyes between thumb and forefinger. Across the lawn over the gentle sound of the rain comes the brawling noise of the piano and the unified voice of the Ladies' Guild in song. Why do they sing? he wonders. Why do they bother? They never do anything but practise and Lord knows the practice doesn't seem to help. Monday noon and already they're at it.

Pell knows he has things to get on with, but he cannot move from his chair. Someone has towed the truck away in the night, and this morning he discovered the distributor cap missing from under the bonnet of his Wolseley. The thud of the football reverberates in the lane and he wonders why those boys aren't in school. He wonders, too, about that feeling, yesterday, when it was as though he stood outside of himself. He had felt it when he shook hands at the door. It was as though he had been cut off, as though he was only partly present but still observing.

Coupar said something about that feeling once, he thinks, or something like it. He said it was like a retirement of the spirit. And I thought he was just making excuses for himself, for his self-exile. Goodness, he was a younger man when he said that. And so was I. The other night — hell, it was weeks ago — that night near the Hacker he had that desperate pensioner's look, as though he wanted to come out of retirement. But he looked helpless — half dead. It's been a long retreat for him all these years. No, I don't want that. Just because they give my job to someone else and I go on the pension doesn't mean I retire. Never.

He sits listlessly in his chair, wishing that Daniel Coupar could be here with him, that they could share a cold leg of lamb and a bottle of beer and a verbal wrangle. Idly, too, he wishes Daniel Coupar could once again shake this town by the ears, seize people's imaginations and make them see and act; but he knows those days are gone for Angelus and even for

158

Coupar. He remembers the days of the boys' camps out at the old quarantine station before the wars, when the young Coupar had been a fiendish if sullen storyteller frightening the younger boys in their camp beds with tales his mother had read him from the Bible. Coupar rearranged details to his own purposes, a fault of his public addresses years later; but the stories were superb.

I remember that one about Jonah—oh, there were a dozen variants—where Jonah is swallowed by the whale and in the whale he meets the Devil himself and the fight is on. It's the violence of the fighting that makes the creature spew Jonah back up on the beach. A neat little ending with the Evil One dragged off into the deep, still a captive. I lay still as a lizard all through it. And the language of the fight! I'd never heard such filth in all my life—the things Satan said to Jonah and the words Jonah chucked back—and I've never heard them used so well since. I can't think what the masters would have done to him if they'd heard. Ah, he was a wonderful liar, Pell thinks. Always used the truth when it suited him though. And I s'pose the truth always used him when it suited itself. Always whales with these Coupars. And Jonah's a wretched vice with them.

Wearily, he reaches across to the coffee table where one of his Bibles lies, and he drags it into his lap with a sigh.

But God said to Jonah, 'Do you do well to be angry for the plant?' And he said, 'I do well to be angry, angry enough to die.' And the Lord said 'You pity the plant, for which you did not labour, nor did you make it grow, which came into being in a night and perished in a night. And should not I pity Nineveh, that great city, in which there are more than a hundred and twenty thousand persons who do not know their right hands from their left, and also much cattle?'

He sighs. And he starts at the knock on the door. With a feat of will he rises to answer it. Miss Thrim stands on the veranda with a Pelaco shirt box in her hands and behind her, shifting from foot to foot, are several other members of the Ladies' Guild cricking their knuckles like street fighters.

'Mr Pell,' she says, 'these are some scones baked by us all as tokens of what you have meant to us over the years.' She hands

159

him the box and there is a shuffle of sensible soles and a low murmur of approval.

'Well,' he stammers, unable to look Miss Thrim in the eye, 'I'm sure the Ladies' Guild bakes scones as well as it sings.'

'Flattery, Reverend.'

'No, indeed,' he mumbles.

Umbrellas bloom. The Ladies move off the veranda into the rain, and Pell regrets that he has not asked them inside for tea or thanked them more effusively. He stands alone with Miss Thrim at the threshold. She clears her throat, a bird-sound.

'Don't you worry, Reverend,' she confides, 'it's not over yet.' Then she is gone, wrapped in a mac, across the lawn before Pell has time to answer. He watches her disappear into the rear of the church hall.

Taking his Pelaco box of scones inside William Pell thinks: Good Lord, whatever does she mean? Old Thrim! As he sits back in his chair he pulls the greased paper aside and surveys the golden backs of the fresh-smelling scones. Looking across the room to where the cardboard box of notes and cheques and record books stands in the open near the dark timber of the bookshelf, he muses, Old Thrim? Old? Hell, she's no older than me! And I can't ever remember her being young. Wonder what she was like?

He bites into a scone. Over the sound of the rain the singing resumes.

V

The paddocks shimmered at sunset. Daniel Coupar saw the ripples, their unrefreshing streams of movement, and he was not satisfied. Something hurt him deep in his chest; the open graze on his arm had hardened like the crust of a creekbed and flies sucked on it.

Coupar had slept beneath the toppled tractor, that night almost a fortnight ago, until the barks of crows woke him in the dawn. Above him, full of dried crud, the great rear wheel shaded him from the first rays of sun. He smelt rubber and axle grease and diesel. The arm of his suit was torn away and he could see the grey flesh of his belly between the tears in his shirt. Somewhere, he could hear the aimless feet of sheep. From the almost perpendicular axle a snake of wire lolled, its barbed head turning; slivers of wood were caught up in the tangle that stretched like a train behind the tractor, twisted and full of those small things it had netted in the journey across the paddock. To his surprise, Coupar found that he was able to drag himself out from under the hollow of the fallen tractor and into the open where he stood in stages, experimenting with back and limbs. With the taste of old vomit in his mouth he set out, stiff and bent with the pain in his belly and side and head and arm, for the house across the way with its black shawl of dead vines and its cluster of falling sheds and emaciated fowls.

He spent that day in bed sleeping and waking to stare at the webs in the corners of the ceiling, observing the dark spots that were once spitballs—paper chewed to a pulp and catapulted with a steel rule—he had sent up on those dull afternoons when his father locked him in his room. Or were some of them Queenie's? He wondered how many spitballs she had sent up to join his there. And his own daughter? The only sign of his daughter having ever existed in this place was that . . . thing he found behind the wardrobe, that sanitary pad, black and hard as a biscuit, wedged in and iced with tiny and delicate spiders' webs.

The next day, rested but still in pain, Coupar rose and went out to the nearest shed and seized a hen from her brood behind an old Coolgardie safe, feeling its awful lightness—what do they eat? he thought—as he took its horned feet and searched for the axe. It took him the whole day to kill and dress the hen; it hurt him to split wood and kindle the fire, and he scalded his hands in the boiling water. Feathers gummed themselves to him. The bird, when dressed, was small enough to hold in one hand. He basted it hastily and roasted it the way his wife had. He ate the old boiler in one sitting without accompaniment and took to bed again, nursing his pain and, soon enough, his indigestion.

This past week Daniel Coupar had been sitting out on the veranda, eating an occasional boiled egg, noticing how little different it was to look out onto his own paddocks and know

161

they were not his own, not his family's. Makes no difference at all, he thought. It's not that I miss. It's that bloody Queenie. And her idiot.

To pass time one morning he counted from memory the pubs in Angelus, naming their proprietors and their premier drinkers. Then he counted those neighbours whose sons had grown strong and stupid and moved away to the city where no one would recognise them in the street. He was glad he had had no sons because he knew he would hate his own reflections and the young sound of his own voice in them. Ah, at least Queenie's fifty per cent mystery, he mused; it's the unknown half in her that's the hopeful part. Coupar had never wondered who her father might have been. It suited him not to know: knowing would inevitably be a disappointment. Sons. He shrugged. He had never got used to having a son-in-law, let alone a son of his own; he saw too much already in other people's sons. That's why, isn't it? he told himself. Because he's like you were — rootless, falling into place somewhere, blundering from shadow to shadow, shying at expectations, disappointing yourself, stumbling onto someone good, extinguishing the good in them, the calm, the freshness, the . . . restless good in them. And under that searching, earnest surface — nothing.

Carefully he had counted the days since he had become an official sojourner on his own land — eleven days. As the tide of heat shook across the earth in the sunset he held in his hands the pages he had torn from the journal of Nathaniel Coupar, and rolling them into a funnel he held the end to his eye and scanned the paddocks and the rim of sea, catching tufts of veldt-grass and loping kangaroos in the circle of vision.

He recalled the time when he first read his grandfather's journals, the long nights after he had given up fighting Benjamin Pustling, when Maureen waited for him in their bed tired from calling until she slept without him. He still remembered the excitement of being in another time, somewhere away from his own disappointment, where every now and then, in those frightening few moments, he had the sensation of writing the journal entries as he read them, of reading them with recognition as though he himself had written them a hundred years before. And he remembered the

162

pursuit of loose ends, the atmosphere of mystery and the sense of dissatisfaction throughout. For a great time afterward, even after he had bought back his father's land in '39, he had a sense of unworthiness, disappointment in his reluctance to come to easy agreement with his grandfather's conclusions. If I was a greater man, he had thought then, these conclusions wouldn't bother me, I'm sure: the greatness, the noble, reasonable part of me would respond. But only in his worst fevers of desperation and anger, when grief and rage blinded him to everything—his wife, his God, himself—could Coupar ever accept: then the journals rested easy with him. Then there was no God, no Grace, no purpose—only betrayal and deception. Justice was an illusion. He had no need of them. He would have to be his own judge and saviour, and tell God to go to Hell.

'All those years of ancestor worship,' he muttered. 'Never even thought he might be wrong.'

Light had gone altogether. Coupar hugged himself in his chair, listening to the sounds of the night.

'He was a stupid bastard. And my father followed. But not me. Not always. Oh, God. Come back, someone.'

He looked across and away to the hill and saw a full moon creeping upon its back.

VI

It is dark, four o'clock in the morning, Tuesday, 21 June 1978, and the *Paris IV* slips her moorings at the town jetty in the cold silence that is broken only by the faint sounds of wind and roosters. Aboard the whalechaser as it leaves Angelus harbour, lights burning, newsmen stand beside their bundled equipment staring nervously out into the darkness beyond their rim of light as the chaser passes out of the narrow gap between the heads. Swell thrusting under them, they joke, smoke and wonder.

Middle Beach, a white crescent like a reflected segment of moon in the darkness, is blotted with scurrying black figures.

163

An outboard motor cuts the silence and then another comes to
life and the two Zodiacs, invisible except for their wakes, bunt
their way out into deeper water, motors running rough and
cold.

Outside Angelus harbour in the belly of the Sound the three
craft sight each other, the chaser idling low in the water, the
inflatables mewling at top throttle, and before long the Zodiacs
have reached the *Paris IV* and are turning circles about her as
she gathers speed and slices up a bow-wave leaving the small
craft to plough her wake in chase.

It is only five minutes before one Zodiac drops behind with
engine trouble, the crew waving the other on. The other
inflatable catches up to the lights of the chaser, riding the
phosphorus chop. The chaser and its remora pass the
lighthouse on Coldsea Island and in time both vessels leave the
sheltering arms of the Sound altogether and strike out into the
rearing Southern Ocean.

At dawn the *Paris IV* and the Zodiac plunge on into the rising
swell. Aboard the chaser newsmen erect tripods and load
cameras and take light readings, shuffling about the deck to
avoid the grumpy seamen who scuttle past. They avoid, too,
the landless horizon to the north-west whence they have come.
The chaser's crew are ill-at-ease with the men the company has
invited aboard; they step around them warily, taking solace
only in the unmistakable hints of seasickness visible already.

In the tossing Zodiac Fleurier and Brent brace themselves
against the loll and jolt of the swells, their ears plugged with
the whine of the outboard. Brent holds his camera to his chest,
waiting for the light to improve.

Two boats pitch on towards the continental shelf, only
specks. An hour later they pass a long white launch trundling
between swells a thousand yards off. They cross a wide path of
whale-oil trailing for miles from her stern. Ted Baer, deeply
preoccupied, does not wave.

Angelus wakes and the townspeople go about their business. At
breakfast they are greeted by the headlines: DOLPHINS STEAL
SHOW AT WHALE RUCKUS and they are reassured. Early in the

morning a film of high cloud smothers the unexpected sun and the grey day wears on.

Shortly before noon, her decks cluttered with seasick reporters, the *Paris IV* eases off power and heaves to. Cameras swivel drunkenly as the Zodiac, unsuspecting, overshoots and skids around, jacking up white water in a circle about them. After a few moments the Zodiac cuts to an idle and Fleurier steers in beneath the chaser's port side. Brent points his camera back at the gallery of lenses. The chaser's skipper brings a loudhailer to the rail and declares himself lost. The chaser's crew laughs, making threatening gestures behind the press cameras.

'What are you going to do now?' the skipper calls, winking at his first mate.

Fleurier in the Zodiac squints up at him. 'Us? We'll lead you home.' He puts the motor in gear and opens the throttle, veering off.

The men on the chaser guffaw; the Zodiac, unaware of the chaser's subtle changes of course over the past two hours, is heading towards Antarctica. *Paris IV* steams out in three long circles, leaving the Zodiac outside her boiling circumference; and because he is well and truly lost Fleurier waits, riding the turbulence. Within five minutes *Paris IV* heads south. Brent and Fleurier glance at one another, surprised and a little proud of their guesswork. But ten minutes later with a blast from her horn the chaser turns seventy-five degrees about and makes north-west for Angelus.

All the afternoon the cameras shoot. The swell chases the two craft until just before dark when they pass Coldsea Island inside the Sound and separate, the chaser entering the harbour and mooring at the town jetty and the Zodiac skittering in behind the point to beach in the cold surf of Middle Beach.

At their evening meals the people of Angelus hear of the seven whales taken by *Paris II* and *Paris III* elsewhere.

VII

Voices were raised in one wing of rooms at the Ocean View Hotel. Surf beat upon the beach across the road and rain fell in intermittent rushes. Queenie listened as Fleurier, pale, spoke with a tired anger.

'They led us on a wild goose chase. The other killer boats were working all the time. The *IV* was just a decoy and a news stunt for the whalers. They made us look like fools and they got it all on film.'

Marks scowled, angry about the failure of his outboard and the fumes that had made him sick. He and his crew mate had returned to Angelus before dawn and a handful of cameras had flashed in their frustrated, nauseated faces as they waded in. 'Hey, come on, Brent,' he said, 'you're supposed to be making this a media event. It's a circus, *their* circus.'

A dozen of them sat around a tiny coffee table, fidgeting, drinking, blaming.

'Allright, allright,' Brent said, looking sick and feeling worse. 'Even when they have all the coverage they've still put the place on the map — and we're the ones on film. Yesterday's dolphins and rainbow got onto national television last night. People didn't even know this goddam place existed. Now they know about us. They're doing our work for us.'

'Lucky for us. What if they weren't?'

'Hey, now —'

'That deputy President, Prime Minister or whatever — he was a dud. A farce.'

'How did I know?' Brent shrugged. 'He's very popular with the local eco-groups. They have him at festivals and things. Angelus doesn't seem to have heard of him.'

'Yeah, well.' Marks looked broodingly at Brent. 'You get any photos out there today?'

'Hey, man, are you trying to tell me what my brief is? You stick to the whales.'

'Well, we haven't done much for any of those poor buggers,' Queenie said. 'Bloody film and TV and newspapers. Images! How many whales have we saved, eh? None.'

All faces turned. There was an awesome silence for several moments.

'Bullshit.'

Queenie turned to face Brent who fidgeted with his cameras, eyes downcast. 'What?'

'I said bullshit. Georges and me held off the *IV* for a whole whaling day.'

'Because they wanted it that way.'

'But we were instrumental in them not killing.'

Oh God, thought Queenie, what am I doing here? 'So,' she said, 'we didn't actively *save* any but we didn't let them kill any more than seven.'

'We put one boat out of the chase. That's something. That's news. I've released it like that. We're amassing our own partisans in the press and TV, don't worry. The visuals are the most important. Saturation. Awareness. We prevented the kill total from being twelve or fourteen. That's effectiveness.'

'You talk another language, mate,' Queenie said.

Brent looked her up and down without replying. He raised his Leica to his eye and focused on her. The flash made them all flinch and for several seconds Queenie saw only white.

Queenie slept poorly that night, disturbed by dreams of almost-forgotten things and a squeamishness within her as though something had penetrated her and was disrupting her insides.

She woke at 2 a.m. and rushed to the lavatory where she vomited, hugging the bowl for thirty minutes with no one to hold her hair back while she retched. She crept weakly back to bed, conscious of its emptiness. There was no one to wipe the balls of sweat from her brow and she felt through her cycles of nausea a disappointment far removed from the day's debacle. I'm home, she thought bitterly. And you'd never know it. A hotel room. Part of her longed for the excitement of confrontation — any confrontation. Surely by now Cleve would know she was back? She was grateful that he had not come, and a little disappointed. She toyed with the idea of seeing him, and she felt tweaks of dread and excitement.

There was no one to hold back my hair, she thought as she

167

slid into an exhausted sleep. 'Granma, Poppa, Cleve . . . they
. . . .' She rolled away into the breathing dark.

Although it was still dark when the Cachalot Zodiacs were
dragged down the beach to be launched, the white sand gave
contrast to the steamy-breathed silhouettes of bodies and most
of the Cachalot people managed to go about their tasks
without falling or stumbling into one another. The sixteen-foot
inflatables were placed on the sand and fuel drums were
crammed into them, and then they were floated in the shallows
and the outboards were fitted and fuel lines connected.
Queenie carried a plastic drum of fuel on her shoulder and set
it down beside the bulbous silhouette of Brent.

'God, I'm sick,' he said. 'Someone said you were too.'

'Yes,' she said. 'Only a bit, it's nerves.'

'Hell, I was doubled, man. I think the hotel staff are trying
to poison us.'

Queenie laughed.

'I mean it.'

'Food poisoning?'

'Maybe. You know how they feel about us.'

'They think Americans are gods. We're all taught that.
They'd never poison anyone with an accent like yours.'

'I'm Canadian, goddammit.'

'Makes no difference. That's the way we're brought up
here.'

'I still think they'd do it. Marks and Georges had a fun time
of it out on the pier that night.'

She shook her head in the dark and moved away from the
confusion and the fumes to stand alone on the white sand. A
dog barked somewhere in the distance. She felt familiar with
and estranged from this beach where she had learnt to swim
with Education Department classes in the mild summers of her
childhood.

Resisting an urge to strip and dive frivolously into the cold
white shorebreak, she walked back, sandshoes squealing on the
sand, to join the others.

When the Zodiacs were in the water, pushed out past the
break into the still deep behind, each of the crews tried to start

168

their motors. Those on the beach could hear the curses and the slaps of starter ropes. One motor turned over and hawked awake, running rough. Fleurier pulled away and opened up across the bay. Marks wrestled with his motor and his Australian companion fiddled with the throttle and choke without success. At length Marks called out to those listening on the beach: he wanted a tow in. Queenie stripped, glad of the excuse, stuffed her clothes and her shoes inside her greatcoat, handed them to someone and waded out.

The water was stingingly cold. It hurt her, finding its quicksilver way into the space between her legs, shrivelling her bladder and tightening her breasts like fists until she became hot and numb. She struck out past the shorebreak in the direction of the curses. Her abdomen tingled as she shoved forwards in the dark, *toes out, right out, just like a frog, out and around and around, head out of the water, that's it, swim* . . . and she smiled at the memories that came out of the dark at her. In a few moments she saw Marks's white cap and altered her direction slightly.

She came up sternwards and called to Marks to throw her a rope. When eventually he saw her he hurled a nylon line that landed beside her.

'Why didn't you use your auxiliary?' she called, breathless.

'Now there's a point,' the Australian said.

'Bright boys,' she called, coughing as a small wave clipped her on the chin. The Zodiac was surprisingly heavy, but her feet touched bottom within a minute and she heaved and felt the Zodiac glide in.

Ashore she became aware of her nakedness and the improving light and the others staring at her curiously.

'Bloody dills,' she said, for something to say.

The Zodiac was hauled up out of the water. No one present knew much about motors. Marks was cursing. An auxiliary motor, a 9.9 horsepower was too small to use alone. Four or five males crowded round the bigger motor flashing torches in each other's faces.

Fifteen minutes elapsed before Fleurier and Brent came buzzing back into view after seeing *Paris II*, the last chaser to leave the harbour, surge away in the distance, fully lit and gathering her fifteen knots.

169

'Missed the mothers,' Brent called out as they glided in, motors cut. A groan rose from the beach.

Back at the Ocean View Queenie lounged about before breakfast, trying to warm up again after her swim. The mood in the rooms was tense. Some of the Australians passed her in the corridor with contemptuous looks. Bloody friendly, she mused, shutting her door.

After dawn and breakfast Queenie sat for a while with Fleurier who smoked quickly and distractedly in his room littered with stacks of folders and loose papers. Blue moons suspended themselves from beneath his eyes; his small mouth was tight with frustration.

'What's all this?' she asked. 'The bloody library?'

'Yes,' he said without looking at her. 'My information bank. Sometimes it seems as overwhelming as my other resources. If only my mind was up to them. How to make people achieve. To make them do what they know. Optimism. Leave things up to the winds, the Fates, the gods, whatever. If we have to live on optimism why don't Brent's gods wake from their divine coma. The only thing more puerile than Man himself are his gods. Sorry. I'm being the philosophic Frenchman. Straight from the comic books. It happens when you're angry enough to explode.'

Queenie knelt on the carpet. 'More scrapbooks. Do you mind?'

'No, go ahead,' he waved. 'Hardly classified information. Information seems such useless shit, sometimes.'

She opened a folder and read: 'The whale's first parental duty is to aid the newborn calf to the surface to taste the air for the first time. Danger and distress ... calves often rescued by being seized in their parents' mouths. . . .'

Queenie, looking up from the mass of dog-eared papers to ask Fleurier a question, found that he was gone. She went to the door but hesitated and returned to the scrapbooks. Outside it was raining and the swimming pool hissed. She picked up a few more folders and skimmed through: 'Rescues ... very good indication of refined social sense ... although it is often maintained that whilst males will come to the aid of females, the reverse does not apply.'

At this, Queenie raised her eyebrows in displeasure but read on.

Twofold Bay, NSW, Aust. Killer whales documented as helping whalers trap humpbacks by preventing them from sounding, jumping on their blowholes and alerting whalers of their presence in an area. They were rewarded with the tongues and lips of killed humpbacks.

Strandings (*a*) disease, (*b*) sonar fault, (*c*) loyalty, (*d*) distress signals, (*e*) stress, (*f*) *other, unknown.*

Even though in a mass stranding the cause of whales returning to the beach once rescued can be attributed to the leader's distress calls, on other occasions a lone, apparently healthy whale will strand on a safe beach and on being towed out will deliberately return to the beach. The reason for this remains a mystery.

. . . a testis from a blue whale can weigh 100 lbs. and be difficult to manipulate . . . a heart = 1000 lbs.; liver = 1 ton; ovaries like volley balls. . . .

Difficult to manipulate, thought Queenie. Hell's bells! Rain continued to fall and she heard cars passing on the esplanade below.

As whales were flensed, scientists delved into the depths of their carcasses . . . drenched in blood, often buried and sometimes suffocated in avalanches of entrails.

. . . the intercourse itself is brief, perhaps a few seconds. Whales lie horizontal or vertical, belly to belly. Loveplay or foreplay precedes this at great length. Some whales like humpbacks caress and slap each other. Such extended foreplay is necessary in an environment where scent is of little consequence. The male gauges the female's readiness by the tone of her responses. If fertilised successfully, the female carries a single embryo back to the cold feeding waters of the Antarctic where the foetus is fattened. After 10–12 months the cow (whalebone and rorqual) returns to warmer waters and gives birth, force-feeding the infant calf with a muscle-pump teat that emits milk.

Cow with calf were easy prey for bay whalers because the

cow was slowed by her offspring and often ensnared by her own maternal instincts. If a calf was harpooned and towed in, the mother would follow and be slaughtered.

Sperm: polygamous
Whalebone: monogamous
Male Sperms fight each other for supremacy during the mating season and victors secure harems.

Queenie dropped that file and took up another. How do you take it all in? she wondered. How can you ever know it all?

She left Fleurier's room and went downstairs to the bar where several of the others were drinking and watching the rain sluice down the plate glass. Brent and Marks, they said, were up in their rooms, feverish and vomiting. A mass of Australian newspapers lay all about, on the bar, tables, stools, and the floor. Cachalot members from Sydney and Melbourne guiltily read the sports pages of the *Age* and the *Herald*, feeding their homesickness. The campaign was now page-eight material in that part of the country. In the city to the north it was page three, and in Angelus it was still front page news. ROUND ONE TO WHALERS, the headlines said.

The afternoon wore on in Angelus, passing like a heavy fogbank indistinguishable from the dusk when it finally came. Winds swept a chill off the harbour that seeped into homes and buildings and numbed those caught outside.

VIII

The beer is free for an hour tonight at the Bright Star and the place is full. Ernie Easton is there, shouting until his eyes ache. Ted Baer has his own ammoniac corner of tall tales, and the crews of the *Paris IV* and the other two chasers are there with spirits and voices wound tight. They tell old stories: about the flenser who tied the whale's penis to the back of a tourist bus, about limbs and lives lost, the old days hunting humpbacks

172

before the ban, and they bring scars for a show-and-tell of proof. More seamen come in, greeted by the woman drumming up custom at the door. During this free hour the darts teams take a sixty-minute recess for some hard, fast drinking. Workers from the abattoirs and the cannery—big meaty men and women fresh from the shift still wearing their hairnets and gumboots—fantasise about having their hands on one of those long-haired poofters from out of town. Hassa Staats sweats, feels the beer slop bubble on his forearms. Celebrate! he thinks. Celebrate! A school of reporters slides through the doors and Staats holds a jug high to them.

And at the end of the hour Hassa Staats watches them settle back into the blue cloud of smoke and some thrifty drinking. He notices the tightness is still there in his chest and he has to fight back the compulsion to cough. It has been with him for weeks now and he has been consulting his old school friend, Doc Duffield, who, days ago, beat gobs of sputum out of him into little yellow-lidded jars for scrutiny. Next Monday he is due to visit Duffield again to get an opinion. He hopes his childhood asthma is not returning.

Cleveland Cookson, conspicuously alone at the bar, with his haunted, amputated look, catches Staats's eye as he passes. Staats also passes his wife Mara but he avoids her eyes and looks away from her thin, pruned frame and that tight mouth which never opens on his account. He makes his way to the WC; he cannot hold it back; a great racking cough bursts out of him and it all moves and he coughs and spits and coughs. I've got the bogger going now, he thinks, seeing spots in his vision. He coughs with greedy satisfaction and a sense of doom.

IX

Next morning the town wakes to an extraordinary phenomenon. Soon after dawn scores of townspeople gather in the drizzle to watch. Whalechasers remain moored at the town jetty and for an hour the two Zodiacs hover about just outside the entrance to the harbour before they give in and return to

Middle Beach behind the headland. Later in the morning, townspeople in their hundreds picket the slope above the harbour mouth to see the right whale and her calf lazing in the channel, lolling flukes, blowing mist from their spiracles. The whalers have given up trying to lure them into the shallower waters inside the harbour and the whales refuse to be frightened outside and away from the narrow entrance. Skippers and crews argue helplessly. The right whale is an endangered species and protected by law. There are too many spectators for harpoons to be deployed secretly. The water either side of the whales is much too shallow for them to pass safely.

Joining the throng on the hill, some members of Cachalot & Company wince, imagining the headlines WHALES DO THEIR OWN FIGHTING. They are eager to avenge yesterday's embarrassment. Telescopes and binoculars glint in the dull light. Hearing the news on radio wealthy tourists take their launches across the harbour to see; they are booed and hissed by the burgeoning crowd as they take their vessels close. The dimensions of the whales come as a shock to many of the townspeople and the out-of-towners who continue to stand in the rain for much of the day; many of them would never have believed that anything on earth could be so big. The cow sometimes has the appearance of a capsized tugboat animated by some unseen current below the surface. Once, only once, she turns a tight circle in the narrow gap and tosses herself in the air, landing with a bellowing crash to the sounds of wild applause from the hill.

Outside his home above Angelus harbour after dark, the town's rotund and powerless mayor has a bucket of pigs' blood emptied on him as strobe flashes blind him. Two stocking-headed persons escape in the oystery night.

Two women give birth in the Angelus Regional Hospital. Fingers and toes are counted, limbs joggled.

Towards midnight women lock their drunken husbands out in

the rain while their children snuggle deep and curl their toes at the sound of the rain in the gutters.

After midnight four Aboriginal boys aged thirteen hot-wire a mini-moke and drive it four hundred yards uphill before it runs out of petrol and rolls back to where it was parked.

Wind strengthens. Out beyond the Sound the ocean mashes itself. By the time dawn comes the storm will have intensified and no craft will leave Angelus harbour. The gulls have already flown inland to roost.

X

In the hours before dawn on Friday, 24 June, after the previous day's storm had finally abated leaving a steady south-westerly swell in it wake, it became apparent to the Cachalot party that Brent and Marks were too ill to ride in the Zodiacs and replacements needed to be chosen. The company bickered in the lobby of the Ocean View Hotel as rain spattered in the darkness outside. Moving around their stamping feet, a porter sucked cigarette butts up with a vacuum cleaner. Even in the lobby their angry breaths blossomed steamily. The argument grew bitter and personal. Two Australians were chosen to crew one boat, and Queenie Cookson, the only other Cachalot member ever to have been in a boat, was made crewmate to Fleurier.

As the Zodiacs were dragged down the low-shelving beach to the water Queenie drew in long breaths to ease her anger and her fear.

Over the low tuttle of the small auxiliary engine she could still hear the arguments in the dark as she rose and fell in the sharp inshore swell. Fleurier engaged the bigger motor and gunned the inflatable out across the south towards the headland light to meet the whalers emerging from the harbour. Queenie settled uncomfortably in the bow

175

surrounded by plastic fuel drums, heavy in her layers of wetsuit and outer clothing, clinging on as the flimsy bows quivered on the tops of the swells. The engine roared in her ears and the whole ocean seemed alive with vibration beneath her.

Paris II heard them coming and surged out of the harbour, quickly coming up to her steady fifteen-knot chase speed, and the Zodiacs never caught up. A few minutes later, however, *Paris IV* cruised up behind, bunting out an audible bow-wave, lights swelling as she closed up to them, and as she passed the Zodiacs fell in behind and followed with ease. Fleurier kept to one side out of the immediate turbulence of the wake, and the two Australians in the other Zodiac followed a hundred yards farther behind for a few minutes until the gap between them widened suddenly and they lost sight of one another. Fleurier cursed and hesitated, then throttled on. Queenie braced herself uneasily as they passed the sombre outline of Bell Head and the swells became longer and deeper and her stomach revolved with the steady undulation.

An hour passed.

Queenie Cookson had never been in such an expanse of water before, and although she couldn't properly see it she sensed its vastness and felt the absence of land in every pore, and was afraid. Yesterday she had told Fleurier and the others about the sharks and for a moment he went pale before his features resumed their grim set and nothing more was said. Queenie had sat alone at the bar for an hour afterwards, hearing them gasping and murmuring amongst themselves.

Grasping a loop of rope for a handhold, she now held herself tight to prevent undignified yelps of fear escaping her. She knew that a white-pointer the size Ted Baer was after could bite an inflatable in half, could swallow an outboard engine, could pierce an aluminium hull. She felt the Zodiac, small and pliable, almost hugging itself to her as her mind filled with newsreel images of launches being towed about by threshing monsters, their sterns battered by caudal fins that looked like huge, honed gunmetal hatchets. She imagined the serpentine copper eyes and the belly full of refuse: sheep, steel cable, anonymous flesh, nylon line, and she felt the panic of nightmares seeping into her.

As dawn came, Fleurier's face was revealed, set hard with

176

purpose and preoccupation; the roar of the big outboard discouraged even the thought of conversation. There was nothing in sight but the flaking rump of the *Paris IV* ahead. She wondered, without cynicism, what Brent's gods had in store for her.

Aboard the *Paris IV* the crew woke their captain, a big, heavy man, and the chaser prepared itself for the day's hunt. There were no pressmen aboard this morning and the atmosphere above deck was jovial. The deckhands threw a few goodnatured obscenities in the direction of the Zodiac as the tiny craft came abreast with a camera. The harpoongun was unsheathed and swivelled and elevated a few times by the first mate who, it was said, appreciated a bit of drama.

Queenie took photos with Brent's big camera until her arms became wooden with cold and her fingers could not adjust exposure or shutterspeed, and for another three hours she rode the movement of the water and listened to the harsh melodies within the larger noise of the engine. Whales no longer claimed her attention; she was busy feeling cold and alone and afraid.

Near eleven o'clock she vomited messily. Fleurier wiped it from his shoulder without expression, gazing ahead towards the black flanks of the chaser.

But Fleurier came back to life when the sloping spout of the sperm whale erupted near them, so close they could both smell and feel the fine vapour of its breath as the long, sleek shape glided forwards lifting its flukes nonchalantly. The Zodiac swerved and moved along the swells coming from the south, and there were shouts from the chaser's bridge that Queenie heard above the engine noise.

The lumbering cachalot left flat patches of water in its wake and sounded again. Queenie felt the Zodiac rear at the tip of a swell that lifted them sideways; the bow yawed across. A short breach; the sperm showed its breakwater back and continued ahead. Twisting round, Queenie saw the skipper moving along the catwalk to the gun.

Oh God, no, she thought. Please.

Fleurier swung the inflatable back round into the swell and Queenie rose high above him as the Zodiac climbed a crest, perched there for a moment, until they climbed down its back with the propeller screaming, out of the water for a moment.

177

The chaser bore down on them. Fleurier held back from the whale and drifted across and under the bows of the *Paris IV*. Crewmen waved fists and shouted. Queenie's body went rigid. The bow-wave hissed at her back.

The whale surfaced to starboard and ahead, blowing shallowly. Queenie felt a sudden lurch of speed. She saw the long, wide, slick back and felt an almost maternal protectiveness, and as she turned to raise a finger of contempt at the bows of *Paris IV* she saw a puff of smoke from the end of the catwalk.

The next ten seconds plodded past unnaturally. First the hair-prickling feeling of the projectile and the wind of steel cable and manila rope passing overhead, then the thunder and, in the ensuing deafness, the silent shower of flesh and blood. Then time was fast. The cable reared, twanged tight, and on it the Zodiac ascended, caught up in its bar-tautness, lifted out of the water. Fleurier fell on the stalled engine, tilting it and the Zodiac jerked free, slewed sideways and fell back into the water as the cable sang above their heads. From then, as she bellowed at the slate sky, Queenie felt time faltering. The whale flurried at the end of the line, throwing blood and water into the air until the second shot passed overhead and there was a muffled crump and it went still. Queenie only half saw the carcass inflated and marked; it made no sense to her. She heard the chaser sound her horn as she cut away, leaving them drifting near the bloated hulk with its slick of blood and the garlands of white excrement that fell from descending seabirds.

Fleurier started the outboard and steered them away from the whale before the sharks came. He had not spoken to Queenie in the eight hours since leaving Angelus. He took the compass from her stained coat and steered north-west.

By the time the lighthouse of Coldsea Island and the muted glow of Angelus came into view, many things had passed through Queenie Cookson's mind. It was as though the gunshot over her head that morning had set her mind in motion like a sprinter under a starter's gun. Vomit swilled about in the bilgewater with the frozen white petals of guano.

178

Several times in the hours she saw herself between the grey knees of her grandfather who held a heavy, benign object which whispered with a soft flurry of ricepaper, and she saw his big, battered hands turning pages, felt against her ear the deep wheeze and warmth of his chest. *The burning sand shall become a pool, and the thirsty ground springs of water; in the haunts where jackals once lay shall grow grass and reeds and papyrus . . . .*

She saw the submarine blue of the pool and the distorted forms of the school sheet squad at the edge. *Swim, swim, swim, go, go!* Where? she thought, where to, where to go?

The first real swimming lessons were those her grandfather gave her before she was old enough for school lessons. He rowed out into the bay and tossed her over the side and rowed towards the shore, always just out of her reach, calling, 'Swim, Queenie, swim! It's the only way!' And sometimes between desperate strokes she saw the tears glistening on his face as he rowed. Swim, she told herself, it's the only way.

Skittering in the face of those long, deep southerly swells with the scream of the outboard in her head, Queenie made herself imagine the swim to land. For ever, she thought, it would take for ever ploughing through those swells with no sense of direction, no clear blue, only the long, long slog, arm after arm after arm . . . stroke . . . stroke . . . .

Looking back, it seemed ludicrous to teach little girls to do the dead man's float; it had been so hard to imagine being dead then, harder to imagine being a man.

Swim, swim . . . .

I could never be anything else, she told herself.

The only time she had come close to being someone else was one day in the bottom of a boat on the Hacker River when she saw herself behind the eyes of Cleveland Cookson beneath her. Him, she was in him, inside him, of him, was him, and yet she had never been more herself, more distinct before in her life. She was herself reflected, still, not thrashing, not swimming. Dead man's float? Two and one in the patchwork paperbark light.

Queenie hugged herself in the dreamy nauseous solitude of the ocean.

Fleurier touched her on the shoulder and she saw the lights

on the beach: headlights, floodlights, camera flashes, television lights, and she closed her eyes to protect herself.

XI

During the day Cleve kept himself in the creaking house, needing somehow the protection of its sturdy old walls and the comforting monologues of shifting timbers to stay calm. His savings were low and the dole had not arrived and he was loath to spend money on petrol, though he longed to drive out along lonely roads allowing the actions, the automatic responses, to absorb his attention, to make him feel active and functioning. Instead, he slept, on his face, the blank sleep of the tired and destitute and the truly unconscious; he slept for most of the day with drizzle crawling down the window that overlooked the agitated surface of the harbour.

At 4 a.m. he had been awake, barely conscious but standing at the window to see the low, lit shapes of the chasers gliding out of the harbour towards the sea. He felt no excitement at the sight, no gooseflesh as he might have felt even a week before. As the lights slid out of the harbour and out of sight Cleve's mind was flat, untouched, and he fell back onto the bed. Before he slept he had a series of short, racing dreams which ran through him like a badly chopped tape. He saw the patronising and angry faces of teachers, foremen, contractors, lecturers; he saw the dew on the windowsill on a winter morning and his faceless mother and father waking him. The last dream was longest. A girl passed him a note in class, sticking the cone of paper in his inkwell and thinking it was a love-letter, he opened it and read it quickly. *You are a dumbhead. Pass it on.* But he was at the end, last desk before the wall, so he put the note in his pocket, shamed.

Late in the afternoon Cleve shuffled about the house listening to the radio, shambling upstairs to look out at the harbour from the bedroom window: the mudflats at the northern end, the Yacht Club at Fill Cove, the squat outline of the quarantine station ruins at Pinter Point, only to shamble back down to the kitchen window to look at the same things with his elbows propped on the table. The radio played Charley Pride and Queen and Slim Dusty. He drank his Bushells tea, waiting for something, anything, to happen to him.

The metallic lights of the wharf came on. Out near the end of the dog's leg that was the deepwater jetty a tiny yellow light germinated. The radio played local news. The lead story ended his waiting.

'. . . . that the inflatable dinghy used by the antiwhaling lobby group Cachalot & Company lost contact with the chaser *Paris IV* around noon and has not been sighted since. The chaser has reported an incident of interference where a harpoon had to be fired over the protesters' heads to secure a catch, an action local CIB spokesmen say is completely defensible in the circumstances. There is also a report that one of the protesters involved was a woman. . . .'

Cleve switched the radio off and sat with his cheek against the cold glass of the window, thinking for a while, mulling it over, before taking up the keys to the Land Rover and leaving.

Despite the cold and the darkness the car park at Middle Beach was full. Geez, Cleve thought, the whales really bring 'em out of the woodwork. He recognised the ABC van across the way and some men setting up lights on the grass. His windscreen wipers groaned across the glass, he waited, irritable, jittery.

Thirty minutes later he heard the whine of an outboard motor. Everyone in the car park responded to it. Floodlights and spotlights played out on the water a few minutes more until a black shape with two yellow marks within it came into view, attracting long, sweeping beams of light.

As the boat slid in on the sloppy surf, people raced into the water, tilted the motors, and dragged boat and occupants up to shore, A faint cheer. People stood about in the rain that slanted, lit in the moving pipes of light. Cleve got out. The two yellow figures in the midst of the crowd were hard to keep in view. Cleve jogged towards them, collar up against the rain, moving in certain, measured steps, closing on them until he

181

saw in the sudden brilliant illumination of a camera flash the pale, worn, frightened face of Queenie Coupar. His pace faltered; it shocked him. It was as if her corpse was being manipulated up the beach by some clumsy puppeteer. Cleve came to a halt in the sand and the apparition passed by in the midst of the crowd and he was left alone by the water.

He did not light a fire to warm the house. He opened the last flagon of invalid port. He wanted to speak with her, to coax the sound of her voice from those chapped lips. Driving home with the image of her death mask still before him, he knew, finally, deep in him, that she would not always be; the thought twisted its way down into his belly. Danger. She had been in danger.

He drank small amounts of port for an hour and began seeing himself again in his mind's eye. He saw himself on the road again with the pleasant drone of the Land Rover in his ears and the long stretches of straight bitumen shimmering, deep valleys with gravel coiling through karri trees tall as the sky itself, his senses absorbing, absorbing; and he saw people who did not know that his mother and father were shadows in the shade, people who had not worked with him, schooled with him, had never seen him smiled about, people with whom he felt equal, even superior. He saw himself walking towards a glittering pool on an empty, blinding beach and there was a face. That face. Alive. Wanting.

Using precious fuel, he drove down to the Ocean View on Middle Beach. He left the flagon of port on the seat and went in.

In the bar he slowly and deliberately drank a glass of beer and watched the glass doors of the lobby. He also kept an eye out for the bouncers. Twenty-five minutes later, for the sake of appearances, he bought another beer. A beanied man beside him at the bar cornered him into conversation. The man looked as though his nose had been broken several times in the past. He was no older than Cleve and certainly less sober. There was a menacing comradeliness about him as he asked rhetorical questions about the protest.

'I'm no expert,' Cleve said, wondering how much the man knew. The whole town must know about Queenie, he thought.

'You tell me what would've happened. If they hadn't been lucky enough to find their way back, I mean.'

'They would've been drowned or ate by Noahs,' the man said, moving his big, cracked hands on the bar. 'Or they would've got lost and we'd've had a big search on our hands and the whole town'd go lookin' for 'em. And the whalers would've took the blame. You think the shot over their 'eads was any bigger danger to 'em than their own fucking stupidity? They don't know their arse from a hole in the ground. People comin' from other countries, other places, to tell us what to do with our town. Our industry. Our jobs. And they roam around — professional protesters — livin' on the dole. They don't need jobs. They 'aven't got families to feed.'

Have you? Cleve wondered, looking at the man. He looked barely adult. It was only his hands that made him look a man. 'Well I suppose that might be true of some of them,' he said. 'You know, over-educated bored romantics and everything, but they're still people doing something they believe's right. I don't know if you — we — can write them all off.'

'Bloody hell I can't,' the man muttered. 'A woman out there, too. You shoulda seen it.'

'Seen it?'

'Bloody stupidity, that's what it is. Miles out over the shelf in a rubber-bloody-duckie. You'd think a shot over their 'eads might've scared some sense into 'em. This dumb bitch looking up with a camera, makin' out she's stoppin' the end of the world. My Gawd, it gets my goat. Ah. But nothin' a good screw wouldn't put right. Eh?' The man shrugged and seemed to cheer up a little. He bought Cleve a drink to stand beside his untouched other one.

Cleve, shuddering, nodded. Be resigned, he told himself, you can't do anything. 'Yeah, I s'pose.'

The man eyed him. 'You don't reckon, do ya?'

Cleve took a token sip of beer and replaced the glass with an agonised steadiness. 'How do you mean?'

'You reckon I'm talking bullshit.'

'Well, not —'

'Carm on.'

Cleve watched the man's big meathook hands and searched himself for safe words. 'Well —'

183

'I mean people can't just turn up and decide for other people how they're gonna live, how they're gonna do their job and *if* they're gonna do their job, now can they? I mean if I went into Woolworths and sat on the girl's cash register and said I thought it was cruel to wrap toy kangaroos in plastic and that all plastic kangaroos should be set free, the cops'd drag me out by the balls, wouldn't they? They'd say I was crazy.'

Cleve nodded emphatically.

'Some French bastard and his girlfriend shouldn't be able to do it either. Stupid slut.'

Cleve sighed. It wasn't just honour; it really hurt. Only words, he told himself, they're only words.

'Well?' the man said, shifting his feet on the bar rail.

'Well what?' Cleve said.

'Do you reckon?'

'It's hard for me to talk about it in those terms, that's all.'

'Why?'

'Because....' he sighed, incapable.

'Because what?' The man turned to face him directly.

Something's gonna happen anyway, Cleve thought, regardless of what I say. You tell him. Cleve took a gulp of beer. 'Because the woman you've been calling a stupid slut is my wife.'

Cleve's head swept along the bar, uprooting towels and glasses and small change; he watched them pass and then his eyes focused an instant later and he was amongst the cigarette butts and gobs of spit in the tray beneath the footrail. Moving. He saw the legs of chairs pass. Feet and trouser legs. Then he was floating.

'Lettin' 'is wife be spoken about like that ... shoulda killed 'im. And all that time 'e was one of 'em.'

Cleve felt his head bunt the swing doors open and then he was floating again, renewing his acquaintance with the grass, only this time it was wet. It went very quiet.

In time Cleve's head stopped its gyro-compassing and his vision cleared and he became aware of a circle of faces hovering over him. He stirred and twisted into a protective ball on the wet grass until someone laughed and, with great caution, he sat upright. The faces were dark.

'Kick you out too, uh?'

184

'Yeah,' Cleve said. Say yes, he thought, say anything.

'You got a dollar?'

'Twelve cents, sorry.'

The Aborigines shuffled about in the rain. One wore an old navy greatcoat, another a chenille dressing-gown, another a green garbage bag with a hole in the top for his head.

'I got some port, though,' he said, wanting to please.

'Gawd, no complain' ye'll 'ear from us.'

Ten minutes later Cleve was sharing his flagon of port in the concrete entry of the men's toilets over the road with five dark faces. The surf mushed below and the grass outside glittered with the light from passing cars. The smell of urine, Cleve found, was not overpowering, and the cold was held at bay by the sweet warmth of the port. He passed the flagon round quickly, afraid his drinking mates might suddenly turn on him. He felt sorry for them—all Aborigines—particularly those in Angelus. They looked sick and listless, like undernourished dogs whose coats had lost their shine, but he was afraid of them too, their eyes, the pinkness of their palms, and he could not trust them. As the port loosened him, he spoke more to them.

'You know, I thought you blokes—youse cobbers—were gunna beat me up when I first saw yers. A skinny whitey like me sees a group of blokes like youse, he just expec's to get his head beat in. Yer scary buggers, you know.'

They laughed, embarrassed.

'Why'd you want the dollar?' he asked.

'To buy a plagon,' the one in the chenille dressing-gown said. 'We 'ad seventy-five orready.'

'Well, we cut out the middle man,' Cleve said, tipping the heavy bottle back.

'Yairs,' they all said, solemnly waiting their turn. They spoke quietly amongst themselves until the drink made them relax.

'What d'you do?' the boy in the greatcoat asked.

The question was a surprise to Cleve. Even they've started to think like that, he thought to himself. Why don't people ask what you like, what you want, what you are, instead of what your job is? 'Nothing,' he said.

'Whitey bludger.' The other laughed.

'What about you?' Cleve asked him.

'Worked on the wheat bins once.'

185

'E's a bludger, too,' the boy in the plastic bag said.

'You c'n bloody talk. Bit of ol' rubbitch in a rubbitch bag.'

They all laughed and shifted their numb buttocks. They're kids, Cleve thought, just kids.

'Where you blokes sleep?' he asked.

'Sleep where we sleep.'

'Everywhere,'

'When it rains?' Cleve asked.

'Somewhere.'

Cleve took his turn at the flagon. Geez, he thought, geez.

'You fellas know Abbie Tanks? Best centreman I ever saw.'

They laughed, elbowing each other in the ribs.

'Our cousin,' the boy in the dressing-gown said. 'Just Abbie.'

'Just Abbie,' Cleve said, passing the bottle. It went round and round and round and round until he was dizzy. The six of them laughed at each other laughing. They gargled the port and it ran down their chins like blood.

'What about the whales?' Cleve asked, spinning. 'What do you think about them whales?'

'Wadda we want wiv whales?' one said.

'Fuck d' whales,' one said.

Another yawned. 'Whales are nice.'

'He thinks it's a bank. Wales.'

'Piss off.'

'You never seen a whale.'

'Seen a snail.'

'Fuck d' snails.'

'Yeah, fuck the snails,' Cleve said, rattling the nearly empty flagon. His body moved in concentric spirals.

The night slipped by with warmth and songs and then sleep.

Well before dawn Cleve was woken by the cold and damp and he stole away from the sleeping youths. He didn't want them to know where he lived, so he did not wake them and he made his way in the darkness and the drizzle to the Land Rover over the road. And he fell asleep trying to start the engine.

He woke on the front seat, cheek against the cold buckle of the seatbelt, when a group clattered past carrying big, heavy things, shouting instructions at one another. Through the misted window he heard the voice of Queenie Coupar and, fumbling with the door handle, fell out onto the wet bitumen, picked himself up raggedly, and went after her.

Queenie's yellow figure bobbed about in the swirl of silhouettes on the beach. Zodiacs were pointed out to sea, noses in the water. Cleve merged with the steam-snorting crowd, trying to locate her by homing in on her voice and following brief glimpses of yellow. He saw his own feet against the white, hard sand and knocked elbows with others who swore and lit red eyes of cigarettes.

'Queenie?' he called out, gingerly.

'Huh?'

'Queenie,' he called louder.

'Oh, God.' A pause. The crowd hushed for a moment and someone asked her if anything was wrong. 'Go away, Cleve.'

'I want to talk to you,' Cleve said, frightened by the sudden silence. 'Can I talk to you?'

'No,' she said, after a pause.

'Just for a moment.'

'Look, I'm busy.'

'Geez, can't you — ?'

'Cleve, piss off.'

'You're, going out there again today, aren't you?'

There was no reply, only a murmur of embarrassment and disgruntlement vibrating from the group. Someone coughed.

'I don't want you out there again.'

'Hey, listen mate,' an Australian voice said.

'No, you listen. You're not taking my wife out there in one of those rubber duckies.'

'She decides that, Mr Cookson,' the voice of Fleurier said.

'Piss off, Cleve. Please.'

'Oh, come on!' Cleve said, angry, helpless. He began to push his way through the shadowy bodies until a large hand gripped his left shoulder and he stopped. 'Orright.' He surrendered, fearing more violence. 'Okay, okay.' He went back through the bodies, up the beach, climbed the retaining wall and crossed the wet grass. An outboard sputtered.

He sat in the Land Rover, shivering with cold and a deep, sustained fright. He wondered whether he was afraid for her, or frightened that she would not come back. He noticed in the

187

dull twilight the group of youths emerging from the public lavatories and he sank in his seat until he was sure they had gone. Poor buggers, he thought. Small mushrooms of mist sprouted from the wet grass. A haze hung over the white of the beach. Gulls, sluggish from the night, cartwheeled cautiously and a man with a lumpy bulldog thudded down the footpath wearing only shorts and sandshoes. Somewhere, the other side of Mount Clement, a foghorn sounded.

The wail of outboard motors faded into the distance. Cleve sighed. The light was curious, as indefinite as moonlight. In an hour, he thought, the town will be awake. Angelus, town of my dreams.

It wasn't long before Cleve thought he heard the sound of outboards again. He sat up with a start and bumped the horn with his elbow. He jumped out, embarrassed.

Down on the grass he stood beside a resinous pine that reminded him of disastrous woodwork lessons — rapped knuckles and bent nails — as he listened to the approaching sounds. He ignored the cold and gazed out into the grey mass of conjoined sea and sky. In time two small bow-waves showed and he watched them grow as they approached until he could see spots of yellow and the engines cut and the inflatables drifted in on the shore break. He heard voices. Some people waded in the shallows. Torches dissected the gloom near the water. He heard them talking.

'What happened?'

'Too rough. Even the chasers turned back.'

'Not our day.'

'No, not today, dammit.'

'Someone make me a Milo.' Queenie's voice.

Someone make me a bloody Milo, she says. Cleve almost laughed. He turned and walked towards the lit frontage of the Ocean View Hotel.

He was sitting on the kerb outside the hotel when the group came across the road. Some pulled small trailers with the inflatables on them; others carried plastic fuel drums and cameras and bags. Queenie stopped at the kerb, pulling the yellow hood from her head. Her breath steamed out before her, lit pink by the overhead neon sign.

'What do you want?' she asked quietly.

188

'To talk.'

'I don't really want to.'

'We haven't talked about anything.'

'I'm not sure I want to.'

'I'd love a Milo,' he said with a grin.

'You bloody look like it. Been sleeping in the park by the looks of it.'

'Yes,' he said.

'Bull.' She wiped her running nose on the back of a woollen mitten. 'A quick talk and a Milo and that's it.'

He got up and followed stiffly.

Queenie flicked the lid of the Milo tin with the edge of a teaspoon and made two mugs of it, filling them from the electric jug on the table near her bed. Her hands were steady, her face crimson from the cold. Cleve sat on the end of the bed, nervous and fatigued.

'I thought some bugger was going to slug me earlier on,' he said.

'You were lucky. They're pretty edgy at the moment.' She stirred with the spoon. 'Georges and Marks got beaten up once, too, you know.'

'I haven't forgotten.'

'No.'

'Thanks,' he said, taking the mug from her.

'You've been drinking.'

He looked at his clothes; there was a vomit stain on his sleeve. 'Yeah.'

'What for?' Her voice was timbred with severity.

'Oh, had a rough time these past few weeks.'

'Why weren't you at work earlier on? It's not ... oh. I should've known.' She sipped her drink, disgusted.

'Yeah. Sacked.'

'You look so bloody awful.'

'Sorry.'

'Not me you have to please.'

'Oh?'

'Back off, Cleve.'

Cleve sipped the hot drink. Down the back of his neck he felt

189

a hot-cold prickling—he was sweating. Both of them felt the discomfort of an unalterable propinquity that made being rude as difficult as being sentimental.

'Sorry again.'

'So you're a drunk now as well.'

'No,' he said, rubbing the coarseness of his chin. 'I'm not a drunk.'

'What is it, an act then?'

'No. What d'you mean?'

'Pale and haggard. Win the lady's heart back.'

'No, I'm going to a fancy dress ball looking like Dylan Thomas.'

'You're pining then.'

'Pining? Whimpering on the end of a leash?'

'Maybe.'

'Okay, so I'm a dog. I confess.'

Queenie smiled; Cleve took careful note of it.

'You smell like a dog.'

'I know. Do I really?'

'Yeah.'

'Can I use your shower?' he asked. 'Clean up a bit?'

'No.'

He hooked a sneakered foot through the strap of a bra that lay on the floor with a heap of other clothes. 'Your friends'll think poorly of you, leaving me helpless, treating me badly, letting me go round like this, like some bloody . . . widower.'

'I think they've enough of a poor idea,' Queenie said, her voice rising. 'They think I'm a cretin to have married you. And I agree.'

'Then why did you marry me?'

Queenie did not look at him. 'Hell, I dunno. I thought . . . there was something about you, something good, something not ready yet, but kind of . . . promising, I guess. I thought you were bloody marvellous. I wanted to be that with you.'

'And neither of us are that.'

'No.'

Neither spoke for a full minute.

'I've finished your ancestor's journals,' Cleve said, at length.

'Oh, great. Glad to see you finish something,' she said flatly.

'Not a pretty picture.'

190

'Forget it, will you?' she said, her voice beginning to break.

'I'll have to understand it before I'll forget it. You know, you're a real Coupar, never mind the dubious parentage. Stubborn, idealistic, self-righteous.'

'What else?'

'Strong. Capable of great good.'

Queenie shrugged, finishing her drink, and she took his half-full mug from him. 'Are you going to try to sabotage us?'

'Our marriage?'

She flinched. 'No, Cachalot.'

'No, I don't give a stuff about that any more.'

'Because your side is losing.'

'My *side*? My side's aching from sleeping on concrete.' She did not respond, so he sighed and continued. 'Anyway, everyone's losing. And I've withdrawn from the competition.'

'You were never in it, Cleve.'

'True, but I don't want any part of it, not even an attitude.'

'You still think the whalers should be allowed to continue then.'

'No. Probably they should go before the whales. They will. They can't last much longer. I think the whales will outlast them. Anyway, I think the whaling should stop.' He paused, looking up at her to see the annoyance and pleasure in her face. 'Looks as though I've still got an attitude. Shame about that.'

'You've changed your mind. Why?' Queenie strode across the room to take up an interrogator's stance above him.

'A whaler called you a slut and gave me a thick ear.'

'My God, is that all! Is that the stuff that makes up your mind for you?'

'A thick ear seems valid enough to me.'

Queenie sat across the room from him trying to relax, to calm herself. It seemed valid enough to me once, too, she thought to herself. 'Well, why don't you do something about this new conviction of yours?'

'I don't feel that strongly about it,' he said with a flick of his shoulders. 'Because it's not as important as some other things.'

'So you join the silent majority.'

'And use soap and fertiliser and margarine and ice-cream and candles and lipstick...'

191

'Big deal. You are so inconsistent, Cleve.'

'Like you. Like your mates. Only I'm not pretending to be. *I'm* not pretending.'

'At least we're confronting the issue.'

'No, you're confronting the media. It's all play-acting. You're no different from the whalers or anyone else for that matter. Think you're bloody crusaders. And how many whales have you saved?'

'It's not as simple as that.'

'Okay.' He shrugged. 'I'm not consistent. I can't see anything through. I'm not even very nice.' He stood up and jabbed a finger at her. 'But I'm not pretending. Your whole little campaign is crook, it's as dishonest as hell, as fake as this whole town.'

'No, it's not true,' Queenie said, trembling with feeling. 'It's an honest, meaningful thing. We're trying.'

'Trying to manipulate people, being manipulated. Oh, you're trying.'

Queenie went to the window; rain was falling. She put a hand up to her face, ran the back of it across her cheek and a quicksilver flash, a tear, fell from her.

'And I'm trying,' Cleve said. 'I need you.'

'Get out.'

'Why? Why Queenie?'

'Because you're as much a manipulator as any of us.'

Cleve got up, began to say something but left off, suddenly windless. She closed the door as soon as he was in the corridor. He walked like a man with artificial limbs.

Outside twilight gave landmarks a weepy, grey look, the sadness of the night before an insubstantial dawn.

'Bitch,' he said aloud, opening the frosted door of the Land Rover. His breath floated from him.

XII

Traffic streams into town from the north. The low sky promises rain. Goormwood Street is congested with tourists and journalists, and the town's hotels and motels are booked out by early afternoon. Latecomers are forced to find accommodation in on-site caravans, chalets, tents and sleazy harbourside guest houses. Public telephones grow appendages, queues of journalists and representatives making reports. The three whalechasers moored at the town jetty are photographed and posed in front of. Enterprising locals, realising that the chasers will not work today because of the sea conditions, organise impromptu tours, and every historical monument, every ramshackle old building rumoured to be consigned to the National Trust, every natural and unnatural marvel, has its hungry pilgrims. The *Advocate* comes out with the headline MAYOR IN BLOODBATH. Nine political counter-factions sell badges on the street in competition with the tin-shaking old women from the Salvation Army and the Daughters of Charity. Behind a warehouse on the waterfront the crew of a national current affairs program takes an aerosol can of paint, sprays WHALING IS MURDER on a blotchy wall and films the slogan from six different angles.

The telephone exchange is in an uproar. By dusk Angelus makes news in Vancouver, Baltimore, Leeds, and Brisbane. In an upper room of the Bright Star the Sesquicentenary Committee meets and a round of drinks is bought and backs are slapped.

At seven o'clock the news of the Angelus Party has got around and the Angelus Oval hall begins to fill. Hassa Staats's, free kegs hiss open, greeting the tourists and mediators who pour through the doors. Two journalists dressed in fashionable war surplus are attacked in the dark as they pee behind the hall, and as they leave their assailants shout 'Greenie pigs!' and disappear into the night. There is, too, a minor clash between the Leninist-Calvinists and the Libertarian Revolutionary Front, and for an hour the Wimmin's Left Front occupies both the male and female toilets. The Protestant Free Commerce Association distributes pamphlets outside in the rain. A dance band grinds away at one end of the packed hall, and the odour of sheep dung from the agricultural show is slowly but certainly conquered by the sweet stink of human sweat, while outside the southerly storm redoubles itself as it moves in off the ocean, wedging open the sky with its puce lightning.

As Desmond Pustling drives through the rain-filled midnight streets towards Middle Beach, he marvels at his acumen. Monday's embarrassment seems far behind. His new secretary has pleased him thus far; she is frightened and ambitious and vain. I've rallied, he thinks, as my old man would have rallied. When you get hit, even if it only stings a little, you come back hard and enthusiastic. Something this whole cretinous town could learn from. You have to remember who you *are*, who you have, who you want. Remember what you control.

Halfway home, Pustling veers around and points his BMW back into the centre of town. Goormwood Street is absurdly crowded. Milkbars and public bars have closed and the newcomers are drifting back to their accommodation. He makes a slow pass of Pell's manse, taking a long glance as he passes. Lights are on in the house and uncurtained windows illuminate the diagonal rain. When he is past and half a block away, Pustling swerves over to the kerb outside the Richardson Bakery and parks. He gets out into the rain and walks unhurriedly back, his three-piece woollen suit soaking up the moisture. He passes shops and the familiar old office fronts before he reaches the hedge-lined driveway whose potted gravel is awash. His shoes slish through the lawn as he crosses towards the nearest window and, stealthily, moves across the frame to look inside. An empty room, much dust and a few balls of paper. The light burns from its unadorned fixture. You're a wastrel with the electricity, Pustling thinks, confirming some deep suspicions. With his head below the level of the window he runs in a crouch to the other front-facing window and slowly straightens to look inside. Pell sits in his chair, big white feet on the hearth, some books open in his lap, dressing-gown firm about his lumpy frame. A bottle of port sits corked on the little table beside him. Furniture glows with reflected firelight.

An old man, thinks Pustling. He's just an old man, look at him. What's he reading, I wonder? Ah, tomorrow, the last sermon. Thank God. What is it about you, Pell? What *is* it?

Rain pours from the rusted gutters and the sky murmurs as Pustling stands outside the manse window feeling the moisture lining his collar.

This is my town, old man, my inheritance. Old man.

194

A car passes on the street. Pustling falls to his knees in the flowerbed with its smell of mulched blood and bone.

Skippers of the chasers do not even bother to try the seas outside the Sound next morning. The current forcing its way into the harbour can be felt as far in as the town jetty where the Paris boats and Ted Baer's launch and the tugs jostle at their moorings.

At dawn the lobby of the Ocean View is crammed. Cachalot and Ted Baer hold independent press conferences at either end. Brent, Marks and Fleurier, greyfaced, try to rally support for their cause. The sharkfisherman, too, has a desperate look about him, cursing the inopportune weather.

By mid-morning cars are leaving Angelus in tiny convoys. The remaining, more dogged, observers fill the lobbies or tax room service in their hotels.

Just before noon William Pell finishes delivering his sermon, an unremarkable twenty minutes on the Parables, and he shakes hands at the door with the same half-absent feeling of last week, feeling or imagining the intense cold in the palm of Des Pustling as he shakes his hand and nods in greeting.

'Fine sermon, Reverend,' Pustling says, grinning widely.

It is late afternoon when Pell sees Queenie Cookson sitting on the retaining wall above the sand on Middle Beach. He has been walking, alone, his big shoes under his arm, watching the gulls twitch nervously in the trees contemplating the sea weather, feeling his toes in the cold, white sand. He remembers summer mornings here in his youth, the giggling of girls, the smell of coconut oil, the sounds of people scrunching by in the sand as he sprawled on a towel, wondering what lay beyond the surf-white dome of Coldsea Island, what made women walk the way they did, what made the short swells falling lightly on the shore with that whispering: *yes, yes, yes, yes.*

Always the sea we come back to, he thinks to himself, even a farm boy like me.

The moment he sees Queenie Cookson she turns her head. Pell hesitates, faltering in his steps. Round on the headland

195

boys fish from the rocks, rugged against the cold. A man jogs past close to shore. Pell goes over to the retaining wall.

'Queenie?'

She looks up at him with an audible sigh. 'Hello, Reverend.'

'Hello. I was just walking. I—'

'Yes.'

Pell scrabbles up beside her, feeling graceless and intrusive.

'How are you?' he asks.

'Oh . . . .' Her voice trails off.

'Not going out today?'

'No, too rough. You know, then. About me.'

'I should think the whole town knows the whole of everything. Everything unimportant.'

'Cleve and I aren't living together at the moment.'

'The whole town seems to know that as well.'

Queenie looks up at him. He winces inwardly, knowing he has let his disappointment show.

'Well.'

'Even your grandfather knows.'

'What? Oh, shit. Sorry. Oh, hell. How is he?'

'Bad, I should think. Or maybe good—who can tell? And you?'

'Can't tell either. Don't come on pastoral, Reverend, okay? I know you did marry us and everything, but it's . . . .'

Pell nods, forces his hands down into his pockets. The wind is cold, gusts hard and sharp as blades. I just haven't got room for it, he thinks. God, I just can't feel concerned enough about it. Look at it. Young love. Convenience. How can I? I've got my own worries. Make them see!

'. . . he's so, so damned stupid. He can't *do* anything, he won't. It just hasn't been what—I dunno. And this is so important, the whales. And he doesn't understand, he won't. Jesus, it's so frustrating!'

Pell claps his shoes together to shake the sand off and he digs his grey socks out of the toes and begins putting them on. Old feet, he thinks. She's repelled by them. To hell with it.

'Who do you want?' he says, lacing up his black shoes.

'What?' Queenie looks at him, a hint of irritation in her tanned, hair-blown face. The face of a child, Pell thinks. The hair of something out of ancient history.

'What do you want?'

'I don't know,' she says, pulling her hair aside.

At six o'clock in the evening in a glittering glass unit in the city's biggest hospital two hundred miles away, Abbie Tanks dies from a brain haemorrhage. The nurse who plugs the orifices of his body marvels at how pink he is in some places.

XIII

But no rain fell on the land at Wirrup, though sometimes waterspouts and rain squalls were seen or imagined out over the sea as the weather passed. It was unnatural, as though God Himself steered the weather away. Every mile east from there the land was drier still and all but lifeless. Bushfires erupted in isolation. In the farthest recesses before the gazetted desert, birds fell from the sky. There was no winter.

In pain, Daniel Coupar lay on the wide brass bed he had once shared with his wife. It was big, softquilted and dusty from neglect. Sleep would not come to ease his pain and he was disturbed by the silence from the bay, the absence of the whales that had long moved farther west and north.

It's bloody shameful, he thought, the upbringing a man has that'll keep him awake at night. All night a man lies here remembering Sunday School texts and cooking recipes and the best way to polish boots, and maps and blokes he met in pubs. What day is it? What'm I lying on?

On his side, Coupar dragged the big box shape from under him. It was his Bible, the one his mother had given him. He turned pages and saw it was an edition of 1901, the year of his birth, and written on a blank leaf in ink that was almost grey:

A poor woman's gift to her son, the things she knows. Be a servant of others, Daniel, and be a fool for God the Father. Remember Romans 13 and remember I have loved you.
Mother 6/1/02

Ah, mother, he thought fondly with a sadness that all but enveloped his pain, you were a wonderful woman. A lot like my wife Maureen, you know; you would have liked each other. You'd have got on like a house on fire. *Romans, Romans ...* thirteen. Ah, now how does it go, ah ... *therefore love is the fulfilling of the law. And that, knowing the time, that now it is high time to awake out of sleep: for now is our salvation nearer than we first believed.* My God, twelve years of Sunday School—all so a man can recite to himself in his senility. Awake out of sleep be buggered. I haven't had a decent sleep in a lifetime.

In time, Coupar slept, discomforted by the black lump of ricepaper that worked itself under him in the night.

He woke in the cool period foreshadowing the heat of the day, not rising for several hours. Far off, in the trees it seemed, a bantam rooster crowed. Coupar ached. He wanted to tell so many things. Before he could even rise the heat of the day defeated him.

XIV

At four thirty next morning the swells reared up out of the dark to meet them. Queenie's cheeks chilled in the drizzle. Past Coldsea Island the swells ran high and deep from the south like a mountain range proceeding from an unseen horizon. Fleurier bent his head to the cold; she could see his teeth flash white in the dark. The *Paris IV* cut open the swollen shoulders of the swells and the Zodiacs followed in the wound of her wake, keeping bearings by her lights.

Queenie braced herself between the fuel drums, letting her mind wander, welcoming any distraction from this menacing darkness. For a while she saw the whiteness of Ted Baer's launch in the distance as it cut away to the south-west. Behind, Brent and Marks, ostensibly recovered from their illnesses, sat low and just visible in the other Zodiac. Weak but determined, Queenie thought: like the rest of us. And aren't the Aussies pissed off.

Queenie had fresh in her mind the renewed arguments in the lobby an hour ago where Brent and Marks had talked their way back into the water to the disgust of the Australian crew. Queenie's position was now impregnable; she was a veteran of the Friday shooting incident and, too, she had Fleurier, the patron, on her side. Two Australians had left town immediately. The women argued for equal representation. Accents were mimicked, people accused of bad manners and bad breath. The number on the beach launching the inflatables in the cold rain was depleted; they were outnumbered by irritable, foot-stamping journalists.

Queenie thought of yesterday's headlines, ANGELUS ENTER-TAINS, with bitterness. They even bring out an *Advocate* on a Sunday, she thought. A circus, a stupid circus. It's as though nothing can stop it, nothing can happen outside of it. Oh, how long can we last out in all this? God, I'm so tired. It's all buggered around. We're just another town entertainment, middle billing on the Angelus Show. Nobody even bothers to threaten us any more — they want us around all of a sudden for the media. And Cleve . . . oh, that word makes me mad. He looks so sick and awful. He's not even eating properly, his last consistent function — he can't even commit himself to do that. He looked so frightened. God, what am I supposed to feel?

Queenie still had that fork of emotion from Saturday morning: the disgust and loathing, the compulsion to strike him, to beat the frightened, vulnerable look off his face, to bend his fingers back, make him denounce himself, make him someone else; but also the rooted desire to tear the raggedy clothes off his back and the blue stubble from his chin, to bathe him and cover him with her big, tanned limbs and to beat that grubby hide of new experience from him with her fists, to open and ventilate his skin with her nails to make him young and fresh-faced and hopeless again, the Cleveland Cookson she had locked in her thighs in the waterfall when summer was a corroboree of cicadas in the ear. He was somehow changed, and it frightened her. But she wanted him. Some of him.

Fleurier's hand on her shoulder roused her from her thoughts. He pointed. The crew of the chaser was visible in the twilight, moving about on deck, and as Fleurier steered the

Zodiac out to starboard and abreast of the ship the first mate could be seen uncovering the gun at the bow, elevating and swivelling the barbed snout. With a quick rap on the throttle Fleurier sped them out ahead of the chaser and across under her bows, lifting his finger in the by now customary salute of contempt. The chaser sounded her horn. Queenie managed to take a picture as they raced down the port side, jouncing in the bow-wave, though she held out little hope for it in that light.

Paris IV mustered speed and the Zodiacs fell behind and to starboard.

At nine thirty the three craft came upon a large pod of whales which sounded shallowly, giving short, excited blows, riding the swells that mounted their flanks.

Paris IV steamed away at full speed, rolling in the swell as she turned to give chase. With the swells rolling them sideways, tossing them aside and off course, the Zodiacs could not keep up.

Queenie, low in the bow, shook the spray from her eyes, felt the shuddering vibrations of motor and sea. *Swim, swim!* Swells came abeam. *Go! Go! Swim!* She caught sight of the skipper of the chaser moving out along the catwalk to the harpoon gun as she had seen once before. They followed. Fifteen minutes of following and lurching behind and seeing, from the top of each sea, the breaches of the whales and the manoeuvres of the chaser obscuring the view each turn; and each minute compounded the feeling in her of something slipping from her grasp. They were too far behind. She motioned to Fleurier for speed, but at the brink of each tilting swell the outboard's propeller ripped out of the water leaving them no purchase. They lost ground.

Then as they went down into the chesty trough of a big swell where there was only sky and water and the vomit swilling in the bottom of the boat to see, the crack of the gun shocked across the water, and as they climbed again and nosed into the air Queenie craned and saw the eruption in the water two hundred yards off where the harpoon ricocheted off the glossy back of the whale. They're hurrying their shots, she thought; we've unnerved them.

The chaser drifted, reloading, and Fleurier gunned the Zodiac until they came abreast of the bow and the men reloading the gun shouted and gesticulated, and Queenie caught sight of the stunned sperm again and pointed and held on and the Zodiac bucked across to the wide, flat spots of water that stood out on the swells like footprints. She believed again. She saw Brent standing in the other careering Zodiac, battling to adjust a lens. He and Marks broadsided under the bows of the chaser. The horn sounded.

Swim, she thought, *swim whales! Dive! Go, fuck you!*

The whale breached briefly in front showing the streaming wound in its back and its breath-vapour wafted across in the wind. Queenie stood to see the flukes breaking water. It was beginning to meander, too tired, too winded, and Queenie heard the sound behind, the hiss of the bow-wave. Fleurier tried to get closer, but it was hard to judge in the swell. The horn sounded. And Queenie saw Brent and Marks almost foundering in the bow-wave, right in the shadow of the ship, and over all their heads came the crack and the cable and, ahead, the smattering impact of steel and blubber. The cachalot cleared the water in a brief, blood-spraying flurry. The flukes battered the water, interrupted by another shot. Fleurier was shouting, shouting over the idle of the engine. Queenie looked away. The whale was still, being drawn in abeam. Other shouts. Brent stood in the other Zodiac, drifting across towards her, calling. The two inflatables rubbed gunwhales and Brent held up his camera.

'I got it!'

'You mean they got it, you stupid bastard!'

'No,' Brent yelled, 'I got it on film. Godammit, I got it for ever!'

Queenie put her head on her knees and covered her face with her hands. She saw through her fingers Fleurier's legs trembling.

'It was worth it, then,' Fleurier said, engaging the motor and throttling away. There was a small spot of blood on his chin, already dry.

Queenie settled in the space between fuel drums and held on as the Zodiac skittered with the swell astern. They could not follow the chaser further; it was outside their range already. Every now and then, on a rising swell, the bridge of the *Paris IV* came into view as it moved farther east looking for the rest

201

of the pod. She held on, heady with nausea, restraining herself from screaming. At least we'll be back by dark, she thought, no before dark, before dark. Oh, why won't they stop it?

An hour later the outboard cut out, running down to a murmur and then nothing. Fleurier and Queenie looked at one another in horror. The others came up beside them.

'It just died,' Fleurier called.

Queenie began to cry.

'Just stopped?' Marks called, ignoring her.

'Yes. What now?'

'Have a look.'

Fleurier lifted the cover inexpertly and poked about inside for a minute.

'How's it look?' Marks called out, impatient.

'I don't know what I'm looking for,' said Fleurier, panicky.

A moment later Marks fell into the bottom of the Zodiac at Queenie's feet and climbed over her to the stern and the hatless motor. He cursed and checked as many parts as he had become familiar with during the constant breaking down of his own motor. It was ten minutes afterwards, when the nausea had almost overcome Queenie completely, making her want to die as the boat pitched and rolled, that Marks cursed and held up a hand as if to strike Fleurier across the face.

'You've used up one of your drums, you asshole!' he screamed. 'Unhook the line, clip it on. Right! Simple. Even a half-ass goddamm French playboy can do it!' He bounded out of the inflatable and into the other alongside. Brent was leaning over the far gunwhale with his heaving back towards them. In a few seconds the outboard came to life and the wind blew fumes back into Queenie's face and she too vomited over the side.

The Zodiacs skittered northwards until mid-afternoon, when through a blur of nausea and seaspray Coldsea Island, its flanks creaming with surf, became a mark on the unsteady horizon. Queenie found herself yearning for Angelus, that dirty smudge intermittent in her vision.

XV

Ten minutes before the Zodiacs flounder onto the sand at Middle Beach, Ted Baer arrives triumphant at the town jetty with a 2,700-lb. white shark lashed alongside, and within minutes the jetty and the foreshore are packed with onlookers. The twenty-five foot shark is hoisted with pulleys and tackle onto the groaning timbers of the jetty, jaws still flexing despite the nest of bullet holes in its head, and then tail-up onto the gallows where it gushes and bleeds, stretching under its own weight. A representative of the International Gamefish Federation fights his way through the jostling journalists, half blind with camera flashes, to announce the catchweight to Baer, still on the bow of his bespattered launch, all his muscles jerking and seizing. A great cry goes up and the crowd echoes it. And then begins the long night, the frenzy of relief and adulation. The town can forget whales and protests. Tonight Angelus is the home of the biggest sharks in the world. There is something to celebrate.

Just before dusk Cachalot & Company retire to their rooms at the Ocean View. Few words are spoken. They pester room service. They sniff their food, scrutinise the colour of their orange juice. The lobby is empty.

As night falls, the floodlit monolith on the town jetty draws more light, more noise, more beer-spray about it as it drips and groans at the end of its chained tail. Cameras, eskies, eyes glitter as the drizzle falls and is ignored. Ted Baer's night becomes fragmented: his own unfinished accounts, flashes of light, bursts of music, and the delirious blare of car-horns. Bikies embrace blue-haired matrons. A helicopter descends and lands on the foreshore, disgorging the current affairs team. 'Auld Lang Syne' wends it way round the harbour from vessel to vessel and an atmosphere of carnivals and armistices, elections and football finals, seizes the townspeople, rugged, collared and coated, at the edge of the water. One by one the

Paris Bay chasers glide in to dock, horns baying, and the crews, who have heard the news already, join the celebrations. Des Pustling mingles with the mob, winking, smiling, squeezing hands.

Confused by the frenzied throngs outside the pubs, the falling beer cans, hats, shoes in Goormwood Street, Marion Lowell shoulders her way to the lane beside the old church and walks, valium-light, along the ragged hedge towards the manse. The house is partly obscured by the church but she can see a strip of guttering in a warm flicker of light. Even the hedge winks. Shadows shrink and bulge weirdly. And as she comes round the hedge feeling her head moving away from her body she sees the fire.

'Reverend Pell?'

'Yes?' He looks at once stricken and triumphant.

'What are you doing?'

'Come closer — oh, Miss Lowell. Burning a few things.'

Marion Lowell puts her palm to her mouth to stifle a sound. Neither of them knows if it is a cry or a guffaw.

'The money?'

Pell rakes the blazing mound at his feet. 'The lot.'

'My God, isn't that illegal?' she says.

'God knows.'

'Cash?' Marion Lowell comes closer to the warmth.

'Yes. And cheques.'

'Think of it,' she whispers.

'It hurts for a while, you know. But then it gets easy. We suspend our disbelief to make the paper valuable, and then we have to find our disbelief again to burn it.' He bends down, knees cricking like brittle cane, and fists more paper onto the fire. From the street comes the sound of breaking glass. Marion stands close beside him. Their faces soften in the orange-red light. Pell fights off the urge to embrace her; it seems so long since he has felt the touch of another person. Wind rattles in over the rooftops bringing cheers and car noise, eddying around the little mound of smouldering ash and sputtering flame, and a burning curl of paper rises in its tiny vortex, lifted above their heads for a few seconds, pirouetting, rocking,

204

before dissipating in a shower of smuts.

'I bet that was a thousand dollars,' Marion says, stifling a giggle.

'I don't believe so,' he murmurs.

'We can't beat him, you know.'

'We can try.'

'We won't win.'

'Neither will we lose.'

She shakes her head. 'I—'

He smiles and lays a big arm about her shoulders, feels his own body trembling as he rakes the embers with the other hand. She smells the smoke in his clothing, feels the heat on her shins. He stoops to put the last of the papers on the fire, then the cardboard box, and the flames force them back, lighting the whole yard with their incandescence, and the wet lawn glitters like tinsel.

'But I'm nothing in this town now,' she says. 'No one will employ me. No one'll want to know.'

Pell shifts his weight from foot to foot. Yes, he thinks with some relief, both of us nothing.

'Where will you go?' she asks.

'Nowhere.'

'But what'll you do?'

'Oh, nothings are useful for other nothings, you know. There's lots of them.'

'There's someone coming.'

'Yes,' he shrugs, not bothering to let her go. He keeps his eyes on the faintly wind-stirred mound as the figures advance across the lawn into the circle of light.

With the big manila envelope under his arm, Hassa Staats leaves his hotel where men and beer-spray hit the walls, where whistling, singing, shouting, smother his voice — his screams for attention — and where his wife Mara shoves him aside, afraid of the look on his face that threatens to dissolve these precious moments of celebration. Cold, benumbed, horribly sober, Hassa Staats reels into the street. If I had the guts and if there was any point, he thinks, I'd go back in there with a shotgun and drive 'em all out — Easton, the whalers, the women, the

205

spongers, the drunks, that bitch of a wife—just so I could see it for myself, that cloud, that blue smoke they've killed me with. Just to point to it and say *there*, that's what's done it to me. I hate them. I hate it. *Hate.*

He throws the X-rays into a bin as he staggers down the street, gradually recollecting his gait. *Those areas, Hassa,* he says to me, *do you see them?* I can't even say the bloody word. Other people's smoke, for Christ's sake? My lungs. Mine.

He walks down towards the waterfront, not feeling the light southerly. Music and laughter float up. Calmer, he strides down, hands in his coat pockets, and sees down along the town jetty the floodlit shark and the wild mob. Two days ago—two hours ago—Staats would have fallen to his knees at the sight; he would have poured beer into all those open mouths, rubbed it into their cheeks; but now he feels nothing. There is no room.

He walks along the port road leaving the carnival behind and in the wind he hears car horns and bugles sounding in the streets above. He walks. Me. Me. Me, he thinks.

He walks slowly on the deepwater jetty, mindful of the black water far below, hearing the rats ricocheting about the superstructure beneath.

A light leads him down to a landing where a thickbacked figure with two heads hunches over the edge, intent on the aquamarine water and the two thin lines rippling in the wind. He stands behind, is not seen, and leaves.

He sticks his head in the door of the watchman's shack, thinking of a sudden that he might strike up a conversation with that young fellow Cookson. The man's head is on the desk, a crescent of drool on the record book, a bottle of White Horse on the table, and a small rat perches, nose in the air, on the back of his chair. Staats closes the door.

He walks, then, past the security signs and the encrusted cyclone wire and out along the hulking side of the tanker against the jetty. Exposed by its bright lights, he hurries its entire length nearly at a run, conscious of his suddenly unrestricted chest. Out of the amber wash of light he walks more slowly out to the end where, behind the row of bollards, there is only the dredged water below. He hears the chop-chop of waves against the piles and, far away, a car horn, as he sits

206

on a rusted bollard and unloops the belt from his trousers. His big belly sags out into his lap and he is ashamed.

'It's a boong's life,' he mutters, strapping his left foot to his right hand.

It is some moments before Pell recognises Billy and Clara Tanks and the others of the clan. Their dark skins hold firelight, their eyes have lost some timidity. An old, white-haired woman is wailing. They have come to ask him to bury Abbie Tanks and Pell knows it before they ask. Boys pull pickets from the church fence and add them to the fire. They are all sitting, Pell and Marion Lowell included, around the spitting fire speaking quietly, when, from the church, another group emerges and crosses the lawn.

My Great God, Pell thinks, staring at the slight figures joining them by the fire. I'm dreaming, the Ladies' Guild . . . with scones. . . .

By midnight the shark catch celebrations have become mobile: convoys of cheering, can-throwing people move from house to house, thinning towards dawn. Outside the pubs Ted Baer wakes groups of Aborigines, shakes hands with them, presses warm cans of beer into their hands, thumps their backs and receives their dumb, frightened looks and moves on. The convoy becomes a racing, haphazard tour to every tourist spot known to those still able to remember and think and speak. Ted Baer, staggering, incoherent, is rushed to the site of every man-made and natural marvel within fifteen miles of Goormwood Street, trailing a motley of locals, media personalities, lushes and wildflower tourists. Near dawn he is nauseated with speed and exhaustion and coastline and he has a manic urge to vomit or to sleep or to do something spectacular.

On the jetty in the bleary light before dawn, the huge, groaning cadaver of the shark, torn through by its own weight, falls to the boards with a thwacking gout of spray, sending a single beam into the air.

207

Before this, though, to avoid the Zodiacs in the Sound, the *Paris IV* slips from the harbour early, her skipper and crew tired of the duelling and the publicity and the shooting over people's heads. Within twenty minutes *Paris III* follows.

When the Zodiacs skim out from Middle Beach and wait in the Sound for the chasers, none appear. They wait thirty minutes, rocking on the abated swell. Another thirty. The crews confer, alongside one another, bickering in the dark. They will wait until dawn.

It is barely dawn when *Paris II* surges from the harbour at full speed, cutting through the gloom. Her crew, only minutes before, have seen the shark fall to the jetty and spring the great plank that spun high in the air and came down onto Ted Baer's launch, piercing the bow. They are late because they have been attempting to contact Ted Baer via the police. Two salvage operators were already at the jetty when they left. *Paris II* takes only minutes to sight the Zodiacs as they speed towards her, skipping across the tops of the swells. *Paris II* is barely out of the Sound when she receives the message of emergency. The Zodiacs follow as she makes a wide turn east around the Head.

Dozens of townspeople and tourists and reporters know that a man has fallen into the sea beneath the Natural Bridge because they were there when it happened. A man, drunk, excited and foolhardy enough had climbed down at dawn underneath the towering granite structure and was quickly claimed by the swell. He was not sucked beneath the shelf at the base of the cliffs as is usual, but tumbled out seawards in a rip.

Twenty minutes after receiving the distress call, *Paris II*, wary of king waves, heaves to a distance from the cliffs and commences to lower boats for a search. The crew is hastened by the sound of outboard motors nearing. A spotter-plane banks away above and comes in low to the water, close to the cliffs.

The crews of the Zodiacs, without radio equipment, are puzzled, only beginning to comprehend when they see the crowds lining the cliff and the boats being winched down from the chaser. At full throttle they scud in close to the cliffs, teetering on the crests of swells until one crew sights the white spot in the grey-black water. And above them, the crowd, ennervated by the dregs of alcohol, finds new stimulation: a race has begun. Hungover journalists collect their wits and their cameras and notebooks. The race lasts two minutes.

Ted Baer, almost dead, is pulled from the water by Queenie Cookson who, when she finally has him on his back in the bottom of the inflatable, gives a cry of recognition. He has been in the water forty minutes, floating stubbornly at the petering edges of the rip, and he is aware of no irony as he is rescusitated in the bottom of the Cachalot Zodiac. Queenie hears her swimming teacher's voice again as she tilts his head and pokes in his throat with a finger.

Before he is conscious, before he is even transferred to the *Paris II*, headlines have been made, and the next race is to the nearest telephone.

XVI

Music and car engines reverberated in the rain-slicked car park of the Ocean View. Queenie Cookson stood limp and somehow guilty by the window of an old station wagon. It was Friday, 1 July 1978, and she felt sick and had been crying and her throat was sore from shouting; the rolled *Advocate* in her hands was blackening her fingers and smudging her jeans with newsprint.

'Well,' Fleurier said, head and elbow out of the car window. 'See you some time, Queenie.'

'Yeah, no hard feelings,' Marks said from the passenger seat.

Loaded cars were leaving, some sounding their horns as they pulled out onto the road. Some had left days ago after the outboards were stolen.

'Yeah,' she said. 'The gods're on your side.' But Brent was

asleep already on the back seat and she was robbed of a parting shot.

'Look after this town,' Marks said. 'Put a match to it.'

She nodded. She shook hands with Fleurier. And when it became evident that nothing else could or would be said, Queenie shrugged and let the last cars leave. A horn or two sounded, fading up the esplanade.

Queenie walked out onto the esplanade and saw gulls huddled on the beach where she had learnt to do the dead man's float. Mothers with prams moved along the footpaths and small children screamed gleefully, rocketing up on trampolines. A cluster of truants' bicycles, all fallen together like an obscure sculpture, glinted in a brief showing of sun. An old man fished with a long rod off the beach. Retired couples strolled along the beach picking up shells, pointed, held hands. A cormorant alighted on the roof of the public toilets. A baby cried. A motorbike passed with a train of two-stroke fumes that reminded Queenie of outboard motors and seasickness. Two truanting girls compared winter tans on the lawn in the heatless sun. Queenie Cookson wanted very much to go down to the beach, but after a few minutes of wistful observation, she went back into the smoky hotel to pack.

BAY OF WHALES

WHEN at first Cleve became hazily aware of it, he thought the knocking sound he could hear was the thud of his own pulse in his ear; but as sleep left him and his head cleared and his eyes opened to behold the morning light it occurred to him that the noise might be from outside him, from outside. Someone was knocking at the door downstairs. He gave out a short cry, sprang out of bed, fell down the short, steep stairs and opened the front door in his underpants.

'Hi.' Queenie stood inside the timber porch, eyes swollen and sick-looking. Over her shoulder, boats crept across the surface of the harbour. 'You look dazzling in your jockettes.'

'Yeah,' Cleve stammered, looking at the suitcase and the bags. 'Anything for attention. Thought it was Miss Thrim for a moment. We've become very close.' His tongue rattled on independent of him.

'Hnn.' She looked at him nervously, not daring to look anywhere for more than a moment. He was shivering, she could see. Tell him, she thought. Words, words. 'Two things to tell you.'

'Yeah?' Cleve rubbed his chin, dazed.

'Firstly, I want to come back here and live—'

'Well, it's your place after—'

'—and secondly, I'm—'

'Kicking me out,' he sighed.

'No, better. Worse. Better. God.'

'You what?'

'I'm pregnant.'

'Come in and shut the door. I'm cold. Coffee?'

She followed him in, dragging her luggage, to the kitchen which was crowded with bottles and plates gummed grey with fat and newspapers, where he filled the kettle and stoked the night's coals, adding kindling. She sat at the table next to the big window, made room for her elbows, looked out across the harbour and thought: be calm, don't let him see you go beserk.

'Did you hear me?' she asked.

'Yeah,' he said with his head in the door of the woodbox.

'Well?'

'Well what?' His mouth seemed dry enough to crackle; everything in him raced. What does she want me to do? Laugh? Explode?

'I don't know.' She smiled self-consciously. There was a silence between them when only the flames of the fire could be heard.

'The others then? Is it all over?' he asked.

'Yes. But that's not why I'm back.'

'I don't believe you.'

She smiled. 'Maybe you're right.' She looked round the room at the motley of old furniture and the precipitous stairs and the familiar tones of wood and worn polish. 'No, it wasn't just that they're gone. I've got money to pay for accommodation. No, it's lots of things. God, I love this house.'

The kettle began to stir.

'So do I.'

Their eyes met for a moment.

'I embarrassed you the other day,' Cleve said, still poking at the fire. 'I'm sorry.'

'No you're not.'

'No, I suppose not. It was embarrassing as hell for me, too. Well, I'm a bit sorry,' he said, grinning.

'Well, I s'pose it's an improvement.'

'I wouldn't know.'

The kettle ticked and creaked and they both watched its burnished heating. The kitchen felt crowded to Cleve with another person, but to Queenie, after the smoky hotel rooms, it was expansive and even the smell of it was beautiful.

'Is all the news about the rescue true?' Cleve asked, pouring the coffee. 'About Ted Baer?'

212

'That I was the one who rescucitated him? Yes. We got to him first. And I damn' near threw him back.'

'Was it the rescue that made you all give up?' He saw her head rear a little in surprise.

'ANTI-WHALERS SAVE SHARK KILLER. Worldwide. It killed our PR. And somehow it was my fault. But it wasn't just that. It was going off anyway. Someone stole our motors the same night. People were just leaving, the rest of us fighting like dogs. And I wanted it to work. And then — bang — it's over. All that effort.'

Somewhere in him Cleve sensed and felt himself sharing her immense frustration and he wished he could tell her.

'Go and put some clothes on,' she said, 'before your balls go blue.' As he went upstairs Queenie looked out over the harbour where the wind coddled craft along the top of the water, and thought: he looked as if he wanted to cry. Or to run.

All day Cleve stalked about the house, stunned and uneasy. He kept out of Queenie's way, did not even stand close for fear of touching her. The very way she moved, the words she used, told him that she had been away, she had been places, met people, done things without him. There was a sadness in her voice despite the new hardness of her that suggested new hurts, new growths of which he knew nothing, that left him with the inferiority of not having been away, of withering a little. He paced, ashamed of the state of the house, the colour of the sheets, the putty look of his own face, the gracelessness of his pacing. At noon he took baskets of dirty linen from the bedroom and, while she lay in an exhausted sleep curled on the sofa, he opened her suitcase and pulled out her soiled, sour-smelling clothes stained with vomit and her sweetish perspiration. Fearing discovery, he crept out the back door and coasted the Land Rover down the street until out of earshot.

When he returned he found her on her knees scrubbing the kitchen floor, and the look in her eyes made him refrain from protest. He hung the washing out, conscious of the neighbours' scrutiny even though he could see no one.

At tea, which he cooked before she could stop him, he gathered courage enough to ask questions. Queenie ate quietly, with her elbows confident on the table, pouring cabernet distractedly.

'You're sure you're pregnant?' he asked her, every word causing him to wince inside.

'Duffed. Well and truly.'

'Well. . . .' He worried his moussaka.

'Yours,' she said.

'Oh.' He caught himself sighing.

'What did you think?' she asked him, turning a fork in the light.

'I just. . . .'

'Georges?'

'I don't know. Jesus, how'm I supposed to know? You're enjoying this, aren't you?'

She gave him no sign, knowing it was true. Cleve stuffed his mouth full of moussaka, furious with himself.

'I'm sorry,' he murmured.

'So'm I.'

'What are we going to do?'

'I dunno. Talk?' Consequences loomed like shadows, incoherent shapes in her mind. Cleve felt the urge to touch her reddened cheek, to fall into her lap, to do something vicious, run away.

II

For five nights, in his brief sleep, Daniel Coupar had the same dream: he dreamt he was a boy again camping at the old quarantine station with his friends, goggling in the bays there for mussels and whales' teeth and abalone. They dared each other, dared themselves to dive deeper than they could bear, down into the greenish depths, further into the dark chill until the greyness of death reached out and brushed their skins. It was as if they willed themselves to death in order to feel alive; they toyed with life and did not understand it, felt no need to. They locked one another in the convict-built cell out on the point, and were thrilled by the dimness, wishing somehow the tiny cell window could be blocked off and the darkness made complete.

Images distorted and passed him in his dream. Once he lay a whole night on the mortuary block in the quarantine hospital with two shillings and a piece of mirror in his hands that he earned from the dare. In his dream, Coupar saw his boyish, strong body on the block and he called out in exasperation at the frightened, stubborn boy; but he, the boy, didn't seem to hear staring up into the sky through the rotten roof, waiting for first light. Coupar shouted himself hoarse and then the dream took its crazy course. He had dreamt it so many times it was difficult for him to distinguish it from memory. The sun rose like a thrown ball. It was suddenly day. He was outside in the sun and his skin, his tanned boy's skin, shrivelled and burnt hard on him; he saw it flaking off like ash. He stood still, shocked, as Job might have stood, waiting for explanation. But then he began to feel pain and he wanted relief and he sought shelter from the sun in a low crack in the granite near the water's edge. Inside, he found it was a cave and the farther he went the cooler it became and the less his flesh tormented him. And then he realised that there was darkness, real darkness, so dark that he could not see his fingers before his eyes, could not hear his own voice when he cried out, and all sensation was gone, as if all his nerve-ends had withered in his hollow body. It was not uncomfortable; it was not anything. Until he saw, in a glow, a skeleton, luminous, limp, far below him. He called out to it, but no sound came. Then there were others, other bones, messes of bones with no integration, no order, no coherence: fingers, skulls, teeth, and he called out again without voice. For a moment his bodily sensation returned and he was wading through this sea of bones, and the sharp pieces pierced his hands and feet as he stumbled, and the pain grew in him until he found he had willed sensation away again and he grovelled on and the bones became rubble to him, and then dirt, then cool beach sand; he smelt salt and seaweed and felt the shell-grit moist and cool beneath his feet, comforted by the earthly smell of his own sweat. He stood still, content. And then in the distance he heard the great thunder, not like the blue cracking thunder he had heard as a child, running to his mother's bed, but the sound of mountains moving. He called

215

out at the shock of it and then he knew it was the thunder of water, water mountains, and next second it milled about his shins, storming out of the dark from where he had come through the crack by the sea. He could not go back out; the water was already up to his knees. He called out again, hoarse with panic, and his voice mocked him from all directions. Blindly, he struck out, groping ahead with the water at his back and darkness, all darkness ahead, and he woke in a sweat.

The dream terrified Daniel Coupar. He did not, would not, allow himself to understand it. He only knew it would visit him again and he feared sleep because of it.

III

The first small group of humpback whales rounds the western capes of the continent, instinctively moving southwards and eastwards. Some are old, and a few are strong and young and lean from a warm season without mass feeding. The land stays at their left and moves slowly past. Each humpback, flanks tough with barnacles and tiny parasites and old weed, sounds shallowly, surfaces, spouts, and cruises on the surface for a time before repeating the motion almost without volition, following the flukes of the tail ahead. The water vibrates with the oscillation of their sounds. The Antarctic, nameless and timeless, only a colour, a temperature and a density of food, draws them on.

They are months early. A thousand miles behind, others follow.

IV

The first morning, after waking in the old mahogany bed with a sheet of winter light warming the quilt, Queenie opened all the wardrobes to smell the familiar fragrances, pulled open drawers and secretly pressed Cleve's shirts to her face. Through the window she saw the still water and the steady clouds reflected in it. Saturday's yachts becalmed. She pulled on an old windcheater and found a clean pair of jeans folded at the end of the bed. Her limbs were still tired and her head still heavy with the long night's talk. Down in the kitchen she found the stove embers still hot and she rekindled the fire, casting stealthy glances into the living-room where Cleve slept still on a mattress before the fireplace. He slept on his back with his mouth open, hair askew, an arm flung behind, and he looked as though he had struggled in his sleep. She cooked him bacon and eggs and brewed him some coffee, knowing it would make him feel guilty, knowing, too, that she wanted to do it regardless.

During the day they did not talk much.

In the afternoon Cleve watched her washing her hair at the kitchen sink, the bread colour of it all forward, the curve of her brown neck agitating him until he rose from where he sat pretending to read and, from behind, wet his hands in the warm, running water, and kneaded with her. At first he felt tension in her neck and in her back at his touch, but in time, without a word spoken, her body relaxed and Cleve buried his hands in the lathered hair, looking past it, every now and then, to the empty sails on the harbour.

With the water cascading past her cheeks, Queenie felt his hands on her and felt her own hands tight on the marble edge of the sink, and she wondered whether her tension was fear or wanting. She was glad he did not speak, frightened his words might give her an answer.

In the evening they talked — safe talk about external events, a little gossip, some deliberate abstraction, and they went to their separate beds burdened with the caution of it all.

Cleve, on his mattress beside the subdued fire, lay awake wondering how much of the past month he would share with her. He had already locked the journals in a case and returned them to the attic and he wished he could have deposited some of his memories likewise. He wondered if he could ever tell her about the kangaroo, or about the speargun he had dropped into a street bin on his way to the laundromat yesterday. No, he thought, at least not yet.

Before Queenie slept she was disturbed by a sense of shame

217

as insistent and discomforting as nausea. She, too, wondered how much she would tell, when she would trust him enough, when she would forgive herself. She knew Cleve had told her nothing; she could see in his face, the hesitancy of his voice, that he had things to tell, and for a few minutes she toyed with the notion of another woman, torturing herself pleasantly to sleep.

In the morning they collided, creeping in the kitchen. It was an overcast day. They joked and kept their distance, argued gently and light-heartedly about the whales that had sojourned in the harbour entrance nearly a fortnight ago. They were like a modest courting couple: good-humoured, eager to please, wary.

A wind arose from the south-west in the afternoon and, suddenly tired of confinement, they walked to the top of Mount Clement to the lookout. The walking relaxed them. People saw them together and it made them smile, carefully. From the top of Mount Clement the harbour became a fortified tear-drop and the town seemed to crowd itself between hills, perching on the water's edge. The great light patches of mud-flats blemished the rich deepness of the harbour, beyond which the quarantine ruins could be seen and behind, obscured by the curve of the protective peninsula, Paris Bay was sensed rather than seen.

Wind gusted in their clothing, buffeting their hair. Queenie was the first to speak. She looked east, over the outer fringes of Angelus, past Middle Beach towards Stormy Beach, a haze between coastal hills obscured in the distance. Closer, the Hacker River cut its way to the ocean between slight hills and patches of cleared land.

'When I was a little girl,' Queenie said, smiling, 'I wanted to swim away.'

'Why?' he asked, imagining he could see Wirrup Hill in the distance.

'Because I thought there was somewhere else to swim to. And I was a hell of a good swimmer.'

You still are, he thought, wishing he could tell her. 'And now?'

'Maybe I know better. You want so many things when you're a kid. You want so many things and the most important ones you can't name. You just want. And it stays with you. Even when you know you can't have. Maybe because you can't have. You want *all* of something and then you don't like it, but you still don't want *all* the opposite. You think that's crazy?'

'No. That's what you're like. Like your grandfather and you. You liked it when he got old because then you were the strong one—the boss; but then I reckon you started to hate him being helpless and you wanted to hear him tell you what to do every now and then. But if he did, you got pissed off.'

Queenie looked out north towards the geometric patterns of farmland and roads, not speaking, but thinking. It frightened her, Cleve saying things like that.

'With me it's different,' he said. 'I never even knew that I was wanting.' He laughed. 'Stupid.'

'And you were never much of a swimmer.'

He glanced at her, unable to catch her eyes to see if she meant hurt. 'No.'

That night after dinner they splashed about in the kitchen making a steam-pudding. They ate it by the fire in the living-room picking out its soft, gluggy centre with their fingers.

'Let's do something,' he said, licking his fingers in the firelight.

'What do you mean?'

'I dunno. Let's just do something crazy—spontaneous.'

'Let's plan something spontaneous?'

'Tomorrow. Let's drive up the coast. Camp. See the beaches.'

Queenie, near him, but not touching, looked at him. 'Yes, let's go away for a while. To think. Something.'

A light rain fell. The fire burnt down. They separated for bed.

V

It is Monday, 4 July 1978. The most persistent journalists take their leave of the town, returning to their cities. They are only

219

a few; the majority have been gone for days. Later in the morning, others will arrive to find they are a week late. They will sulk in public bars, then make a hopeful trip out to Paris Bay before leaving town in disgust. Out past the continental shelf the chasers from Paris Bay plough about in the grey swell which mounts their foredecks drenching gunners and crews.

Mid-morning, Ted Baer leaves Angelus with 2,700 pounds of frozen shark. The only townspeople to see him leave are the dozen in the funeral procession on the road north to the cemetery. Since Friday's report by the coroner Hassa Staats has remained uninterred, refused Christian burial by his church. William Pell conducts a brief service in the grey light, speaking out over the neatly pared hole in the earth which the mourners can hardly bear to see. There are eleven mourners, all members of the Ladies' Guild.

In the classrooms children are still whispering about the body dredged out of the harbour: it astounds them to know that it was once Mr Staats, the big, round, red man who stood outside his pub on Saturday mornings smiling at their mothers, and to think what he must have looked like after two days in the water, bloated, blue, nibbled.

All morning, her mind straying, Marion Lowell reads to her mother from the *National Geographic*. She finds herself looking out of the window, wonders why.

At noon a talent scout from the Metropolitan Football Club checks in at the Bright Star. He is met by Rick Staats and his mother who welcome him and show him to his room overlooking Goormwood Street. Down in the public bar the regulars are eulogising.

Down on the foreshore work continues on the replica of the *Onan*; a mast is raised, teetering on deck, to the sound of buzz-saws and electric planes. The siren wails at the canning factory. On the deepwater jetty Dick and Darcy, cocooned in a blanket, stare reproachfully at the water. It has been days since a flagon was last brought down and there is apprehension in their crusty faces.

And in the afternoon there is another funeral. Abbie Tanks is buried in the new cemetery on the northern outskirts of Angelus and his family and their friends and the Presbyterian Ladies' Guild listen to Pell's words as the wind whips about

220

them. He prays. They stand with their faces downturned. Their only comment is a murmured *Amen* and for some minutes they do not disperse.

Although he is in no hurry, late that afternoon Des Pustling drives fast along the peninsula road back from Paris Bay after his very pleasant meeting out there. In an hour he has a sesquicentenary meeting and a few backs to thump. Then Rotary. It is time for taking stock, he thinks, time to assess the exposure. He does not see the small kangaroo as he takes the bend, but when it catapults through the windscreen of the BMW he hits the brake instinctively, feels the bilious slide in the gravel at the roadside, the not-stopping, the hiss of stones, and he cannot believe the left side's impact with the marri tree. He is upright at the wheel in the ensuing silence. He sees bluemetal, sky, the ice-cubes of windscreen in his lap, and the long smear of blood down the walnut dashboard from the animal's mouth. In the rear-view mirror he sees a spot of it on his chin and he tries vainly to reach for his handkerchief, wondering about insurance.

VI

The night before, afraid of sleep, Daniel Coupar forgot his pain and climbed the hill in the dark to stand on its smooth brow and smell the dryness of the land. The sky above him was a featureless black and the stars seemed to him more like aberrant spots than other worlds. Sweat moistened his body and the pain returned. July, he thought, and no rain, no winter. He breathed in the dry air, felt it on his tongue. He sat on a flat piece of rock and got to thinking about the whales. All his life they had puzzled him as they came each year to sojourn in the bay and to move north and pass again later, faithfully tracing out the ancient cycles of moving, feeding, mating. Scuffing the granite with the back of his hand he remembered the time when he was a boy that a whale stranded itself on the beach below the farm and his father organised a flensing and the men from neighbouring farms came and worked inexpertly on the huge, stinking carcass, talking as they did about the way it had thrown itself upon the beach. He heard them mutter 'mindless suicide' and he mimicked them, dashing about in his patchy shorts calling 'mindless silverside' at the gulls hovering above. The whale putrefied. The little oil they gleaned was unmarketable, and the men kept it for years, using it for fishing and for lubricating old machinery. There was still an old drum of it out in one of the sheds, full of the embalmed bodies of drowned rats.

'No such thing as mindless suicide,' he said aloud. 'Only suicide. When you know what you're doing.' That moment he envied the whales their unalterable pattern. They don't know, he thought, they just *do* and it's enough. Why do we have to know? Why can't we be innocent? I'm a man and I'm s'posed to *know*, but where is it? Where's what I know? Those whales. Loyal to their own, loyal to the cycle and to the Creator. And me? Loyal only to this body, this shell of memories. Innocence. When was the last time we saw innocence? Gawd, not in this family—not even Nathaniel Coupar, the first. Not his bloody pretence at innocence. Ah, the Coupars—the firm fruit. Hah! Rotten to the core with pride. And when they saw it—phhtt! Blame someone else, pretend to escape and leave someone else to labour on. My God. I want to open a door and just step outside into something else. It's not right! It's not.

At that moment he stood and brought his hands up past the height of his shoulders as if to summon, to shout at the sky, the stars, the darkness, the light, but he shoved his hands abruptly into his pockets and made his way incautiously down the track.

VII

Moving from one warm body of shallow water to the next in the pattern imprinted upon their brains from millenia of repetition, the small and solitary pod of humpbacks moves slowly east, propelling their bodies in light and darkness, clicking and shrilling opaque melodies as they move, pausing

222

at intervals for those cows with young, occupied by the singularity of their hunger.

VIII

Although it was noon when Queenie and Cleve left Angelus on Monday heading east, it might have been mistaken for early morning or late afternoon, such was the dullness of the sky and the thinness of the light. The Land Rover, winding through the swampy bush on the grey strip of road, was just another moving component of the drabness. The Cooksons sat watching the land come to meet them, blur in the corners of their eyes, and fall behind. Neither spoke. Queenie sat with an army surplus blanket over her jeaned legs to ward off the draughts. Cleve drove idly, bunched into his corner.

They felt speed and flight, and they tried hard to feel married again.

At the Hacker rivermouth the inlet was like stone, without birds, without reflections. No boats lay trustingly upside-down and the paperbarks seemed an impossible way away and stooped and scabby. The whole scene seemed to have dissipated with added space; memory had compacted and condensed, fitting everything too easily, identifying, giving meaning, but now the scene was vacuous, expanded from their reach. On the sand-bar the Cooksons stood vainly trying to re-live it. They were as resentful as the bereaved.

They walked without intent up the long beach towards the cobalt pools where they had once swum. Sand ground away beneath them. At odd moments they caught each other's eye. At some stage during their walk a small pod of whales came into the bay. Both saw, but neither mentioned it to the other, and they continued to stroll. Then one of them took the other's hand; it was impossible to tell who was the initiator.

'Shame about the estuary,' Cleve said.

'Yeah. It all seems different. I thought when you got older all the things you remember seem so much smaller, you know, everything shrinks.'

223

'You saw it too, then. Everything is too ... big.'

'Yes.'

'A shame you know, because. . . .' Cleve could not finish his sentence; he grew suspicious of himself.

'God, I feel so old,' Queenie said with a bleak sign. 'You feel old?'

'I suppose.'

Queenie felt a grief at this; he still looked a boy and she sensed her own incongruous youth. It's fatigue, she thought, not age. Age is different. 'Imagine what it's like to be old.'

'The last thing I want to do,' he murmured.

'Hnn.'

They walked ahead in silence, and after a time Cleve chuckled. 'Old.' He looked out across the water. 'Once, when I was a young kid I had a good look at my grandmother and said to her, "Gee, Nanna, but you're getting old under the arms." I could actually notice she was ageing. The first time I ever noticed that old people used to be young.'

'I would've smacked your bum if I was her.' Queenie laughed.

'She burst into tears.'

Queenie did not let go his hand. It was the first time he had ever mentioned his grandparents. He sounded sad. She watched his toes digging into the sand. She stopped and scooped up a handful and let it filter through her hands. 'Look at them,' she said, not needing to point.

'Yes,' he murmured.

'They're early. Very early. Humpbacks.'

'Hm.'

'Beautiful.'

'Yes,' he said, 'they are.'

'So much more than us.'

They stood by the cobalt-coloured pools for a while, marvelling at how cold they looked, how different they were; they were still young enough to be amazed that things changed. Returning along the beach they walked in their own footprints, sinking their toes where their heels had been. The rest of the afternoon they wandered along the edge of the estuary and back into the paperbarks, catching glimpses of their reflections in the water, privately wondering.

That night the Cooksons risked the appearance of the local ranger and pitched their tent in amongst the trees by the inlet. The lamp hissed, hanging from a tree limb and the fire's limpid flames hung in the cold air. Whale sounds came to them every few minutes from in the bay.

'Mascots,' she said.

'Us or them?'

She shrugged, smiling. They ate tinned salmon and salami and sipped claret. In bed they listened to the sag of canvas and the whale noises from the bay. Cleve found himself wondering: what are they saying? He felt Queenie's hand on his back and he flinched.

'Yeah?' he asked, full of doubt.

'Do you mind that I'm having a baby?'

'Course not.'

'Good.'

'You?'

The question took her by surprise. 'No. Not really. It's just that I don't know what we'll be like. As parents.'

'Hm.'

In the morning the whales were gone. The Cooksons dismantled camp after breakfast and kicked their fireplace in and moved east.

The road to Stormy Beach uncoiled ahead of them and lashed up at the belly of the Land Rover with spits of gravel. There was a strange closeness, an anxiety between them that thawed some of their awkwardness. Galahs flashed across the road in pink spurts. Trees and stumps and juts of granite became sharp in their perception.

On the flat white sand of Stormy Beach the Cooksons parked the Land Rover and went walking. The sun came out for a while and they lay in the powdery warm sand and slept. Queenie woke, shaking the sand from her hair, when the air began to cool. We're waiting for something, she thought. It was then that she saw the pod lazing in the shallows several hundred yards offshore, lifting curtains of water with their flukes, their backs catching the dull light.

'They're here, Cleve,' she said. 'The whales.' She turned and

225

saw that he was awake. He was smiling.

'I bet they'll be at every beach we go to,' he said.

'As if they're keeping an eye on us.'

In their big sleeping bag that night Queenie felt Cleve's finger in her navel, and knew she was afraid to be a mother, afraid to be a wife again. *Queenie Coupar's got blood!* she heard. Oh, no she hasn't, she thought; not this month.

Basking in the heat of her body, Cleve, too, thought about the child. He felt helpless, so removed from it. He couldn't even recall the last time they made love. Wirrup? he thought; that far back? In the stagnant pool? It seemed so long ago, seemed impossible, even a little ugly.

'Queen?' he murmured. 'You awake?'

'Yeah. Thought you were asleep.'

'About me hitting you that time.'

'Yes.' Her body tensed; both of them felt it.

'Well?'

'Well, what?'

'I dunno.'

They shared a silence.

'Well, it didn't help things much, did it?' she said.

'Do you hate me for it?'

'Not now. I don't think so.'

Cleve sighed and scratched the fabric of the tent. 'Do you love me? At all?' His voice was pathetic; it embarrassed them both.

'I don't know. It's not the same.'

'That's not necessarily bad.'

'No, I suppose not.'

Weariness did not blunt their excitement as they drove hard along the highway to the east. The whales had been gone when they pulled camp at dawn and they had occupied all their thoughts since. The land on either side of the road was flat and shrouded with a fine mist that moved low and sluggish over its surface. Black arrows of crows emerged from it and disappeared again without sound. A wallaby tripped out of the path of the whining Land Rover and stood at the edge of the mist as it passed.

As they sped eastwards the country became drier and paler and starker in its starvation, but they saw only the creeping strip that blurred beneath their feet. Silver-eyed mileposts marked off the distance in units that seemed unreal.

At Teal Beach the Cooksons set up camp away from the cleared paddock the Angelus Shire had called a caravan park, and waited in strained silence for signs of the whales. They lit a covert fire and cooked and ate without speaking and, without discussing the idea, they went walking. They went down the gravel track, passing unlit squatters' shacks with their fallen, rotted watertanks and boarded windows, and past the long, warped rails where the salmon fishermen hung their nets, down a grassy trail to the hard, flat sand of the beach. An ivory moon hung over the blank sea. They walked for an hour, earnestly, as though there were a destination ahead. On the return lap they recognised the sounds of the humpbacks, the slaps of vast bodies against water, and they whistled and hooted, cavorting in the moonlight like excited children.

IX

The same night, Daniel Coupar slept for an hour and woke, damp as usual. For the first time in a long time he went down across the thin, hard ground, through the baked flats of the swamp where kangaroos had been felled with musket balls, and made his unsteady way down the lightening sand track to the beach. Dunes crouched luminous, shoulder to shoulder. He moved off the rutted track between them.

Harder than he remembered, the sand squealed beneath his boots as he scuffed along it holding a thin curl of paper in his fist. He moved towards a place he had not visited since he was a young man. It was at the end of the beach behind a thick nest of vegetation in the lee of the headland and he watched for it in the stark monochrome of night. His moonshadow skimmed beside him. Although he was hard-set with resolve, navigating himself by the lumpy shadow of the headland, he found time between his old man's breaths to be wistful.

227

He thought of his granddaughter; he wished he could see her again. He felt strong things about her. He wished with the fervour of a man in his last momentum that he could somehow inject his granddaughter with some tonic, some drug that would make her *see*. She was strong and mostly honest and capable of good, he thought, but foolish. He wished he could breathe into her all his years, his knowledge, the things he had touched and smelt and heard and seen and tasted and truly sensed, wished that his experience would be hers, prayed that some measure of understanding might seize her and save her from his own confusion. God, I'd take her pain, her life's pain upon myself, her confusion even, if only you'd give her understanding now. I could suffer anything for that and die without waste and tragedy. I'd be nothing. Less. For that.

But near the end of the beach and close to his destination he realised the meanness of his offer. It would be an easy sacrifice, he knew, to die for someone now, to suffer a little in the short time left. There were more costly sacrifices he would never consider. No, he thought, Queenie will suffer as all of us do. She will suffer herself. And I'm no use to her.

Old Daniel Coupar had some difficulty with the under-growth and debris that protected the cleft in the rock to which he finally fought his way. With some fear, he let his body into the crack and felt his way in. The cave resounded with distant trickles and the skitterings of crabs in the sand. A flurry of wings swept his face, startling him. Bats! he thought, before recognising the flitting sounds of swallows taking shelter in the safer dark outside. Movement became difficult for him. As a boy he had manoeuvred well in this dark, but he had forgotten the terrain. He crawled for a few yards, paper in his fist, and put his back to the wall as his grandfather had done before him, and he lit a match to find fuel, ignoring the white silhouettes opposite. Gathering old kelp and tumbleweed and fingery dried twigs and splinters of driftwood, he scuffed them into a graduated mound and set fire to them. In the improved light, Coupar found two thickish pieces of old wood and kept them at his side until the flames were ripe. He had done this on the beach and in caves many times as a boy, and now it heartened him, the deliberate, purposeful procedure.

Then with a sigh he unrolled the paper he had carried and

crumpled with him. And by the unsteady light of the fire he
read.

August 30th, 1875   All my life I have laboured and tilled
and kept myself upright before God. I have shown
courage and dutiful conviction. Yet God has cursed me
unjustly with a fool for a son and daughters who waste
away my savings in town living. In addition I have a
plague of blacks who persist in returning and being driven
off like locusts from the land for which I have laboured,
fought and suffered, and my body has grown old too
soon, a disgrace to its Maker.

Oh, my son Martin will cause grief, I see it now. I will
bear no more grief from him.

September 1st   Had I eaten the flesh of other men in an
unholy Communion, had I raped native women and
mutilated them, raped men of my own kind, tortured,
enslaved, cheated, besotted myself with drink — *then* would
I be unworthy.

Where is my Blessing?

Today I cease from work.

10th   My family have left. Forsaken me. Am I unclean?
Where is respect? If I am cursed, then let them be too.
Angelus, the barren. Let them go there.

Eli, Eli lama sabachthani? I have done nothing wrong,
and what others do is their own sin, their own salvation,
their damnation.

September 12th   I too am angry enough to die. Will I
ever be spat from this great void?

No work.

I have been deceived. God has deceived me. I have
deceived myself. God is nothing, worse than evil.

19th   Pieces breaking in my head this morning. Smash
these very ideas smash this very God and other. Sometimes
in the cool of the evening I hear noises and I call out
Abba but no one is there. But I call out. Had that dream
again last night. I was resting under a tree and I looked
up and saw a piece of food falling and I opened my
mouth in shock or to receive it and it caught between my
teeth, between your teeth yes. Then with great weight it
forced itself down my throat and my belly bloated and I
burst and sat with my guts in my lap and woke hungry.

I spit in the face. Adam and his slut.

20th   Remember when you were twenty, Nathaniel the
prophet Coupar? Had God the power to judge you
innocent. He would have done so. Save yourself. Save
yourself. I shall. No, I shall.

Daniel Coupar laid the pages flat on the flames, watching the
brown heart burgeon until it was fire. Oh, you poor miserable
sick bastard, he thought. And when I was a younger man I
came near to believing you. Pride let me. But never again. The
Father of Lights withholds the rain because of our pride. Our
pride must finish. But pride waits until all else has withered.

The vertebra of a right whale stood end-on against the wall
opposite, grey-white, veined with corrosion, big as a mill-end.
Whisks of baleen lay next to the vertebra and sections of jaw
stood against the granite. Coupar sifted the shell-grit through
his hands and fixed his gaze on the sheep skulls that lay
together on their sides, sockets aimed at him. He had brought
these relics into the cave in his childhood. The cave was once a
hideout. This was the cave his grandfather came to for solitude
when he was a whaler, the cave where Nathaniel Coupar had
found the body of Bale the lunatic. And this was the place
wherein Nathaniel Coupar, in old age, had shot himself. As an
adult, Daniel had stayed clear of here.

Another frame, the tiny skeleton of a swallow, was visible on
the sand. He could have popped the skull into his mouth like a
gravelstone. He moved over and touched it and it became dust.
Then he picked up a sheep's skull with trembling fingers and
looked into its cavities.

'Here's your bloody Blessing, Nathaniel Coupar. To know
that I beg mercy for you and for me and ours. Why is it so hard
to love? To be loved? To fulfil the law?' He felt a great weeping
shout well up in him. 'I came here to lie with the bones of my
fathers like the men of old. Seems so bloody ludicrous now.
Bones arise! Makes you laugh.'

Then the shout burst from him, a great guffaw, and he felt
his stomach unknot. 'I've changed my mind. I'm not dying
here with you poor buggers.'

Still laughing, he groped his way out of the waning light of
the cave and into the fresh darkness of the night outside,

carrying his old frame up the beach.

He collapsed at the bore with the insistent cries of animals in his ears.

X

Late in the morning Cleve and Queenie slithered out along the gravel of the Teal Beach road towards the highway, weaving between the lumpy carcasses of birds and rabbits and kangaroos. On the sealed road neither spoke, leaning into the curves. The engine lulled them into a trance, a dull fixity of purpose. Cleve sat at the wheel counting the carcasses as he had done when a boy. Queenie concentrated on the blur of the road just under her nose, thousands of tarred stones becoming one ribbon of grey. *Flog a dog!* she recalled bus rides, the winding trip home after school, and the showers of boys' spit raining into her lap from behind. *Queenie Coupar, Queenie Coupar, swim!*

The turn-off sign for Wirrup was visible for miles on the flat stretch of tinder plain. The Land Rover slipped back onto gravel. Dead land rushed past unseen.

Before reaching Coupar land at Wirrup, they left the road, opened gates and cut across neighbours' land to get more quickly to the beach. Queenie directed Cleve through farms, across the wasteland of paddocks, to a track that wound down the hill to the bay.

There was no sign of the whales out on the water. The Cooksons drove along the beach, churning through soft sections of sand until they were directly below Coupar land which began at the high-water mark.

'Do you think we should go up and see the old man first?' Cleve asked as they sat waiting.

'Yes. Later. I don't want to miss anything. They might come while we're gone and they could move on and we'll lose them,' Queenie said.

Cleve shrugged and she gave him a tense smile.

At noon they still waited, but there were no whales. As the afternoon wore on they dozed in the Land Rover, exhausted by tension and expectation. When they became hungry they ate apples and sultanas and peanuts from paper bags, and drank from a warm carton of orange juice. Outside, the air was shifting, unsettled. 'We should at least say hello,' he murmured.

'Later,' she said.

Miles back along the coast, bulls and cows, tired from the months of mating and chasing and nursing, keep a steady, unhurried pace. The cows are hungry with bodies within them to be fed in the cold waters of the south. Nothing deviates them from their hunger.

Daniel Coupar woke at the bore, still damp with the sudden dew of the night. He shivered inside his clothes. The afternoon sun was obscured by clouds and did not warm him. His sleep had been clean and dreamless and now he woke to his nightmare. The animal noises returned to him, the weak bleating of the sheep, dry-throated lowings of the surviving stock. Turning onto his side he saw grey huddles, piles, pools of starved animals. Sheep lay quivering, twitching their abysmal mouths. Daniel Coupar saw feeble lambs beside scabby carcasses and whispered, 'My God.'

He stood unsolidly and made steps to the nearest live sheep which lay flat on its side like a tanned rug. He took the emaciated frame in his arms and felt it slip into sections like a thin bag of dirt, and he shook it, but the sheep only opened its mouth at him revealing its wizened throat, so he lay the thing back in its own imprint in the colourless dust; the knocking in its chest stopped. Then Daniel Coupar saw the paddock writhing; it writhed with the heads of stricken animals.

'Oh God.' He wanted to crawl between the legs of his mother and butt his way back into the darkness again. He turned his head, taking in the scene. A steer had fallen on its side with its head near the bore and its weight had dragged it forwards, too weak to move, down the steep little bank until its head was slowly submerged. Coupar's legs moved; he willed himself up towards the house, knowing that there was still some gruelling effort ahead as he stared at the shamefully bald earth and felt

232

his breath rattle in him.

At the house he found the big knife he and his father had slaughtered with. The weight of the knife disfigured Coupar; his right side sagged with it.

All afternoon Daniel Coupar moved amongst his neglected animals with the knife, disconnecting withered throats. He visited each immobile huddle with darkened hands. A black-eyed lamb touched his forearm with its tongue. He was amazed that such bodies still had blood to offer.

Near dusk he lay by the bore again and slept. The water was still and full of bodies. He rested his head on his bloody arm and slept with something moving in his near-vacant body.

Coupar slept the sleep of a man no longer in need of dreams. He woke well into the night, smelling rain. He licked the unearthly dew from his lips, dropped the knife he had clutched all night into the body-bog of the bore and picked his way in the luminous dark to the foot of the hill. Fuelled by anticipation, he made his way up.

At dusk the Cooksons had pitched their tent on the beach and crawled inside. They listened without moving and heard the excitement of each other's digestive systems and the clip of lips shifting. It was humid inside the tent and so different from the freezing nights before; after two hours they became restless and dressed and went outside again. The sky was starless and hot with cloud. It felt low enough to scoop down with uplifted hands. They walked to the shore where the rising swell was thundering down with the force of falling cliffs. Foam lifted like blanched mountains rearing in the night. Every minute it grew; every lumbering breaker seemed bigger. Cleve felt a drop of rain on his arm and they returned to the tent.

'What the hell are we expecting?' Cleve asked the fabric above him as he lay on his back.

'Who knows,' Queenie murmured.

'My God what a swell.'

A raindrop thudded on the fabric.

Utterly spent by the climb, Daniel Coupar lay on his back on the flat top of the hill and stared up into the night. For a moment he was consumed with a longing to see Queenie, but he knew his body was finished and he found himself speaking in low tones to those he had loved and betrayed, as though he was near them. His hands lay on the rock, washed clean of blood from the sweat and abrasion of climbing. He would have raised them had they obeyed him. Just an old gesture, he thought to himself.

Rain began to fall, drops bursting on his brow and cheeks, hitting the rocks hard enough to make sparks.

Labouring in the midst of the storm that sweeps towards the coast gathering force as it comes, the pod of humpbacks moves in closer to the coast, shunted by the wind, barrelled along by the swell, sensing the outer frontiers of the shallows.

Daniel Coupar was buoyant, no longer supporting his own weight. He heard the thickest mass of rain coming, hissing on the water. His mouth was open—he needed it so to breathe—and he felt heavy drops hit the back of his throat and roll into him. *Deep calleth unto deep at the noise of thy waterspouts: all thy waves and thy billows are gone over me*, he thought. Then rain fell without bounds as the sky fell in. Daniel Coupar heard the cries of the whales piercing the deluge impossibly. The pips and clicks twitched in his ears and he knew the whales were back and another season had finished; and then he was skimming in flight over dark like bitumen blackness and swimming and swimming and swimming strongly without fear. Light, immanent, white, speared about him and he counted as his mother had taught him, to judge the distance between light and thunder, and he felt the water at the back of his throat and himself filling and his breath bubbled as he moved with the thunderless light. As he ceased counting, the hill shuddered with a report that shook the birds from their trees and out into the deluge, and the sea flinched.

Daniel Coupar lay shrouded in water.

The whales press on despite the narrowness and the sharp, too-

234

quick return of their cries from the bottom. A ripple of panic and dread moves through them. They continue.

Over the smacking rain, Cleve and Queenie Cookson heard the cries of the whales and were suddenly awake. They lay still for some time, paralysed by joy and disbelief, hearing the sounds come closer every moment as though nearly with them.

'They've come,' Queenie whispered.

'Yes.' Cleve hugged her.

Rapid scalar movements, changes of tone, sounds of unmistakable emotion came to them, and the Cooksons dressed and rushed outside with a torch and ran down the wet sand in the rain and shone the torch and saw the huge, stricken bodies lurching in the shallows. Queenie screamed. Surf thundered and the night was images in torch beams. Masses of flesh and barnacles covered the sand, creeping up, floundering, suffocating under their own weight. A pink vapour from spiracles descended upon Cleve and Queenie Cookson as they moved between the heaving monuments.

ABOUT THE AUTHOR

Tim Winton is the author of several novels, short-story collections, and children's books, for which he has received every major literary award in Australia, including the Australian/Vogel Award and the prestigious Miles Franklin Award. He currently lives in a fishing village in Western Australia with his wife and three children.